Jule McBride

MISSION:
MOTHERHOOD

Harlequin Books

TORONTO • NEW YORK • LONDON
AMSTERDAM • PARIS • SYDNEY • HAMBURG
STOCKHOLM • ATHENS • TOKYO • MILAN
MADRID • WARSAW • BUDAPEST • AUCKLAND

For Karen Solem—for negotiating rough terrain and
helping me hang on to the wheel during the bumpy ride
of this whole last year. Thanks!

ISBN 0-373-16693-1

MISSION: MOTHERHOOD

Copyright © 1997 by Julianne Randolph Moore.

This edition published by arrangement with Harlequin Books S.A.

® and TM are trademarks of the publisher. Trademarks indicated with
® are registered in the United States Patent and Trademark Office, the
Canadian Trade Marks Office and in other countries.

Printed in U.S.A.

ABOUT THE AUTHOR

When native West Virginian Jule McBride was little, she kept her books inside her grandmother Helen's carved oak cabinet, to which only Jule had a key. Only later did she realize that the characters she loved weren't real and that someone called a "writer" conjured them. That's when she knew one day she'd be a writer. In 1993, that dream came true with the publication of Jule's debut novel. It received the *Romantic Times* Reviewer's Choice Award for "best first series romance," and ever since, the author has continued to pen heartwarming love stories that have met with strong reviews and made repeated appearances on romance bestseller lists.

Books by Jule McBride

HARLEQUIN AMERICAN ROMANCE
500—WILD CARD WEDDING
519—BABY TRAP
546—THE WRONG WIFE?
562—THE BABY & THE BODYGUARD
577—BRIDE OF THE BADLANDS
599—THE BABY MAKER
617—THE BOUNTY HUNTER'S BABY
636—BABY ROMEO: PI
658—COLE IN MY STOCKING

HARLEQUIN INTRIGUE
418—WED TO A STRANGER?

HARLEQUIN LOVE & LAUGHTER
23—WHO'S BEEN SLEEPING IN MY BED?

Prologue

Genesis, Long Island
Six years ago

Even without the three-inch platform heels of her char-treuse combat boots, Daniela Newland was still five-nine, nearly a full foot taller than Margie. Not that be-ing vertically challenged was stopping the housekeeper from blocking Daniela's way.

"You can't leave, Daniela!" Margie pressed her del-icate back flush against the stainless steel front door to the Newlands' mansion. "He'll *kill* you!"

If he finds me. Daniela quickly checked over her out-fit—straightening her black opaque tights, tucking a short-sleeved ribbed turtleneck into her lime miniskirt and closing the front of a lightweight black leather jacket that was made mostly of zippers. As she regrip-ped the handles of her two dark leather suitcases and lifted them, her usually heart-shaped mouth flattened into a straight, determined line and one of her Roller-blades—they were knotted by the checkered laces and flung over her shoulder—thumped against her chest. So did her transparent plastic pocketbook, the strap of which was looped over her opposite shoulder.

"I *am* crossing that threshold, Margie." Daniela eyed the door behind the housekeeper, and her voice rang out the proclamation "And I swear to you, I'm never coming back."

Margie wrung her hands. "You sound like Scarlett O'Hara."

"Scarlett O'Hara was a Southerner stuck in a war. I'm a dyed-in-the-wool Yankee trapped in Genesis, Long Island." And the last thing she wanted in her life was a man, something of which Scarlett had had plenty.

A man.

No, she'd never let one near her again. The hard mask of Daniela's face suddenly threatened to crumple, but she willed away emotion. She wouldn't break down now, couldn't. The grandfather clock in the foyer began to chime; it was seven, which meant she was almost out of time. "Please. I've got to go before he comes home from work."

Margie didn't move except to slide her palms nervously down the sides of the starched white apron she wore over her gray uniform dress, and to blow a wayward graying curl off her forehead. "You'll leave over my dead body, young lady."

"Margie," Daniela warned, advancing.

At the last possible moment, a resigned Margie stepped aside, opening the door. Daniela paused just a heartbeat at the doorway, smelling sea salt on the late September breeze, hearing rushing waves break on the nearby beach. Her chest suddenly squeezed tight. Oh, how she'd miss that scent, that sound. Was she really going to cross this threshold, run away to a new life?

When Daniela glanced over her shoulder, sadness twisted inside her and her voice softened. "Margie, you *know* I have to leave. I don't have a choice. And you know why.''

Margie's eyes registered the truth of it. ''Well, then, at least slow down.'' Her serviceable white, nurse-style shoes padded beside Daniela, then Margie wrenched one of the suitcases from her hand with surprising strength.

Daniela sighed. ''I'm not letting you carry my suitcase.''

Margie clutched the handle. ''The doctor said you're not supposed to lift. You shouldn't even be out of bed. Besides, they both have rollers.''

There was no time left to argue. Daniela's heavy boots clomped across the black-tiled veranda, then she hauled the larger, heavier suitcase down the steps to the paved driveway. Crisp, rustling leaves of bright rust and orange and gold caught the twilight, making the long, tree-lined road look like a shimmering gauntlet.

At the end was a vaulted steel gate.

And on the other side of the gate was the yellow cab Daniela had called.

''I hear a motor.'' Margie glanced over her shoulder toward the garage as she plunked down the suitcase she'd taken from Daniela, grabbed the handle and started rolling the suitcase down the driveway. ''Maybe it's Baines, coming with the car.''

''Probably.'' Daniela nodded toward the gate. ''But Baines doesn't need to take me. I called that cab.''

Margie sighed. ''I just wish this was like that trip you took to Oregon. You know, when you told everybody that the logging capital of the country was the perfect place to turn over a new leaf.''

The trip had seemed so symbolic at the time. All

three days of it—right up until Daniela had fled back East. "I wish it was like that, too."

But it wasn't. Childish games were over. The last eleven days had really happened. And the last nine months. And both made Daniela wish she'd never been born at all. When her heart wrenched, she pushed down her emotions again. "Turn over a new leaf?" she muttered. "I should have uprooted the forest."

"It's *his* fault," Margie said, her voice gentling. "He never should have pushed you to..." There was a long pause, then Margie continued. "You're not still...depressed, are you?"

No doubt, Daniela was suffering from postpartum depression. But she gritted her teeth and narrowed her eyes and told herself to hang tough. She was New York born and bred and that meant, beneath her pampered exterior, she was lean and mean and made of steelier stuff than most people on the face of the earth. At least she hoped that would prove to be the case.

"Daniela, just promise me you won't do something crazy."

She'd sure thought about it. Now she swallowed hard, mustering her bravado. "Like what? Jump from the stock exchange screaming, 'See ya later, cold, cruel world?'"

"Well, I don't know," Margie said uncertainly.

Daniela's voice suddenly turned fierce. "Don't worry, Margie. I'll live, if only to spite him."

"I know he cut off your money."

"I'll get a job."

But where? And doing what? Daniela fought the urge to stare down at her outfit. It may have been just right for parties in the Hamptons, but it wasn't exactly secretarial attire, and typing was the only marketable skill she possessed. Unless talking on the phone counted. Maybe she could be a receptionist. She wished she hadn't dropped out of college.

Don't you dare start wallowing in self-pity, Dani.

She fixed her unwavering gaze on the gate ahead, still feeling the empty postmodern mansion she'd just vacated looming behind her. The massive barn-shaped structure was of steel and chrome; glass walkways connected various cylindrical outbuildings. She told herself she wouldn't miss it, this sterile place that housed all the creature comforts known to man—and then some.

Still tears threatened. Not that she'd shed them.

Margie said, "What *are* you going to do for money?"

"I've got my Rollerblades. Maybe I'll get a job in one of those coffeehouses with the skating waitresses."

"I don't think that pays very much," Margie said nervously.

"I don't care." And Daniela didn't. She just had to get away from here. If pure fury or her need for revenge didn't keep her going, she figured her dark sense of humor would.

A horn tooted as Baines pulled the Lincoln beside her and Margie. The middle-aged man tipped the bill of his chauffeur's cap as he powered down the window. "Daniela, why didn't you tell me you needed the car?"

"Because I don't. I called a cab."

Baines hunched over the wheel, crawling alongside her and Margie, peering between the windshield and the passenger window. His voice was cautious. "He's going to be quite upset, you know."

"She knows," Margie said.

"And she shouldn't be carrying that bag."

"I told her that, too."

Tears welled in the rims of Daniela's eyes, but she blinked them back. Baines and Margie. She'd sure miss them. "Please, Baines—" Somehow she kept her voice from shaking. "I just want to take the cab."

Baines hunched further over the steering wheel. "Does that mean you're going into the city?"

Was she? Daniela fought a sudden rush of panic. "I—I don't know."

"I bet he calls the police," Margie warned. "And hires a private investigator."

"No one blames you for wanting to leave," Baines coaxed through the window. "But you *can't* leave right now. We're all so worried. And the doctor said you need to rest."

The doctor. Desperate anguish washed over her, but her voice was resolute. "I'm leaving. I should have left a long time ago."

Better late than never.

For days after coming home from the hospital, she hadn't gotten out of bed. She'd let people push tranquilizers down her throat and baby her, and yet nothing could stop the soul-deep ache for what had happened. Or the fact that she'd never forgive herself.

Then suddenly she'd started getting angry.

Really angry.

And today she'd gotten up.

She'd taken a good hard look in the mirror. At her waist-long hair, its ten natural shades of blond tumbling over her shoulders. At her flawless skin. At the heart-shaped mouth in the heart-shaped face. And the round chocolate eyes and jutting cheekbones that always made people compare her to Lauren Bacall.

Oh, she'd been blessed with stunning outsides.

Trouble was, only insides counted.

Daniela knew that now. Margie's voice drew her from her reverie. She realized Baines had braked in the driveway, letting the car idle, in case she changed her mind about needing a ride.

"Daniela," Margie said, "there must be some other recourse."

Daniela's temper flared, though the anger was at herself. "What? Someone else to pick up the pieces? To make me hot chicken soup? A pot of tea that'll make everything all better?" Daniela shook her head. "Not this time, Margie. I've got to get out of here. And I'm going to find a law—" Her voice cracked. "A law—"

She couldn't even say it. Couldn't think about lawyers yet, any more than she could think about the doctor who'd delivered her baby.

"Wherever you go, he'll find you."

"Maybe he won't look."

"He'll look."

Both women stopped in front of the gate. Daniela put down her suitcase and turned, staring back at the house, taking in the connected cylindrical steel buildings and black-tiled verandas one last time. With a sudden jolt of insight, she realized the place looked like an oversize bank vault. Suitable, since Genesis was the home of New York City's richest banker.

Genesis.

Sometimes, she'd noticed how the reflected blue of a romantic night sky could appear to emanate from within all that shining chrome and steel. Or how the stars twinkled between the outbuildings and how faroff slivers of the ocean's silver surf could be glimpsed between the steel sculptures on the lush green grounds. Yes, sometimes, Daniela saw real beauty in the house named Genesis.

Genesis.

It was the name the architect had given the house, and the name had later been given to the whole surrounding community. Well, leaving it was her genesis. Her beginning. Abruptly she turned—and found herself staring into Margie's eyes.

"Oh, *damn!*" Margie shoved her hands on her hips. "I know I tried to stop you, but I'm glad you're going. I can't forgive him for this, so I know you sure can't."

Daniela managed a smile. "I...I'll be all right."

Margie's voice was so tender it almost melted Daniela's heart. "Good luck."

"Thanks. I'll need it." Daniela leaned and hugged Margie hard. But she wouldn't cry. Maybe she had no real tears left. In the past eleven days she'd been to hell and back. She'd cried enough to last the rest of her life.

"Tell Baines I said goodbye."

Margie squeezed her hand. "Get going."

Leaning toward the gate, Daniela pressed a steel button. Everything—the distant lapping waves, the insects in the air— seemed to fall silent. Then a buzz sounded and, as Daniela lifted both her bags, the gate's sides whirred back, sliding apart on electrified tracks. Daniela walked through, her boots loud on the concrete. Then the steel gate whirred shut behind her and closed with a metallic clank.

It was a sound Daniela knew she'd never hear again.

And suddenly her body wrenched around of its own accord. She wanted to run back home into Margie's arms, into the car next to Baines.

But she didn't.

She turned back around, took a deep breath and then put one chartreuse boot in front of the other. Because life as she'd known it had come to an end eleven days ago—when she'd been forced to do the unthinkable and give up her newborn baby.

Now she had to find Jake Lucas.

Daniela had never even talked to him personally, but already she hated him because he'd taken away her child. Now she was going to track him down. Hunt him. Get some kind of revenge. Even seduce him if she had to.

And, one way or another, Jake Lucas was going to give her baby back.

Chapter One

New York City
Six years later

"Nurse!" Judge Tilford Winslow shouted. "Nurse Dani!"

"I'm a nurse, not a waitress," Dani called over her shoulder. "At least from nine to five," she added, since she occasionally still waitressed part-time at a place called The Roller Derby Diner.

"But Nurse Dani, I am *trapped!*"

Sure enough, the corpulent, balding, red-faced eighty-five-year-old judge had wedged his wheelchair in the doorway again. After his daily constitutional in Central Park, Judge Winslow always insisted Dani precede him through the doorway to his building, so he could enter unaided. Dani suspected it was because he didn't want the desk attendant—a buxom, comely sixty-six-year-old named Evie Pope—to see him being pushed by a nurse. Now Dani glanced over the judge's hemmed pant leg and the plaster cast that covered his leg from his knee to his toes and thought, Pride Goeth Before A Fall.

Judge Winslow raised his voice. "Nurse Dani, may I remind you that it is *I* who pays your wages?"

"Such as they are," Dani rejoined lightly.

"Heartless!" the judge exclaimed. "Simply heartless!"

"I can only do one thing at a time." Besides, weeks of dealing with Judge T. Winslow had taught Dani how to put her foot down without feeling even a pinch of guilt.

"Hi, Evie," Dani said.

The desk attendant lifted her eyes from a romance novel, then chuckled. "You've sure got your work cut out for you, Dani. But one of these days the judge'll learn." She glanced at the people gathered around her desk. "The natives have been waiting for you both to get back. If you haven't noticed, they're all restless."

"Sorry, everybody." Dani quickly started taking clipboards and signing for various items, dispensing with the judge's dry cleaning and pressed shirts, the UPS man, a teenager delivering groceries and a Lycra-clad bicycle messenger who left a manila envelope.

Judge Winslow suddenly shouted, "My dear Ms. Pope, would you be willing to testify in a court of law that Nurse Dani's treatment of me is inhumane?" Still stuck in the doorway, he made a show of trying to roll his wheels forward. Without waiting for a response, he continued. "In the park, we ran into one of Nurse Dani's classmates from a patient dignity seminar. Ha! Patient *in*-dignity if you ask me!"

Dani glanced around. The doorman was on break and Evie couldn't leave the desk. "Did you just say something about *patience,* Judge Winslow?"

"The only thing I've said about patience, Nurse Dani, is that I'm losing mine."

Dani sighed and shook her head. Welcome to New York, she thought, glancing over the pandemonium and grabbing yet another clipboard. "One of you could go help him, you know."

"Oh, I would—" the feminine voice was made softer still by a melodious Spanish accent "—but my car's parked by the back door and I'm late. I'm going on vacation. I'm, uh, Rosita de Silva. Anyway, I just need a signature, it doesn't even necessarily have to be the next of kin."

Dani glanced over the woman's short dark hair and trim pantsuit. She seemed so familiar, but Dani couldn't place her. Reaching past two law clerks in suits—one gray, one navy—Dani signed Rosita's paper. "There. Enjoy your vacation."

"Thanks!" the woman said over her shoulder.

"You're so lucky," the navy suit enthused as Dani turned to him. "I'd *kill* to work for Judge Winslow."

"You won't even help him when he's stuck in a doorway," Dani observed.

The navy suit pinned her with his eyes. "The law briefs we're delivering are highly confidential. We've been instructed by Judge Lathrop to hold them until either Judge Winslow or yourself signs." He riffled through some papers. "Here, here and here."

Dani sighed and started signing.

In spite of their constant bickering, Dani admired the judge. He was eighty-five and temporarily in a wheelchair, but he was still more active than most people Dani's age. He hadn't retired his post at family court until a few weeks ago when he'd broken his leg, and he was still working sixty-hour weeks. Between work and school, Dani only clocked about fifty.

"Yeah," murmured the lawyer in the gray suit. "It must be wonderful to work for him."

"He's brilliant," said the navy suit.

"So erudite," agreed the gray.

"So—"

"As you young men know, there are laws against making the elderly work for free," the judge called out, "so, if you're after pro bono work again, you'd better have brought me some good Cuban cigars."

Dani glanced up at the lawyers, who both looked stunned. "So manipulative?" she suggested with a chuckle.

"Judge Lathrop *did* suggest we bring Judge Winslow a cigar," said the gray nervously.

"But did it really have to be Cuban?" asked navy.

"I thought Cuban cigars were contraband," said gray.

Looking confused, both gave Dani a final, anxious glance, then strode toward the doorway to release the judge. She followed as the lawyer in gray slipped a cigar into the inner pocket of the judge's sport coat.

"In addition to a cigar, I do hope you young men brought umbrellas!" Judge Winslow exclaimed as one lawyer held the door and the other pushed the wheelchair.

"Umbrellas?" The man in the gray suit peered uncertainly through the glass door at the September sunshine.

"Indeed! Because here Nurse Dani comes like a rainy day!"

Dani shot the judge a long, level look. No doubt he was brilliant. But he was trickier than a two-year-old. And he had a twinkle in his blue eyes that said he still enjoyed more wine, women and song than men who were a full half century younger.

Dani shooed the clerks out the door, then automatically turned back Judge Winslow's lapel. "No sugar, salt, liquor or cigars allowed," she said, plucking out the cigar. "And you're not supposed to try walking with that cane you insist on carrying around." Dani stared pointedly toward where the judge had left his cane hooked over the brass knob of the front door.

Judge Winslow scowled. "Oh, why live?"

"Now don't get morbid."

"I don't know why I need a nurse," he grumbled.

"Because you fell down a flight of stairs and broke your leg." Dani started pushing his wheelchair toward the desk. "And I'd like to remind you that there were thirty other applicants for this job, all of whom you turned down."

"One look," Judge Winslow growled, "and I knew it was you I most wanted to torture."

Dani parked his wheelchair and leaned beside him. In a teasing stage whisper, she said, "Since I took your cigar, feel free to flirt with Evie while I retrieve your cane."

"I warn you, Nurse Dani," he intoned as she headed for the door, "I, too, can play matchmaker. I *will* get rid of you one way or another. Humph. By marriage or murder, it's all the same to me!"

"From what I've seen of most marriages," Dani called over her shoulder, "murder might be kinder."

"Believe me," the judge assured. "I'll keep that in mind."

Grabbing the judge's cane, Dani took a satisfied look outside. It was Friday. A sunny September day of the sort that made her glad she lived in Manhattan. Across

Fifth Avenue from the judge's venerable old stone building, with its respectable green awning and gargoyle cornices, were teeming crowds milling on the Metropolitan Museum's steps, hailing taxis, glancing curiously inside passing limos or strolling toward Central Park where the leaves of the trees had turned sunny yellow and burnt orange.

A little blond girl skipped into Dani's line of vision. She was about six. Dressed in a plaid school uniform, she crushed a notebook against her chest and clutched a fistful of pencils. As the child bolted up the museum's steps, Dani felt the past six years slip away like a veil. Even though she hadn't actually seen her baby, she'd always felt sure she'd given birth to a girl. She had no idea why. Labor had been long and hard, and her eyes were blurred with tears when she'd tried to sit up on the delivery table, desperate to catch just one glimpse. She'd strained with all her might—to this day, she could feel her aching muscles stretch—but she hadn't been able to rise. Not even an inch. Not even when she heard a wail, just one, and then felt her baby go forever, an absence from her womb and heart.

Even now, Dani couldn't stand to think about it.

She watched the girl vanish inside the museum. *Did my own little girl start school this year?* Dani wondered, her insides twisting into knots. *Is she still here in New York? Or did Jake Lucas move her out-of-state?* A sudden, crazy urge to chase after the little blond girl seized her. What if *that* girl was hers?

She's not. Of course, she's not. But knowing that didn't stop the pain. For six long years, Dani had searched the faces of strangers' children, hoping to see some mark of resemblance to herself, hoping to find her child. And during all that time, she'd worked two, sometimes three, jobs trying to turn herself into a woman her daughter would be proud to call "Mother."

Daniela Newland, the flighty party girl, was long gone. The serious woman now reflected in the doorway's glass was in her final semester of nursing school. She wore no makeup with her practical, all-white uniform dress, cardigan, hose and Reeboks. Her hair, cut to manageable shoulder-length, was held back by a serviceable plastic clip. Not that all the hard work in the world could have numbed her pain. Six years may have passed, but all it took was seeing that one little girl and Dani's wounds gaped open, hurting as though they were fresh.

If only Jake Lucas had told me where she was.

Dani had traced the adoption lawyer to Big Apple Babies, the private adoption agency he owned and ran in Greenwich Village. Since the agency was Dani's only connection to her baby, she'd even taken a nearby apartment. With reason prevailing at the last minute, she'd hired an attorney to approach Mr. Lucas. Not that it helped. The adoption was final, the records sealed. Only the child she'd given up could access the files, if a request was made someday. Meantime, Dani would be charged with harassment if she further pursued the inquiry. Apparently she hadn't just given up her baby. She'd given up every last one of her rights.

So, six Septembers ago, she'd spent long, grief-stricken afternoons standing vigil outside Big Apple Babies. She'd come to recognize some of the employees—an urban cowboy, a Latin woman with big hair and a larger smile, not to mention a lean, rangy, raven-haired guy with a mustache who had to be one of the most mouthwatering men she'd ever laid eyes on.

And then there was Jake Lucas.

At least Dani thought she'd heard someone yell "Jake" at him one day. He'd been a dead ringer for Lou on the "Mary Tyler Moore" show—middle-aged, balding and powerfully stocky. *Jake Lucas,* she thought now. The man who, to this day, could tell her where he'd put her little girl. A man for whom, right or wrong, she'd let hatred fester these past six years.

"Nurse Dani!"

Dani turned around and frowned. Someone, no doubt a harried mother, had momentarily parked a stroller next to Judge Winslow. He looked murderous, but then he usually did.

"Hurry!" Judge Winslow roared.

Dani stopped in front of him, raising her eyebrows. "Is something wrong?"

The judge's piercing blue eyes cut her to the quick. "I should say so." He wrenched his cane from her grasp and, using it as a pointer, directed it downward. "*That* is what's wrong."

Dani's eyes followed the length of the cane and landed on the stroller. It had navy canvas seats stacked two across and two-deep. The two front seats were occupied by exactly identical blond, blue-eyed girls who suddenly bounced up and down, giggling as if Dani were the funniest-looking person on earth. The back seats were empty.

"Who are they?" Judge Winslow demanded.

Leaning forward, Dani scrutinized the pink-beaded bracelets that graced their wrists. "Lyssa and Kirby." Judging from her textbook training, Dani decided the girls were probably about one year old. She could barely look at them without wondering about her own little girl at that age. Had she been happy or sad? Active or peaceful? She forced herself to squint at the two empty back seats. "I guess they usually travel with a couple more."

Judge Winslow crinkled a piece of paper. "Indeed! Two that probably look exactly like them. While you were signing for law briefs and laundry," he thundered, "didn't you even *realize* you'd signed for quadruplets?"

Dani gasped. "What?"

She snatched the paper from the judge's hand. Scrawled across it were the words, "Quads. A year old, to go to Winslow at 82nd and Fifth. Think he's next of kin. Rosita, please handle." Rosita? That must have been the dark-haired woman. Suddenly Dani's pulse quickened and she realized why the woman had looked familiar.

"Oh, no," she murmured. Six years ago, Dani had seen that woman outside Big Apple Babies! Oh, Rosita de Silva's hair had been long then and she'd been inclined to wear jeans, not suits, but it was definitely her.

Dani whirled around, but the woman was gone. Even worse, when Dani's gaze returned to the paper, she recognized the letterhead. A festive left border was formed by assorted apples of green, gold and red, some with bright white bite marks or cute smiling worms. In tiny letters was the motto Big Apple Babies Are Babies Of All Kinds!

At the top of the stationery was a large old-fashioned safety pin, the head of which was shaped like a red apple; the pin skewered a swath of diaper cloth which bore the words *Big Apple Babies* in bright red.

Dani's heart was beating so hard she was breathless. Was she staring at Jake Lucas's scrawl? Was this, somehow, her excuse to meet the man who held the key to the whereabouts of her child?

"I am apparently the next of kin to four one-year-olds who have now been left in my custody," the judge was saying. "I would also point out, Nurse Dani, that you failed to retain any documentation which would tell me their full names. Judging from the staple mark in the upper left-hand corner of the paper, other papers were once attached. And having spent fifty-odd years on the family court bench, I can tell you that the form you failed to get is yellow and comes in triplicate with carbons."

Dani forced herself to stare from the stationery to the stroller's empty seats. "But if we were supposed to get quadruplets, then where are the other two little girls?"

"I assure you, I don't know or care." The judge shot her a peeved look. "But at the distinguished age of eighty-five, I for one am far too old to be something so ridiculous as a single father. So, Nurse Dani, I strongly suggest you do something."

"Like what?"

"Like get rid of those babies!"

"BIG APPLE BABIES IS no longer legally liable," assured the representative from the adoption agency.

The speaker wasn't Jake Lucas. All the way downtown to the family court building, Dani had braced herself in case she was about to meet the Lou Grant lookalike. Now she didn't know which she felt more— disappointment or relief. Or cold fury, since this man's attitude was so unconscionable.

"No longer liable!" Judge Winslow shouted.

"That's right," the man said.

Dani sighed. The judge's wheelchair was on her right, the stroller on her left. And how she'd gotten all these sets of wheels into the trunk of a cab, she'd never know. At least Judge Winslow had managed to pull some strings and see Judge Lathrop in his chambers immediately. Because of their work in family court, both judges were already acquainted with the Big Apple Babies representative, at least by heresay. Not that anyone had stopped bickering long enough to introduce Dani.

She stared across the table at the rep again. What a nightmare. She recognized him just as she had Rosita de Silva. He was the tall, rangy raven-haired guy she'd noticed outside Big Apple Babies six years ago. And up close he was even sexier.

Competence clung to him, wrapping tightly around a lean, muscular broad-shouldered body that emanated edgy tension and raw sensual strength. He wore a tan corduroy sport coat over a V-necked sweater, but beneath the layers of clothing, Dani knew his belly would be rock hard, his chest covered with a silken thatch of tangled, curling black hair. The jet hair on his head was so wavy that no matter how often he pushed it back, a wayward lock fell and grazed the thick lick of an eyebrow. He had dimples. And a bad habit of tweaking a mustache that was neither too thick nor too thin and that teased the top of his full upper lip…

His eyes just wouldn't quit.

They were the cool glittering green of emeralds sparkling in bright light, but Dani found the gaze unsettling. It was so…dispassionate. It hinted at buried emotions and angry secrets and, even worse, made her wish she wasn't already hauling around enough excess baggage of her own.

Not that the man was so much as looking at her. He was staring at Judge Winslow.

"No longer liable?" Judge Winslow shouted again, his face becoming flushed.

Feeling determined to ignore the Big Apple Babies rep, just the way he was ignoring her, Dani kept her gaze studiously trained on the judge. She patted his arm. "Now, Judge Winslow, don't get excited. Just calm down."

"Calm down? I'm going to sue! I'm eight-five years old, my leg's broken, and I can't have any babies in my apartment!"

The rep glanced at the babies, then grunted softly as if to say Judge Winslow was being entirely unreasonable. "The nurse signed. You *can't* sue."

The nurse. Dani was getting sick and tired of hearing him call her that. Especially since his voice rumbled in his chest, then vibrated on the air in a way that should have been unpleasant but that thrummed inside Dani instead, stroking her bare nerve endings. *This jerk could be talking about lost pocket change, not babies.* "Excuse me," she interjected. "I have a name."

The man nodded curtly, not bothering to ask for it. When he didn't so much as grace her with a glance, Dani's temper rose. How could one man's mannerisms be so irritating? She just hated how he rolled the end of that silly black mustache between a thumb and index finger. Or thrust out his lower lip to absently toy with it. Or sat back lopsidedly with one shoulder an inch above the other, as if a chip had just been surgically removed, lightening its weight and making it rise.

"Judge Winslow." The man cleared his gravelly throat. "I'm well aware of your excellent reputa—"

"Don't you dare try to flatter me!"

The man's smoldering gaze was like molten green metal. "I'm not flattering you, only saying that you, of all people, should know that since the nurse signed, Big Apple Babies is no longer responsible. If you try to sue, you won't have a legal leg to stand on."

"Leg to stand on?" Judge Winslow's color deepened to purple as he glanced down at his wheelchair. "My leg's *broken!* Which is why I've got to get rid of these babies. Don't you see? I'm in ill health!" As if to prove it, the judge's shoulders shook, racked by a spasm of harsh-sounding coughs. "Pills," he gasped. "Nurse Dani, my pills."

Dani was already clawing through her handbag. "Now see what you've done!" she exploded. As she angrily shook two white heart pills from a bottle, she shot the Big Apple Babies rep her most murderous stare. Not that he noticed. He was too busy rolling those seductive eyes of his toward the ceiling.

"Ga-ga!" Lyssa squealed, apparently reacting to the rattling sound of the pills.

"Ga!" Kirby agreed excitedly as Dani quickly helped the sputtering, gasping judge. When he'd calmed enough to speak, he crooned, "Thank you, my dearest Nurse Dani," as if he'd long considered her his guardian angel. Then the judge pinned the rep with a stare. "Young man, you may have no *legal* responsibility, but what about your morals? *If* you have any." The judge cleared his throat. "Which I most sincerely doubt."

"I doubt it, too," Dani piped in.

Not even that got a rise out of the guy. Well, Dani just prayed poor Judge Winslow wouldn't really be held liable for her foolish mistake. She should have been far more circumspect in questioning Rosita de Silva. But the desk had been so busy...

"The agency will help to locate the other two children,'' the man said. ''But for now, we can't do anything. Rosita left for vaca—''

''You could call her!'' Dani interjected.

The ends of the man's lips curled with displeasure, and he glanced at her as if noticing her for the first time. Whatever impression she'd made, Dani was sure it wasn't good, because he reached up and tugged his mustache in such an irritated way that she half expected hairs to come out. But his eyes—devastating, coolly assessing green eyes—never left hers.

Dani glared back.

Even as she denied her attraction, her breath caught, her chest squeezed tight and her heart pounded dangerously fast. Beneath her skin, heat stirred, seeping into her cheeks until she felt dizzy and weightless and green around the gills.

As if sensing her distress, Judge Winslow patted her hand. It didn't help. In all her nursing studies, Dani had never come across an antidote for lust. Six years ago, after Jake Lucas had taken away her baby, she'd stricken male-female relations from her list of troubles. She'd been immune to men—until now. When the rep's testy voice thrummed her nerve endings again, she had to fight the urge to squirm.

He said, ''Rosita left no number where she could be reached.''

Dani just stared at him. He looked so serious and formidable. And so smart she wanted to shriek. How could a guy who'd just lost two babies look so efficient?

She took two deep breaths—in and out, in and out. But when she found her voice, her words were still clipped. ''I am very sure...'' Dani paused, regally straightening her shoulders and praying this man hadn't

guessed at her traitorous attraction. "I am very extremely—I mean—I'm sure Ms. de Silva's family will
know her…"

Whereabouts.

Dani's voice trailed off as she realized this man saw
her as a plain, uninteresting-looking woman in a
starchy white nurse's uniform. Fleetingly she wished
she hadn't cut her waist-long hair, and that she was
wearing makeup and the kind of clothes she used to.
Curve hugging and stylishly sinful, they'd turned more
than one head in Genesis, Long Island. Not to mention
at every watering hole between there and the Hamptons. Yeah, six years ago, even this guy would have
looked twice.

Now he looked bored, maybe even sorry for her; the
mere thought tweaked her pride. "Excuse me, did you
not hear what I said?"

"Of course I heard."

"Well, weren't you going to answer?" *Damn.* Dani
wanted to clap a hand over her mouth. The man had
flustered her and he knew it, too. He shot her a long,
level look, as if to say he'd continue whenever she
could manage to control herself. Fuming, she crossed
her arms and waited.

"Rosita was having a lot of trouble getting pregnant.
So, she wanted some privacy. She and her husband…"

Sneaked away to make a baby together.

Now color positively stained Dani's cheeks, and she
wished she could simply vanish. What was this man
doing to her? He'd merely alluded to sex, and her
whole body had flooded with unwanted warmth.

Six years ago she'd thought herself so worldly-wise,
though of course she wasn't. But now she was almost
a full-fledged nurse. She nodded in a manner she hoped

befitted a health professional. "If Rosita and her husband are—uh—" Words suddenly failed her. And it was all his fault. Surely she could talk if he'd just quit staring at her. "Are—uh—unavailable..." She paused again, trying to regain her runaway respiration. Then, feeling exposed and furious, she exclaimed, "Two babies are missing in Manhattan! The two in this room need a place to stay! What exactly do you intend to do about this?"

His eyes narrowed. "I didn't even have to come here."

"Your agency lost two babies!"

His voice was unnervingly calm. "You signed for them."

Dani's blood ran cold. Her own little girl had been placed by Big Apple Babies. What if all the agency's workers were this callous and unfeeling? Maybe Jake Lucas hadn't found her baby a home after all, but had simply lost her.... *Dani! Get your emotions under control.* She managed to say, "You don't feel you're at all responsible?"

"Do I really need to repeat it for you?"

"Yes." She glared at him. "I think you should. If for no other reason than to remind us all of what sort of heartless person you really are."

He didn't even bother to hide his contempt. "You signed for the kids. And so now they're the judge's. Got it?"

"Got it," Dani snarled. "And do you know what else I got?"

The lazy lift of a black eyebrow said he couldn't care less. "What's that?"

"The single worst impression of another human being I've ever gotten in my life."

His eyes turned jewel hard. Rapid fire, in that annoying rumbling voice, he said, "The agency's been thoroughly searched, I've filed a report at the Sixth Precinct. Larry McDougal, the caseworker who wrote the note, quit a few days ago, but we're looking for him, and my two best men are trying to track down Rosita. We've contacted airports and train stations. And as soon as I can—probably tomorrow—I'll search *again* for any missing paperwork in the office. In order to ascertain if anyone else knows anything, I've sent around a memo."

"A memo?" The man was beneath contempt.

He threw up his hands and shrugged. "Okay, lady. Actually, it was an E-mail."

"You sent an E-mail?"

"Again, which part couldn't you understand?"

She gaped at him.

"Those kids are only temporarily misplaced," he continued, once again the voice of efficiency. "We do reams of paperwork, and we're all highly qualified." He raised a hand as if ready to make a huge concession on her behalf. "But maybe someone can question Judge Winslow about his relatives, to figure out why he's been named next of kin."

As if this is the judge's fault! Dani shook her head numbly. Truly, it was guys like this who gave New Yorkers such a bad name. "Don't knock yourself out."

His eyes were steely, his voice soft. "I'm not."

When Judge Winslow suddenly grabbed Dani's forearm, she started, inhaling a sharp breath. She'd been so focused on the jerk in front of her that she'd completely forgotten about the judge.

Judge Winslow wrung his hands. "Nurse Dani, I assure you, I have no idea from whom those babies could have come!''

Judge Lathrop, a burly man in his late fifties, cleared his throat. ''We're getting nowhere. And it's imperative we do, because I just got a call from Suzanne Billings. Someone got wind of this and asked her to bring suit against Big Apple Babies for negligence in this case. She's already on the docket. Monday after next.''

Judge Winslow gasped as if *he* hadn't been threatening to sue. ''Suzanne Billings! She works for citizens' action committees. How could she have learned of this? Who could have hired her?''

''I don't know, but she could shut down Big Apple Babies,'' Judge Lathrop said.

Dani couldn't help but groan. ''Well, maybe someone should. They've lost two babies.'' Suddenly she felt light-headed. *Did Jake Lucas lose my baby?* Her heart hammered against her ribs. *No, that's crazy, Dani. Completely illogical.*

The rep was now staring at her with scarcely concealed fury. ''Big Apple Babies helps countless people.''

His rumbling voice had turned venomously flat, and Dani realized he was hardly heartless, just hell-bent on keeping Big Apple Babies out of a lawsuit.

Not that the revelation gave her comfort. Even now she could feel her baby being wrenched away. Whisked from her arms. She could hear the one wail that had broken her heart. Big Apple Babies helped people? No, they'd taken away her newborn. Placed it where she'd never find it again.

The rep was still glaring at her.

And her insides tangled in confusion. Was Jake

Lucas this formidable? In spite of the adversarial nature of the rep's piercing green-eyed gaze, it warmed her blood. Even as her heart ached for her child, her body turned traitor, tingling with sexual longing she'd buried for years.

Fortunately Judge Lathrop spoke. "Well, everybody knows Suzanne Billings can wreak havoc. So, you all had better team up and find those kids." He glanced between the rep and Judge Winslow.

The man's dimples had vanished, and now a tick pulsed in his cheek. "Judge Lathrop, Big Apple Babies is not—I repeat, *not*—legally liable. This nurse signed—"

"I have a name," Dani snapped. "And it's Dani."

"Fine." Shooting Judge Lathrop a thoroughly aggravated glance, the Big Apple Babies rep rose with a long-suffering sigh and, when he was towering over Dani, thrust out his hand. "Jake," he growled. "Jake Lucas."

Chapter Two

Jake gripped the padded leather steering wheel and scowled moodily through the windshield of the Big Apple Babies minivan. Even if he hadn't been waiting for an opening in traffic, he'd still rather stare at Centre Street and the courthouse than at Nurse Dani. Hell, her outfit—the boxy, stiffly pressed white uniform, cardigan, white support stockings and sneakers—was so sexless that she might as well have been *Sister* Dani. God knows, she'd sure made him feel guilty enough to offer them all a ride.

His eyes slid toward her again, then past the carefully composed mask of her face, to her hair. Even a nun's habit wouldn't have helped. Visible comb marks raked through sun-streaked strands that were partially bunched in a plastic clip, and her stiff posture made Jake's own shoulders ache with tension. He could swear he was still cold, too, from the icy grip of her slender fingers when they'd shaken hands. The way she'd glared at him when he introduced himself, Jake personally could have misplaced *her* baby.

Which he most certainly had not.

The judge's voice drifted from the back seat. "Oh, Nurse Dani—"

Jake fought not to roll his eyes. When he'd offered the foursome a lift, he'd known he was bound to get at least one back seat driver. Somehow, he'd just assumed it would be the nurse or the babies. But those three had remained thankfully silent. At least so far.

Judge Winslow waved a heavily veined, liver-spotted hand as if he were a Shakespearean actor in one of the world's worst tragedies. "Nurse Dani," he continued feebly, "if you could just scoot a bit closer to Jake, so I could have a view through the windshield…"

Oh, please. The man made it sound as though he were suffering from lifelong vista deprivation, when anybody who'd ever stepped inside family court, Jake included, knew the judge was richer than Midas and could afford any view he wanted. Including one from a Fifth Avenue apartment overlooking the museum and Central Park.

Even worse, when Nurse Dani pursed her lips with distaste and inched closer, the ramrod-straight set of her shoulders announced loud and clear that she was only doing her duty to her employer, leaving Jake sorely tempted to point out that a few more scoots would land Nurse Dani's dutiful little derriere squarely in his lap.

Already she'd gotten so close he could smell beyond the starch in her dress to her more personal, feminine scent; it was enticingly soft and faintly floral and hinted that somewhere inside that oversize boxy uniform, there was actually a woman.

Not that Jake wanted to know exactly where.

He suddenly punched the gas. As the minivan darted between a taxi and a bus that was transporting recently released prisoners from Rikers Island, the nurse's palm slapped down on the dashboard in a way meant to indicate that Jake was driving too dangerously.

He wasn't. At least not for Manhattan. He shot her a swift, sideways glance. "Where are you from? Vermont?" He'd heard they still had roads there that weren't even paved.

She kept her gaze trained straight through the windshield. "If you'd simply waited, someone would have let you in."

"On Centre Street in this traffic, I sincerely doubt it," he muttered. "And what have you got against me, anyway?"

She didn't bother to look at him. "Not a thing. I just think you should be more careful. We *are* transporting babies."

Jake grunted softly, feeling murderous. Why did she keep insinuating he was unfit to care for children? And how had a woman dressed in that outfit managed to get under his skin? His voice was lower, gruffer than he intended. "I transport babies every day of my life."

"I'm sure you do."

Jake had to fight the urge to mock that snippy little tone of hers. It was positively setting his teeth on edge. He thrust out his lower lip, then worked his jaw, chewing his mustache for comfort and thinking this had to be the worst day of his life.

Not that he cared what a repressed nurse with the worst kind of New York attitude problem thought of him. He was competent. He took responsibility. And the buck always stopped with him. But he was no fool. And in situations like this, it was imperative that he follow legal procedures to the letter. Suzanne Billings might still be able to sue him, but only over his dead body.

Still, he was starting to wish Nurse Dani was at least capable of something resembling normal conversation. If nothing else, it was a long drive uptown. Street noise was pouring through the rolled-down windows of the van, but her stony silence seemed louder than all the jackhammers, horns and shouts put together. Even Jake's ex-wife, Lanie, couldn't seethe so noticeably. And that was saying something. Jake's frown deepened as he realized the two women looked somewhat alike, with light hair and dark eyes.

Of course, Lanie had been a flashier dresser. Face it, Jake thought. A potato sack would be flashier than Nurse Dani's cotton garb: at least burlap had texture. But why were those don't-touch-me vibes rolling off her?

He sighed, glancing in the rearview mirror as he turned onto Canal Street in Chinatown. Catching a last glimpse of the family court building's uninviting black facade, Jake remembered the first time he'd seen it as a child. And how years later he'd returned, dressed in a suit and carrying a briefcase, ready to set the world on fire. A wry smile twisted his lips. Oh, he supposed he'd lit his share of torches, right up until he'd burned himself out as a prosecutor.

He stopped for a light. Assuring himself he was merely bored, he ventured another sideways glance in Nurse Dani's direction. She was still staring intently ahead at some fixed point in the distance. It was as if she were a meditating monk and his windshield was the Buddha. Suddenly, without warning, Jake drew in a breath so sharp it knifed to his chest.

"What?" she snapped.

"Nothing."

But he suddenly realized why he'd been so preoccupied with her. The woman was beautiful. Absolutely, astonishingly, breathtakingly beautiful—and obviously doing everything in her power to hide it. On some subconscious level, he must have noticed.

The light changed, and he forced his attention back to the road. Two hours had passed and only now could he really see her. The vague dark smudges of her eyes were an intriguing smoked chocolate color, huge and haunting and deeply recessed in poreless, flawless skin, above pronounced cheekbones that made her look a little like Lauren Bacall.

She was tall—Jake *had* noticed that—but she'd seemed gangly, not statuesque. But now, beneath that uniform, he'd bet she was stacked. He could just make out high, firm breasts, the full kind that might beg for the touch of a man's hands in the dark. She had a slender waist. Hips a guy could squeeze and hold on to.

All of a sudden, Nurse Dani had gotten awfully interesting. Maybe it was because of her good looks. Or maybe it was because she was hiding them.

Jake's eyes narrowed. Had she been abused? He'd seen such cases countless times in family court—beautiful women who hid their feminine assets for fear of soliciting negative male attention. Maybe this was her way of making men see her in the generic—as Nurse with a capital *N*. He almost groaned aloud. *Don't get involved, Jake.* He already had the weight of the world on his shoulders, with a home life, a business to run. Not to mention a possible impending lawsuit and a hundred kids to worry about, including two missing babies. Besides, Nurse Dani looked like a tougher-than-average case, even for Jake's savior soul.

Flexing his fingers on the wheel, he tried to tell himself there was a simpler explanation for her stylistic choices than personal tragedy. Hell, maybe she was a consumer advocate who didn't believe in wearing formfitting clothes, sexy shoes or makeup. Just thinking that, he suddenly imagined her in high heels and a negligee. And then, feeling as if he'd been doused in ice water, he remembered she had him pegged as a cold, heartless SOB.

"Look," he said. "I'm really not such a bad guy."

Her chin rose a haughty notch. "I'm sure you're not."

Her tone said he was, but he decided to give it one more shot. "I think...you may have caught me at my worst today."

"I'm sure you're right."

He frowned. Now he could swear she sounded...nervous? Had they met before? Maybe in family court? Had he prosecuted a case in which she was involved? Was that the reason for her standoffish attitude? No, he would have remembered.

The judge suddenly called out, "Nurse Dani!"

She scooted again.

A slight smile lifted the corners of Jake's mustache. If he didn't know better, he'd think the old man was matchmaking. *Good luck.* Nurse Dani wouldn't give Jake the time of day if they were joined at the hip in a clock tower. Besides, although Jake had never gone before Judge Winslow during his own career, he knew his reputation. The judge had been accused of many things—being temperamental, willful and manipulative—but never of being a matchmaker.

The nurse suddenly said, "You don't have to help us."

Her tone indicated that the last thing she wanted was

help from the likes of Jake. "I don't mind," he lied. "And don't mistake my lack of enthusiasm for a lack of concern."

"Don't act concerned if you don't feel that way."

"You sure have a wicked attitude."

"I assure you, I'm not at all wicked."

Reflexively Jake's grip tightened on the wheel. Beautiful or not, she was trying his patience. He shrugged, his tone cooling considerably. "The only reason I'm here is that I have business interests to protect."

"Of course. Why else would you be here?"

Because you're beautiful. Jake sighed. "Do you want my help or not?"

"Judge Winslow and I can handle this."

"Right." Somehow Jake doubted the corners of the judge's Fifth Avenue furniture were outfitted in childproof plastic.

"Please, Nurse Dani!"

When she scooted yet another time, Jake felt the heat of her. It took away his breath. He knew he had to see her outside the minivan...to see her move, to watch how her hips and breasts swayed when she walked.

Glancing in the rearview, Jake could swear he saw a faint smile ghost over Judge Winslow's lips, as if the old man had read his thoughts. Then Jake caught Nurse Dani's dark eyes drifting over him. *She thinks I'm hot.* He realized it in a flash and decided her attitude was meant to mask her attraction.

Or maybe not. When she averted her gaze, a twinge of warning twisted in Jake's gut. He said, "Do we know each other or something?"

"No."

He squinted at her. "You're sure?"

She stared through the windshield. "If I'd met you before, I would have remembered."

It wasn't a compliment. Well, he knew he'd never seen her. He wouldn't have forgotten that face. At least not once he'd taken a good hard look at it.

"Quit staring at me!" she suddenly snapped.

How had she even caught him? She sure wasn't looking his way. Feeling annoyed, Jake merely stared harder, knowing the heat of his gaze would unsettle her. Lowering his voice persuasively, he said, "Why should I?"

Slowly, regally, she turned her head, those dark smudgy eyes smoldering with repressed sensuality. And then she very calmly said, "Because, Mr. Lucas, if you don't quit staring at me, you're going to rearend the car in front of us."

His gaze shot to the windshield. "Jake," he growled as he slammed on the brake and swerved to avoid the impending bumper. "Nurse Dani, do me one small favor and just call me Jake."

After a long moment, and when they were clear of danger, she spoke. "I guess you can call me Dani. I mean, uh, instead of *Nurse* Dani."

"Gee," Jake couldn't help but mutter. "Are you sure that wouldn't be a little too forward?"

JUDGE WINSLOW LAID his cane across his lap, as if he intended to rise and start using it at any second, then he gripped the wheels of his chair. "Nurse Dani, I could certainly use a good stiff drink."

She could barely find her voice. "No alcohol. You know the rules."

Judge Winslow's lips pursed in haughty distaste. "Mineral water, then?"

"Sure." Somehow Dani forced herself to look at Jake.

"I'll take a cup of coffee if you've got it. Instant's fine."

Dani's mouth went dry. And she couldn't move. Rather than sit on the judge's overstuffed velvet-upholstered sofa or on the Empire daybed near the French doors, Jake had claimed the only straight-backed chair. His sensual body dwarfed both it and the two blond babies who were happily crawling on the floor, pinching the toes of his shoes.

Dani swallowed around the dryness of her throat. "I'll just run to the kitchen."

And maybe she'd never come back. As soon as she made it down the hallway and shut the door between herself and Jake Lucas, she sagged against it, feeling as though she'd just emerged miraculously from a heap of smoking wreckage.

Oh, God, how could that man be Jake Lucas?

She felt as if he were still right beside her; she could smell the warm, heathery scent of his wool sweater and the shampoo from his thick, wavy hair. Her eyes shot to the kitchen window, taking in the gate and multitude of locks. She seriously considered leaving down the fire escape.

But you need this job. She had bills to pay. Rent. Tuition.

For about two hours now, her raw emotions had been in overdrive. She felt numb, shocked. Her head was spinning, her heart hammering. But now she was finally alone. Safe. And she needed to think.

She'd been so sure Jake was the Lou Grant look-alike she'd seen at Big Apple Babies. She could swear she'd heard someone call his name. How, for all these years, had she gotten things so wrong?

Year in and year out, she'd imagined Jake as that big balding bear of a man with the powerfully rounded shoulders. And oh, how she'd hated him. That first winter in New York, she'd lain awake nights on her secondhand futon, watching snow flurries spiral in the clear cold wind that tunneled down the air shaft outside her window. Millions of times, she'd conjured the image of that big, tough-looking, middle-aged Jake. She'd beat at the lapels of his dark coat with her fists, threatened him with bodily harm and cursed him with sharp-tongued speeches because he was a baby stealer. Oh, she'd made countless plans for revenge.

But *this* Jake?

Oh Lord, it wasn't fair.

She'd been tricked. She hadn't even liked him. But her body had betrayed her from the instant she'd seen him in Judge Lathrop's chambers, reacting to the penetrating slashes of his cool green eyes, the masculine scents of wool and coffee and shaving cream. Her eyes had lingered on his strong shoulders, just as her toes had curled on hearing that rumbling voice. And the second his strong, long-fingered hand folded over hers for a handshake, warmth had flooded her.

And then, only then, had she heard his damnable name.

"Jake Lucas," he'd growled as if it were any name, like John Doe or Sam Smith.

And Dani's whole world had shattered.

No, she hadn't liked him before that. But now she knew the real reason why. And anger boiled up inside her, a dangerous fury bubbling from deep within. Jake Lucas, the real Jake Lucas, was now within arm's reach, sitting right in the judge's living room. Oh, how she hated the power he so unknowingly wielded over her, because he, and only he, knew the whereabouts of her child.

Suddenly she wanted nothing more than to take the judge's gun—she knew he kept one in a bedroom drawer—and simply go get it and point it right at Jake Lucas's annoyingly broad chest and demand to know the whereabouts of her little girl.

Could she do it?

No.

But Dani sure wished she had the nerve.

She blew out a shaky sigh, knowing she was playing this all wrong. She'd been so shocked to find herself in Jake Lucas's company that she could barely speak. But now she had to figure out how to take advantage of the situation. This might be her only chance.

He was attracted to her.

That much she knew. She could even name the exact moment in the minivan when he'd decided she was beautiful. Suddenly those unnerving, perceptive eyes had narrowed, shrewdly undressing her, seemingly guessing at her motivations for hiding her looks, seemingly seeing right through to her soul.

Of course he really hadn't, she assured herself.

But had he guessed she'd recognized him? He'd asked if they'd met, but certainly he didn't realize he'd handled the adoption of her baby.

And he won't.

No doubt, Jake was acquainted with her background and the official name, Daniela Newland. But he'd never expect to find her dressed in a nurse's uniform or living in a Greenwich Village walk-up. Now, if luck held, Jake would only hear her referred to as Nurse Dani.

Besides, Jake had probably handled so many cases in his career that he wouldn't remember them all, certainly not hers. At least not without cause.

Dani fought a sudden rush of guilt. His agency *was* highly reputable. She'd checked that out six years ago. And the missing quadruplets, wherever they were, were probably safe.

But where is my child?

That was all she cared about. Pain seared through her once more as she thought of the missed milestones—the Christmases, the first steps. How, for every birthday, she'd lit a candle and blown it out, making wishes for her baby. Never once had she stopped believing in a telepathic link between mother and child, between her and her little girl. Surely her daughter always felt her love.

And soon, Dani could hold her. Because Jake Lucas was right on the other side of this door. And he knew where she was.

Dani would have to be cunning.

And she could be. For her little girl, she could do anything. Even seduce Jake Lucas if she had to. She'd find out where he kept sealed records. While he helped her look for the two missing babies, maybe she could get inside Big Apple Babies and snoop around.

It was just too bad that Jake was starting to seem like a decent guy. He had driven them all here. He'd gone through the diaper bags, too, then stopped to buy Pampers, bottles, food, extra outfits and sleepers. He'd even changed Lyssa and Kirby's diapers at the courthouse, deftly, quickly, as if he'd done it a thousand times with his eyes shut.

Well, Jake Lucas could be Gandhi.

But Dani had waited six long years to find her child.

She squared her shoulders and took a deep breath. Then she bustled around the island, quickly fixing their drinks. Biting her lips and pinching some color into her cheeks, she headed for the living room.

"Your coffee," she said.

Jake merely nodded.

Was her soft smile overkill? After all, so far she'd only scowled at him. Well, he'd warm to her. Because inside her starchy white uniform was the old Daniela Newland, and *she* could charm the pants off any man.

She watched him test-sip his coffee. Seemingly finding it temperate enough, he then downed half the cup with a gulp. Replacing the cup on a saucer, he reflexively licked at his mustache to catch any excess.

And then he noticed her smile.

His eyes said he wondered when and why she'd changed her mind and decided to play nice. But his lips smiled back.

At least Dani thought that's what they were doing beneath his mustache. Unbidden, she suddenly wondered how it might feel pressed against her lips. Bristly or soft? Coarse or featherlike? Trying to ignore how nothing more than his broadening smile warmed her, she told herself that heat flooded her only because she wanted something from this man.

Edging behind him, she glanced at the legal pad resting on his knee, noticing that his printing was neat, the letters square and masculine. "Who's Grantham Hale?" It was the only name on the pad that didn't belong to a relative of the judge's.

Jake glanced up at her. "Grantham's an ad man. He designed the Big Apple Babies logo, and he owes me one."

"For what?"

Jake shrugged. "He's a widower, but we recently helped him adopt the twins he and his wife wanted. I figured I'd call him in case I need to do any damage control."

"Damage control?"

Jake shot the judge a level glance. "If the judge or Suzanne Billings sue, maybe Grantham can recommend an image consultant for my agency." Jake arched a dark eyebrow. "Would you hand your newborn over to an adoption agency that had lost two babies?"

Dani tensed, her pulse accelerating. *I apparently did.*

"Oh, Jake!" the judge exclaimed. "I'm not really going to sue. I merely want to ensure you're doing everything possible."

The relief in Jake's eyes was unmistakable. "I am."

Dani suddenly realized how tired he looked. Like a harried businessman who was having one doozy of a day. All at once, his broad shoulders seemed to invite her fingers to rub. Quickly she distracted herself by scooping up one of the babies. It turned out to be Kirby, judging by her bracelet. Holding the little girl made Dani ache, reminding her of her own. She pressed her cheek against the few soft, sweet-smelling strands of Kirby's hair. Jake just had to tell her where he'd placed her child.

"Can you think of any other family members you haven't mentioned?" Jake said.

The judge glanced searchingly around his well-appointed apartment, toward the salmon foyer, with its potted palms and Regency mirror, then through the French doors overlooking the museum. Then he gasped. Just as quickly, he said. "Oh, dear, you can't call *her*."

Jake leaned forward. "Who?"

Judge Winslow crossed his arms and shook his head.

"Judge Winslow," Dani warned.

The judge glanced at her guiltily. "I'm sure these are my great-niece Elsie's children. She called once to see if I could baby-sit. In order to discern Elsie's whereabouts, though, we'll need to phone my sister, Gertie."

Dani's eyes narrowed. She wasn't about to let the judge tease her off the scent. "Who else?"

"I am a man of somewhat advanced years." Judge Winslow crossed his arms and furrowed his gray eyebrows. "I've outlived two wives. I have five siblings—two living, three dead. Six sons and daughters, three by each wife. Fifteen grandchildren, at least at last count. That means twenty or so great-grandchildren, and even more great-greats..."

Dani said, "What's your point?"

"That I don't know who's responsible for those...those—" Judge Winslow glared down at Lyssa and Kirby "—horrors."

Jake was clearly losing patience. "You thought of someone. Please tell us who."

Judge Winslow sighed in resignation. "Phoebe. But that great-granddaughter of mine would never have a baby, much less four. She's too unstable. Last I heard she was in terrible trouble. Well—" There was an embarrassed pause. "She *is* from the Rutherford side of the family."

"The Rutherford side?" Dani asked.

The judge merely shuddered.

Jake was scribbling. "Do you have a number for her?"

"Indeed, I do not!" The judge looked appalled. "And you mustn't seek her out. She'll probably ask for money. She's probably been put into jail by now for all I know."

Jake sighed. "I'll try your sister and the other female relatives first, then Phoebe."

The judge paled perceptibly at the idea. "I assure you, Phoebe Rutherford has bounced checks, has points against her license and was once arrested for dancing naked in a fountain. That she could be a mother is entirely unthinkable."

A tiny shiver sneaked up Dani's back. What kind of mother was she, Dani? Probably every bit as bad as Phoebe Rutherford.

The judge suddenly raised his cane and pointed toward the foyer. "Nurse Dani! Get that—that *baby* out of my palm tree!"

Dani ran and caught Kirby's ankle as she climbed into the palm tree pot. By the time Dani turned back, Jake was shrugging into his sport coat. He shoved his legal pad under his arm.

Dani leaned against the door in panic. Jake Lucas couldn't leave. Getting to know him was her only chance of finding her child. Her voice faltered. "Where are you going?"

Jake's apologetic smile deepened his dimples. "Sorry," he said, stopping in front of her. "But I've got to get home."

Home. Of course the man had a home. For so long, Dani had thought of Jake only in his professional capacity at Big Apple Babies that she'd never even considered his personal life. Her eyes darted to his left hand. There was no ring. When she glanced up again, Jake looked faintly amused.

"Divorced," he said softly.

She flushed. What was she supposed to say?

"Great" didn't seem right. Or "That's nice." She nervously shifted Kirby on her hip.

Jake lazily lifted an eyebrow. "You?"

"Me?" The leisurely way his gaze drifted over her filled her insides with butterflies and made her want to say, "Single but definitely not looking." And yet she knew she had no choice but to seduce him for information. "Uh, single, I guess."

When he smiled, his eyes narrowed, crinkling at the corners. "It's usually more clear-cut. And not one of the better things to guess about."

Feeling flustered, Dani glanced away only to find her eyes darting right back to his. Was this the last time she'd see him? To ensure it wasn't, she guessed she had no choice but to ask him on a date. "Hey, uh, Jake, would you like…"

To go out? Why couldn't she say it? Was it because she really did want to go out with him? That damnable, horrible, unwanted heat flooded her again.

He seemed to know exactly what she was thinking. "Like…?"

She couldn't do it. "Like some help getting the babies ready?"

Jake stared at her. "I'm not taking the kids."

She stared back, slack jawed. "The judge can't care for them!"

Jake shrugged. "I'm sorry, but—"

"For a minute, I was actually starting to like you. But I guess Mr. No-Legal-Responsibility has just returned."

Jake had the audacity to smile. "You were starting to like me?"

He was incorrigible. Dani clutched Kirby against her hip. "Believe me, I must have briefly lost my mind."

Jake reached beside her and rested his hand on the doorknob. "Dani, I can't be liable. Even if I wanted to take these kids, I couldn't. Legally, they have to be in the care of the judge or the signee."

Dani puffed her cheeks, then blew out a long sigh. She guessed she couldn't blame him. He could be sued and lose his business. Besides, she didn't want to alienate him; she wanted access to wherever he kept sealed records. "Signee?" she said, wondering where she'd have to take the babies next.

He stared at her for a long moment. "Uh...in legalese, I'm sorry to report that means you."

"But I can't—"

"If it's any help, I'll come back tomorrow. We can head over to the Sixth Precinct, track down the judge's relatives, shop for some more clothes for the kids...whatever you need."

Flinty anger sparked inside her. "What am I supposed to do? Stay here with Judge Winslow?"

"You can't," the judge interjected. "Nurse Melinda—who sometimes lets me smoke a good Cuban cigar, I might add—comes at night, and she needs the guest room."

Dani shot the judge a cold stare. Then her eyes pierced Jake's. "Should Melinda watch them?"

Jake shook his head. "Technically, they're your responsibility. From a legal standpoint, you should take them home."

She simply couldn't believe this. Six years ago Jake Lucas had ruined her life by taking away her baby. And now he was trying to leave two little girls in her care. Not that she didn't want them, but... "I can't stay here. And I can't take two babies to my apartment. I don't even have a crib. Are you crazy?"

"Really," Jake said firmly. "I wish I could stay."

Dani rolled her eyes. "Oh, I'll bet."

"I do."

"Then why don't you?"

"Because I have to pick up my son."

"COME ON…" Jake leaned in the stairway outside her fifth-floor apartment. "At least let me come in and help you set up."

Dani backed against the door, feeling breathless, either from the walk upstairs or Jake's proximity, she wasn't sure which. He'd insisted on stopping and buying her a crib and a more manageable two-seat stroller. But now she couldn't risk having him come inside; he might see her mail or magazine subscriptions, something with her full name on it. "Thanks, but that's okay."

Jake stared curiously at her door. "You don't look like the messy type."

She wasn't. "You never know."

His mouth quirked. "Hiding lovers?"

"The place is too small. More than one wouldn't fit."

His smile deepened, dimpling his cheeks. "But there is room for one?"

Jake clearly meant himself. All she'd done was smile at the guy, and now he'd become an unconscionable flirt. She blew out a piqued sigh. "For all I know, you might be an ax murderer." Actually, he was worse she reminded herself. He was Jake Lucas.

"I look like an ax murderer?"

"No," Dani conceded, "but this is New York City." She glanced at Lyssa and Kirby, who were parked at her feet, then shot Jake another wry smile.

"Besides, I'm not exactly thrilled about this situation, and your son is waiting for you."

Jake shrugged. "Okay, then. See you tomorrow."

With a final, inquisitive glance, Jake headed down the stairs and Dani watched his long-limbed gait, how his thighs worked beneath his slacks. When she was sure he was gone, she pushed the stroller through the door, then hauled the unassembled crib inside.

Jake Lucas has a son, she thought as she pieced the crib together. Dani should have known. All these years she'd been childless, only able to imagine her little girl ripping wrappers off candy packages at Easter and dressing up like a goblin on Halloween.

But all along, Jake Lucas had been raising a child.

Dani didn't know why it hurt so much. Why it made her hate him all over again. But it did. The man had so much love in his life. A son. All those babies at his adoption agency. *And all I want is one baby—mine.*

Finishing with the crib, Dani scooped up Lyssa. "You look so sleepy, sweetheart." Ever so gently, she laid Lyssa down, then placed her sister right beside her. Leaning over the crib, she rubbed each baby until they stretched and offered tiny yawns, their little eyes drifting shut.

"Are you two going to help me study tonight?" she whispered, glancing at her textbooks and wondering how she'd concentrate. "Well, don't you worry. We'll find your sisters. I betcha they look just like you, which'll make it easier."

At least Jake seemed convinced the mystery would be solved by tomorrow. And Dani almost believed him. Beneath his surface edginess, the man possessed a quiet strength she was drawn to, like a moth to flame.

Suddenly panic fluttered inside her. After six long

years, Jake Lucas was finally in her life. Even better, the man was attracted to her. And even worse, he seemed like a nice guy.

At least he would be unless you crossed him.

And Dani was about to cross him, all right.

First she had to get anything with her full name on it out of sight. She sighed and glanced around. Like most apartments in the West Village, hers was tiny. Because the building was irregularly shaped—wedged on the cozy corner where Charles and Waverly streets met Seventh Avenue—her living room was nearly triangular and her bedroom too small for anything more than a single bed.

She began rifling through drawers for NYNEX and Con Edison bills, scanning tabletops, checking envelopes shoved between the books on her bookshelf.

"There," she murmured when she was sure she'd collected everything. If Jake came over, he'd never realize who she was. Shoving magazines and bills under her arm, she headed for the kitchen.

It was the only square room in the apartment, but it still possessed its oddities. It had no sink, for instance—that was in the living room—and the only window faced the neighbor's, over the foot of an air shaft. Not that Dani wanted more usual quarters. At least that's what she always told herself. The city had been her haven, a place to anonymously lick her wounds. Besides, as far as cities went, New York had a lot of heart. Dani opened her fridge, shoving her mail into the vegetable bin.

"I thought you were supposed to read your bills, not chill them. What will the IRS have to say about this?"

Dani gasped, and with her hand pressed to her heart, whirled around. "Trevor," she said flatly.

Both windows—Dani's and the kitchen window opposite—were wide open, and sixteen-year-old Trevor
Marpas was grinning at Dani over the air shaft. He had
beige hair so frizzily curly that it was easy to imagine
his silver mouthful of braces had conducted too much
electricity. He and his mother, Maureen, lived in the
apartment right across from Dani's, and Trevor had a
long-standing habit of unlatching Dani's window
screen and conversing with her over the air shaft.

Dani stared pointedly at Trevor. "You scared me to
death."

The teenager, who was far too smart for his own
good, merely grinned again and said, "True. But at
least I don't freezer-burn my issues of Playboy."

"You subscribe to no such thing."

Trevor merely laughed and stretched a long, gangly
arm over the meager foot of the air shaft. His hand,
holding out a tall plastic cup filled with ice cubes, appeared over Dani's windowsill. He shot Dani another
endearing grin. "For just one glass of soda, I'll read
you your horoscope from the *Post.*" Suddenly Trevor's
brown eyes bugged. "Are those babies?"

Trevor looked so shocked, Dani burst out laughing.
She told Trevor about the day's events as she headed
for the fridge again, got a bottle of soda, then filled
Trevor's cup. His arm vanished over her windowsill
and the cup clunked on the Marpas's window-side table.

"So," Trevor said when she finished. "Tell me
these aren't the kind of babies that cry. You know, loud
and late at night."

"Of course not." Her mouth quirked. "These are
those other kind of babies."

Trevor's eyes narrowed playfully. "And should I be jealous of this guy you just met, Jake?"

Jake. Just hearing the name made unexpected heat coil inside her. Why did he, of all people, have to be the lawyer who'd handled her baby? Somehow she kept her tone light. "Now, Trevor, I refuse to respond." Dani sat at her own kitchen table. "Oh, and while the babies are here, this screen stays shut." As if to prove her point, Dani swung the screen into place and latched it.

Trevor pressed his palms together, prayerlike, and inclined his head in a bow. "My wish is your command."

"I mean it, Trevor."

He threw up his hands. "Do I look like the kind of guy who would willingly endanger rug rats?"

Her lips twitched. "No. I didn't mean to imply you did."

Trevor sent her a mock glare through the screen, then he took his gulp of soda and started turning the pages of the *Post*. "Well," he said. "For once, your horror-scope doesn't say it's the end of the world."

Dani realized she'd been staring at the babies sleeping in the other room again, and glanced at Trevor, feeling almost curious. Lately her horoscope had been the voice of gloom and doom. The *Post* had repeatedly instructed her to watch out for black cats and ladders and to be careful what she wished for. "What's it say now?"

"You mean about you and this Jake guy?"

Dani rolled her eyes. "C'mon. What's it say?"

"It says, 'Tomorrow, all your dreams come true. Expect love to come knocking. If you are ready to answer the door, you will finally find what you have long sought.'"

Dani's throat went dry. *What I have long sought.* The words reverberated in her mind. Soon her little girl would be in her arms. Dani could feel it deep inside her, with the strength of a premonition. And yet she scarcely dared to hope. Her heart squeezed tight and her voice trembled. "And then I win a million bucks in the lotto, right, Trev?"

Trevor shook his head. "Nope. Tomorrow you just get love and dreams."

Love and dreams. *Oh please, God,* Dani suddenly prayed.

It was all she wanted in the world.

Chapter Three

"Love and dreams," Dani whispered the following day, glimpsing Jake through the peephole as he knocked.

Opening Judge Winslow's door, she found herself staring from Jake down to the cutest little boy in the world. With a quick toss of his head, he shook away the shaggy medium blond bangs that dusted his eyebrows, then he squinched up his face and scrutinized her with doe-brown eyes. He was carrying a backpack, so he was probably already in school, and his jeans jacket, tan corduroy slacks and neat plaid shirt looked suspiciously new. Slicking a palm down the side of his pants, he thrust out a pint-size hand.

"I'm Tyler Lucas."

"I'm Nurse Dani." Dani leaned down and gave the small hand her most firm, serious handshake. "But you can just call me Dani."

He looked pleased. "Hey, you can call me somethin' shorter, too. Daddy calls me Ty."

"Okay, Ty."

As Dani rose, she did a quick inventory of his father, her eyes flickering over the stonewashed jeans hugging his muscular thighs, the simple black belt. He wore another V-necked sweater today, this one black, and a tweed sport coat draped his powerful shoulders.

Her voice came out sounding throaty. "Hey there."

"Hey there, yourself."

Nothing had changed since yesterday. His voice still rippled through her like no other man's ever had. Like a jewel being dropped into her bloodstream, it sent waves through her, all the way to her extremities, until her fingertips tingled and her shoulders lifted with a tiny shiver.

Here we go again. Clenching her teeth, Dani tried to stir up some cold-blooded hatred. She remembered how, six years ago, she'd entered a hospital barely more than a girl. And come out a woman. She reminded herself that Jake was the man who'd taken away her baby. That those large, strong hands of his had held her little girl, when her own hadn't. And that she was merely using him.

But it was hard. Especially since his perceptive eyes were taking their own inventory, lazily drifting over her, leaving bold licks of heat in their wake. She told herself that imaginary tongue didn't really graze her breasts, that he was just eyeing the nameplate on her uniform pocket that said Dani.

But she knew better. Even though Jake didn't move a muscle, the burning touch of his hand suddenly seemed to trace the path his eyes had just taken.

It didn't. But it felt that way.

Hours later, in a back corner of the loud Sixth Precinct on Hudson Street, with Ty playing with the babies and uniformed cops milling around them, Jake's penetrating eyes were still on her, making her feel all knotted up inside.

She felt overly conscious of her appearance, too. Of

how she'd worn her hair down around her shoulders today for him. And how she'd put on makeup, just light smears of eye shadow, blush and lip gloss. It had been so long since she'd gussied up that it had taken her a full hour to find her makeup bag. She'd had to go out to a drugstore to buy the lip gloss.

She realized Jake was frowning.

"What?"

"Are you sure Judge Winslow is all right on his own?"

Dani didn't know which warmed her more, Jake's voice or his concern. Either way, she felt as if a luscious, lapping whirlpool had taken up residence in her belly. She chuckled softly. "No. Judge Winslow won't be all right. He'll rustle up the booze he no doubt hides somewhere, fix himself a stiff drink, then crank open the kitchen window and smoke a foot-long Cuban cigar."

Jake laughed. "Why did he bother to hire a nurse?"

Dani shrugged. "He may be eighty-five, but he's not used to having limited mobility. And he's smart enough to know he needs someone to save him from himself. Besides, he's got a cell phone attached to his wheelchair. He'll be fine."

Jake lifted a hand and absently pinched his mustache. "You don't mind doing the legwork to find the kids?"

"He threatened to withhold my paycheck if I don't."

"I guess you did ask the building personnel to spy on him during their breaks today."

Dani laughed, her eyes straying down to Ty, who was amusing the little girls with a rattle. "I said *check* on the judge."

"Maybe, but everybody knew what you really meant."

Dani lifted her gaze again, then wished those dazzling green eyes would quit making her melt. Even as something deep inside her softened, even as she felt heat drizzle at her core, she tried to tell herself it was only because Jake knew the whereabouts of her child. But it was a lie. For the first time in six long years, Dani desperately wanted a man. She wanted him. Feeling sure he could read the naked emotion in her eyes, Dani glanced away.

Jake stared toward a uniformed sergeant's office. "Well, with any luck, they've found something. If not, I can at least give the sergeant all the information we got yesterday from Judge Winslow." Leaning, Jake lifted his legal pad from the rack beneath the stroller.

Dani cleared her throat. "Go ahead and talk to the sergeant. I'll stay here with the kids."

He nodded.

Ty stared up from the stroller. "Can I stay with Dani, too?" he asked, clearly not realizing he was one of the kids.

Jake smiled. "Yeah. On one condition."

"What?"

"You do everything she says."

Ty giggled and pointed to a vending machine near the door. "But what if Dani told me to get ten candy bars and eat 'em all?"

"Every last one of them?" Jake shot his son a wry, lopsided smile. "Well, then, I guess you'd have to do it, Ty."

Ty smiled up sweetly at Dani. "May I *please* have a candy bar?"

He was so incredibly adorable that Dani wanted to

say he really could have ten. Suddenly, remembering his father was in charge, she glanced uncertainly at Jake. He smiled back. Reaching into his pocket, he brought out a handful of change and dumped it into Dani's palm. At the contact, she felt as if a long fingernail had just drawn slow, lazy circles up her spine.

Her eyes found Jake's. "I promise we won't spend it all in one place."

Jake wagged a playful finger between her and Ty. "And you two better share."

Ty jumped up and down. "We will, Daddy."

Affectionately tousling his son's shaggy hair, Jake headed for the sergeant's office. Dani watched him go, her eyes trailing from his long legs to the thick, wavy black hair that brushed the collar of his sport coat. There was tension in his strong shoulders and rangy, roving gait. The same tension she'd seen in Judge Lathrop's chambers, and sometimes in his eyes. It was the sudden unmasking of whatever made him tick. A flicker of anger, maybe. As if something bothered Jake Lucas so deep down that he wasn't even really aware of it.

Feeling a tug on her uniform, she glanced down at Ty. "Hmn?"

"Are you lookin' at my dad?"

"Yeah," she admitted.

"Is he cute?"

"Uh..." While she didn't want to admit her attraction, she could hardly tell a kid his own dad wasn't cute, especially when it would be such a blatant lie. Fortunately, Ty didn't seem to expect a response. Gripping her hand, he tugged her toward the vending machine. "Wait," Dani said, grabbing the stroller and pushing the babies alongside Ty.

"You get to pick which kind of candy bar," Ty announced when they reached the vending machine. "But then you gotta tell me about my dad."

"Well, here. You drop in the quarters."

After Ty did so, Dani pulled the lever for a Snickers bar.

Ty gasped. "How'd you know Snickers was my favorite?"

Dani chuckled. "I read minds."

Ty rolled his eyes. "Do not."

"Do too."

While Ty merrily scooped the candy bar from the machine's bin, Dani glanced toward the sergeant's office. Through a glass door, she could see Jake, his broad back turned away from her. Realizing Ty was watching her, Dani tilted her head this way and that, as if considering.

"Well?" Ty demanded.

"Yeah, he's cute. At least from behind." Then she smiled at Ty and pointed toward some empty chairs that lined a far wall. "Let's sit over there."

Once they were seated, Ty ripped the paper from the Snickers bar. Lyssa and Kirby peered up longingly. Ty frowned. "Can the babies have Snickers?"

Dani's eyebrows furrowed. "I think they're better off with their juice. It's healthier."

Ty crinkled his nose as if deep in thought, then he split the candy bar. For a long moment, he carefully compared his and Dani's halves to make sure they were exactly even. Handing Dani hers, he said, "Why do you get to do everything more unhealthier when you get older?"

"You don't, really. It just seems that way."

"Oh." Wolfing down his chocolate, Ty seemed lost

in thought. Dani decided that Jake's son was every bit as heart stopping as the man himself. Her smile turned wistful, and she realized Jake's wife had probably been beautiful. Suddenly she noticed the little boy's eyes had turned sad.

"You okay, Ty?"

He gazed up at her worriedly, then glanced around the precinct. "If I turn up missing, would Daddy come here real fast and look for me?"

"Oh, honey, of course he would."

Instinctively Dani put her arm around Ty's shoulders and drew him close. He sank against her side, nestling his head against her while he licked chocolate from his fingertips. Sighing, Dani thought of how she'd awakened in the night, holding Lyssa and Kirby when they'd cried, offering comfort until their small sobs ceased. She'd felt so strong and needed, as if she really were a mother. Now she slid her palm down the length of Ty's arm and gave it a reassuring rub.

He looked up at her again. "Could the police put the babies' pictures on a milk carton or somethin'?"

"The police will do everything they can," Dani said firmly. "And don't forget, your daddy's good at his job. Everybody at Big Apple Babies is looking. Wherever Lyssa and Kirby's sisters are, we're sure they're just fine."

Ty looked marginally convinced. "But if we don't find 'em, does my dad gotta get a new job?"

She shook her head. "No. And besides, we'll find them soon. I promise."

"Well, maybe Daddy could adopt 'em." Lifting his chin, Ty smiled bravely. And then, just as abruptly as his mood had darkened, Ty grinned, licking his upper lip for missed traces of chocolate. "Oh, hey," he said in a complete non sequitur, "did Daddy tell you 'bout my new room?"

Dani shook her head. "New room?"

Ty rushed headlong into a description of his bedroom, which had been redecorated with a dinosaur theme. Just as anxious to talk about his dad, Ty said Jake had been divorced forever. He hated to shave, but he liked Yankees games, eating Chinese takeout and reading the *New York Times* in his underwear on Sundays. Rather than having his son for the weekend, which is what Dani had assumed, Jake was a full-time father. About his mother, Ty only angrily said he didn't have one, and Dani guessed Jake's divorce had been messy.

After one of Ty's longer speeches, this one about the rigors of first grade, he stopped breathlessly and said, "I really, really like you a lot, Dani. You *swear* you think my daddy's real cute from behind?"

Dani chuckled softly. "I swear."

A deep voice suddenly rumbled from above. "Cross your heart and hope to die?"

Dani glanced up to find Jake staring down at her, his eyes bright and his lips twitching. Color flooded her cheeks.

Jake raised a dark eyebrow and covered his heart with his hand as if mortally wounded. "I'm only cute from behind?"

Dani managed to shoot him a playful smile, glancing around the precinct. "I'd answer, but somehow this doesn't seem like the place."

"Then we'd better go someplace else." Jake reached down and offered her his hand. Dani let him pull her to her feet and another warm tingle spread through her as she bounced against his chest.

Ty gave his dad's pant leg a hard tug. "Dani invited herself to dinner with us, Daddy."

Dani stared at Ty. "Did not!"

Ty giggled naughtily but didn't retract the lie. Instead, he hiked his pants, squatted in front of the stroller and began studiously teasing Lyssa and Kirby.

Jake's bemused gaze followed his son. "Well, since the police haven't made much progress, we need to pick up some more things for these kids before anybody eats." Suddenly he frowned. When concern touched his eyes, it deepened their color to the green of a thick forest.

"What?" Dani said.

Jake shrugged. "I can't requisition petty cash from Big Apple Babies since the girls aren't legally in our care, but...I can buy a few more things out of pocket."

"Uh, I'm still in school, but I don't mind spending whatever I can."

Respect shone in Jake's eyes. "Of course not. I'll buy the stuff."

The man was definitely endearing himself more and more to her. How could she have hated him all these years? Noticing the collar of his sport coat was upturned, she reached and gently smoothed it against his collarbone, her fingers lingering longer than they should have. "What? Are you secretly a soft touch?"

Jake smiled. "I don't know if I'm a soft touch, but I can sure touch softly."

Dani's eyes shot to Ty, but the little boy hadn't noticed the flirtation. Sighing more wistfully than she'd intended, she said, "Oh, I'll bet you can."

Jake's answering chuckle was husky, inviting. As he placed a warm hand beneath her elbow, he leaned close and whispered, "You don't need to gamble on it. You can be absolutely sure."

DANI RAISED HER VOICE. "What in the world's going on in there?"

There was no response.

Feeling panicked, she hurried from the kitchen toward the judge's living room. Nurse Melinda had called to say she'd be late, and somehow—Dani wasn't quite sure how—the matchmaking judge had wound up inviting Jake and Ty for dinner.

Now Dani was afraid the cartoons blaring from the television would make the judge cranky, and she'd just hate for poor little Ty to get an earful of the old man's surly tongue. *I never should have left those two together so long.* But then it had been so easy—*too* easy, she told herself—to stay in the kitchen, chatting with Jake.

When she reached the living room, she stopped in her tracks. Then a slow smile spread over her lips. She should have known. Judge Winslow was every bit as defenseless against that adorable little boy as she was.

The judge was hunched in his wheelchair, facing the TV and holding a baby in each arm. Lyssa was punching the channel changer to no avail, while Kirby tugged at the judge's nose with her tiny fingers.

Not that Judge Winslow seemed to notice. He was staring down at Ty, who was sprawled in front of the wheelchair, his backpack open, various markers strewn across the hardwood floor. Ty's tongue rested on his upper lip in concentration, and there was a meager inch between his nose and the judge's cast, which was now covered with brightly colored drawings. At the moment, Ty was creating a green-and-purple beast with a giant head, jagged teeth and a big spiked tail that spanned the cast from knee to toe.

Dani frowned, wondering if she should remind the judge that he'd be obliged to wear the decorated cast around Central Park. Instead she said, "What a wonderful dragon."

Judge Winslow tried to shoot her his usual scowl, but failed. "It's a dinosaur," he corrected loftily.

Fortunately, Ty didn't seem to notice Dani's mistake. "Dinosaur," she repeated. Then, raising her voice, "Ready for dinner?"

Ty glanced up. "Judge Winslow says we gotta eat out here 'cause he always watches my favorite cartoons when he eats."

The acerbic judge always ate in stony silence, unless the slow-crinkling pages of his newspapers counted. Dani shot the judge a smile. "Oh, does he?"

Ty started boxing up his pens. "That's what he said."

Dani knew if there was one thing the old man hated, it was being caught in the act of being an old softie. Now his eyes narrowed to bright blue slashes. "Please, Nurse Dani, dispense with these babies!"

Unfooled by the tone, Ty giggled. Before Dani could scurry across the room, he'd hopped up and very carefully moved the wiggling girls from the judge's arms to the floor. Then Ty got behind the judge's wheelchair and, with a great heave-ho, helped maneuver the judge to a desk, where the two apparently meant to dine.

Without me and Jake. Dani frowned as she headed toward the kitchen again, wondering if Ty and the judge had knocked heads and conspired to matchmake. Not that she minded the idea of eating alone with Jake, she thought as he helped her fix two heaping plates.

She returned to the living room, the plates in either hand trailing sweet-smelling streamers of steam. "Here we go," she said.

The judge stared down and sniffed.

"You said prawns and vegetables with Szechuan sauce," Dani warned.

Catching Ty's eye, the judge seemingly decided not to deny it and gave one quick nod of his head. "So I did."

Ty didn't bother to scrutinize his dinner. The instant Dani handed him a fork, he started shoveling in rice and vegetables. Between bites, he said, "I betcha Daddy's getting awfully lonely."

"Nurse Dani," Judge Winslow said, lifting a broccoli top with his fork and peering suspiciously beneath it as if he fully expected something to lunge out at him. "Your job is to help safeguard my home while I'm too immobile to defend myself. So I can't allow you to leave complete strangers like Jake Lucas prowling around my kitchen."

Ty giggled, and Dani glanced sternly between the boy and older man, her own barely suppressed smile tugging at the corners of her lips. "You two should mind your own business."

Judge Winslow merely shrugged and began removing all his snow peas to the side of his plate. "But young Mr. Lucas reported to me that you thought his father had a cute behind."

Ty giggled again.

Dani flushed. "I said he was cute *from* behind. That's hardly the same thing."

"Maybe. But he won't have a behind at all if he starves to death."

Dani turned.

Jake was lounging lazily against the doorjamb, watching her. For a fleeting second, she thought she saw wariness in his gaze and she felt thoroughly unsettled, as if he'd looked straight through her eyes to her duplicitous soul. The very air around him seemed to snap with whatever angry energy he held inside him, but then he suddenly smiled, and the impression was gone.

"How long have you been there?"

Jake shrugged. He'd removed his sport coat, and his black sweater now stretched over his chest, looking as dark and touchable as velvet. "Too long."

She headed toward him. "Well, I'm coming."

"Good, because I'm wasting away."

Dani smirked and gave him a quick once-over. Every inch was rock-hard muscle. "Oh, yeah," she said dryly. "You look like you're about to perish."

When they'd almost reached the kitchen, Jake draped his arm around her, cupping her shoulder with a palm. "I really will perish if you don't let me kiss you."

Dani's mouth went dry. No doubt their easy flirtation made him think she was more experienced than she really was. But she'd only been with one man. She tried to keep her tone light. "Go ahead."

Jake merely laughed, the touch of his palm becoming a slow, tantalizing caress. "You really think your kisses make better appetizers than desserts?"

She tamped down a flush. "Why not a main course?"

"Because I'd rather drive you crazy by making you wait."

She chuckled. "What? You intend to kiss me back to mental health?"

"Or make you crazier."

She couldn't help but shoot him a saucy smile. "I thought a guy's final goal was the bedroom. Not a padded cell."

They'd reached the kitchen door. Jake turned to her, his smile no longer meeting his eyes, the green irises darker, almost smoky. "Just where do you want me to take you?"

For a moment she couldn't find her voice. *Into those strong arms of yours, Jake—and to heaven.* That was her first thought. Her second was, *to wherever you put my baby.*

His voice was silken. "Dani?"

"Directly to my dinner," she said. "I'm starved."

Jake pointed. *"Voilà."* He pushed open the kitchen door, then held it, nodding for her to precede him.

Feeling him behind her, Dani blew out a nervous sigh. She suddenly felt all tangled up again, as if everything were moving too fast. Oh, Jake's kiss would be heaven. But hell was right around the corner. She wasn't exactly lying to him, but she sure wasn't telling the truth. Why, of all the men on earth, did she have to be this attracted to Jake Lucas?

Silently they scooted onto stools side by side at the island table. Dani peered inside the white cardboard containers as Jake filled their plates.

"Chopsticks?" he offered.

She took a pair. "Sure."

Then they dug in, too hungry to talk. They'd almost cleaned their plates before Dani's nerves settled. Then she started going over what they'd done this afternoon: in addition to visiting the precinct, they'd called some of the judge's relatives, including a distant cousin who, to the judge's great dismay, was now planning a Winslow-Rutherford reunion. Phoebe Rutherford was no-where to be found.

Dani dabbed the corners of her mouth with a napkin. "And other people at Big Apple Babies are working on this, too?"

Jake nodded, lifting a baby ear of corn with his chop-sticks, then munching it down. "Winston Holiday's one of the most conscientious employees I've got. And James Sanger stayed until midnight making calls. He'll be the one facing Suzanne Billings in court."

"Not you?"

Jake shrugged. "I concentrate on running the place. And I'm interviewing new caseworkers this week, to replace Larry McDougal."

Catching her worried expression, Jake reached over and squeezed her shoulder with slow, reassuring pres-sure. "We're calling all over town. Those kids are safe. It's just a matter of time until we find them."

"I believe you. I don't know why, but I do." He was so strong. So competent and responsible. Dani sighed. "It's just that I feel accountable since I signed for them. And I feel like..."

"Like we were having fun today while two kids were missing?"

Pushing her plate aside, Dani nodded. While shop-ping for the babies today, Jake had acted more like a kid than an adult in a toy store—playing miniature bas-ketball with foam balls and putt-putt on a pint-size green, buying Ty a stuffed dinosaur that had made the boy's eyes brighten with delight.

Fun? Dani wasn't even sure the word covered what she'd felt. It had been six years since she'd laughed like that. Six long years since she'd let herself go with a man. Lord, she'd forgotten how attractive nothing more than a man's undivided attention could make her feel.

Jake's attention.

It was focused on her now, the searing intensity of those eyes making her blood warm, and suddenly she felt even more—the warmth of his hand closing over her own. She glanced up, startled, but she couldn't bring herself to pull away.

He stared deeply into her eyes. "I promise I'll find them."

"I know."

He leaned closer. "Look, I know you probably think I can seem too…detached."

Dani shook her head in denial. She knew he was the sort of man who could care deeply, with his whole heart and soul. "Maybe at first," she admitted. "But now I know you better."

He sighed. "I didn't want to sound cold in Judge Lathrop's chambers. But in my line of work, you've got to watch it. I actually started out as a family court prosecutor."

Dani had just assumed he'd always been an adoption lawyer. Her mouth quirked. "A prosecutor? A nice guy like you could grill somebody on the stand?" she teased.

He smiled. "Could and did. Was damn good at it, too. Though who knows what might have become of me if I'd ever gone before Judge Winslow. He's got a reputation for making lawyers quake in their loafers."

Dani glanced down pointedly at Jake's Doc Martens. "You don't even wear loafers."

"True." Jake chuckled. "Still, I assure you that beneath my own sweet smile lurks the heart of a killer shark."

Dani tilted her head and surveyed him as if from a distance. "I don't know about your being a killer shark, but you're sure killer handsome."

His grin deepened his dimples. "So they say."

In the pause that followed, Dani became conscious of the TV blaring from the living room. Closer, balmy autumn air drifted in through the open kitchen window. And even closer than that, deep inside her, she felt her own internal weather shifting. Inside, it was more like spring than autumn. Without even knowing it, Jake was making her stir like a bulb in April rain. Listening to the far-off traffic sounds coming in through the window and still gazing into Jake's eyes, she breathed in deeply, smelling the herblike scents of leaves from Central Park.

"Coffee?" she finally asked.

"Sure."

"Black?"

He nodded. "Same as yesterday."

She edged her hand from beneath his, then headed for the counter, poured two mugs and returned. "Why'd you quit being a prosecutor?"

He shrugged. "I prosecuted mostly abuse cases."

"Child abuse?"

"Yeah. That's where I learned the value of detachment. You can't save everybody, and if you don't let go, you just burn out and wind up not helping a soul. Like now, with these missing kids. All we can do is look."

"It must have been difficult," Dani murmured.

Jake shrugged, breaking the mood with a soft chuckle. "No more difficult than anything else."

For a long moment, Dani merely watched him sip his coffee, feeling sure Jake Lucas was everything she'd ever wanted in a man. He was so strong and responsible, but not domineering. And if there was one thing Dani hated in a man—or feared—it was a domineering spirit. She sighed. Jake deserved a lot better than her lies.

But she had to find her child.

She lifted her own mug and took a nervous sip. "I think, uh, being an adoption lawyer could be just as hard as being a prosecutor."

Jake glanced at her, considering. "It's mostly rewarding. People who want kids are grateful to get them. It's only bad when people give up babies then change their minds. Usually they hire lawyers to approach us."

Dani's chest squeezed so tight it was painful. For a second, she could barely breathe. "Well, they deserve to know where their children are."

Jake shrugged, his voice taking on a discernible edge. "I tend to side with the adoptive parents."

Dani wanted to persist, to make Jake admit that biological parents' rights were more important. If only he shared her views, then maybe she could tell him the truth and what she wanted from him. "Well," Dani ventured carefully, "you do keep records carefully sealed."

"We keep files under lock and key."

She tried not to look too interested. "On the premises?"

He nodded. "Sure. But there's never been a problem. I even keep an extra key to the room in my own office." Jake's eyes suddenly narrowed. "Speaking of the office..."

When his voice trailed off, Dani felt the fear of God shoot through her. Had Jake somehow realized who she was and what she wanted? Her voice caught. "The office?"

"Ty's got a karate tournament tomorrow. But if you wanted to go through my office, to see if you can find any papers Rosita might have left..." He shrugged again. "I already looked, but you might find something."

Dani forced a smile. "Trying to put me to work?"

He grinned. "Bad habit."

Her throat was bone dry, her heart racing. "I don't mind stopping by Big Apple Babies tomorrow," she said. "It's right over on Waverly Place, right?"

He nodded.

She knew exactly where it was. To hide her nervousness, she focused on smoothing her uniform skirt. "I guess I could run over in the morning. Do I need a key or anything?"

"You sure? I know it's your day off. Maybe you could meet Ty and me afterward if you don't have to study."

The respect she saw in Jake's eyes actually hurt. He trusted her. Liked her because he thought she was the kind of woman who would donate her time and energy to help strangers. Instead, she was a rotten liar with her own agenda. And tomorrow, she was going to ransack his office.

"I'll be glad to help," she said.

The next thing she knew, Jake was handing her the key to his interior office. On her outstretched palm, the metal felt as cold as the guilt in her heart. But Dani tried to tell herself she didn't care. By this time tomorrow, she'd know the name of the couple who had her little girl.

Somehow she mustered a bright smile. "So, tell me more about your business."

Jake's eyes suddenly twinkled. "Well, actually, Big Apple Babies' initial financial backers are a complete mystery to me."

Dani stared at him. "What?"

"It's true." Jake chuckled softly. "I was at the end of my rope. Burnt out as a prosecutor. And my marriage to Lanie was breaking up."

So Lanie was his wife's name. Dani started to ask what had happened, but it wasn't the right time, so she simply said, "Rough times?"

"The worst. I'd been working fourteen, sixteen hours a day."

Dani groaned. "Well, everybody in Manhattan works too hard. They don't call it the rat race for nothing."

Jake shrugged. "And I loved it, too. But Ty came along and I wanted a life. And then one day—you're really not going to believe this—"

"What?"

"I got an anonymous check for seven million dollars and directions to open Big Apple Babies."

The words were so unexpected that Dani laughed. "You're kidding."

But Jake's eyes were dead serious. "It's true. I got a check and a letter telling me which building to buy. Look on my office wall tomorrow. The letter's framed." He suddenly smiled again, as if the amazement were still fresh. "Hell, I was sure the check would bounce."

Dani had forgotten everything but Jake's wild tale. "But it didn't?"

Jake shook his head. "To this day, I haven't the

faintest idea who gave me the start-up money. Or why.'' He raised an eyebrow. ''Buildings in Manhattan don't come cheap. Of course, now the agency more or less runs itself, though the few times I've needed a cash infusion, it's magically appeared.''

''You just get a check in the mail?''

''Yeah. From some secret philanthropist, I guess.''

Dani squinted at him. ''And the headers on the checks don't offer a name?''

''Nope. None whatsoever.''

Some things really could restore one's faith in the human race, Dani decided. ''Any rich people in your family? Zillionaires you haven't told me about?'' Guiltily she thought of her own privileged background, and realized Jake probably would never guess at it.

Jake shrugged. ''My parents are both lawyers here in New York. And they weren't exactly thrilled when I opened the agency.''

All at once, Dani sensed that edginess emanating from Jake again. Restless and searching, it came from him like heat, like his life force. Just feeling it, Dani tensed, too. ''But you've clearly done so well for yourself.''

His narrowing eyes met hers, and the assessing gaze made her feel as if she were about to be given a test. ''Maybe they thought I'd start looking for my birth parents,'' he said. ''I'm adopted. It's why I eventually chose adoption law.''

Dani tried not to react. So that was it. Like her own child, Jake was adopted. In that flash, Dani understood him. She thought of the children he'd defended by prosecuting abusive adults. Of the full custody he had of his son. Of all the kids at Big Apple Babies who needed him. She hadn't imagined his anger, after all.

Jake had never forgiven the parents whom he felt had abandoned him. That was what drove him so hard, the need to be needed, wanted.

"So, you've never looked for your birth parents?" she probed gently.

Jake shrugged almost casually, as if the thought had never crossed his mind. "My adoptive parents raised me, gave me the world. Helped me in my chosen profession. At Big Apple Babies, I've helped other couples find the kind of happiness my own parents got from me. My birth parents…"

Gave me away.

Dani wanted to deny it, to explain, to make excuses for Jake's biological mother. What if Dani's own child harbored resentments? "And you never looked for where the money came from, either?"

Jake shook his head.

He was a strange man, she decided, forcing herself not to dwell on the many ways in which his life experience touched hers. Trying to lighten the conversation, she said, "How can you live with so much mystery?"

At that, he suddenly chuckled. "Oh, I don't know. How can *you?*"

She laughed. "No mystery here." As Jake leaned closer, her breath caught. With sudden insight, she realized he was going to kiss her. And oh, how she wanted him to. She might be playing him for a fool, but she had to know if this man's chest was as hard as it looked. If his skin was as smooth. If his lips were as soft.

And then there was the fact that she hadn't been kissed in six long years. And never by a man like Jake.

Jake's palm slid up the sleeve of her uniform, then

beneath her hair and cupped her nape. His voice was a low rumble. "Oh, I find that smile of yours very mysterious, Nurse Dani."

Heat crept into her cheeks. "The way you say it, I could have the Mona Lisa's smile."

Jake leaned, nuzzling her cheek. "I knew I'd seen that smile somewhere before."

Just kiss me, Jake. Her heart was thudding. Something that felt like sawdust hit the back of her throat, and she couldn't swallow. Or take this unbearable tension. The words were out before she could stop herself. "I—I haven't kissed anybody in a long time."

"How long?"

"Just a long time." Trying to regain her dignity, she leaned away and smoothed her uniform in her lap, but Jake's free hand caught hers, stilling it, then his fingers twined through hers.

"C'mon," Dani found herself saying nervously. "I know you're going to kiss me." *Let's just do it.* His hand was still in her lap, a warm, living, pulsing weight that made the core of her suddenly ache. When she looked longingly at Jake, he smiled, his eyes so warm now that she felt the gaze touch her heart.

Her voice was husky. "I guess this is what you meant when you said you like to make women crazy."

His eyes sparkled like the devil. "Are you feeling crazy?"

"Yeah, Jake."

"Good," he whispered.

And then he kissed her. Finally that heavenly mustache brushed her lips, sweeping every thought from her head. She shut her eyes, not bothering to hide the luscious shiver that shook her shoulders.

"Hmm," he murmured against her mouth. Then he

pulled her stool closer until their thighs touched. And when he deepened the kiss, all Dani's questions were answered. His mustache could be both soft *and* bristly. His lips were even silkier than she'd imagined, his chest harder, and his tongue like velvet.

Six years of supressed passion surfaced, and Dani's arms wrapped tightly around his neck while his strong corded forearms squeezed, hugging her hard. As he thrust his tongue ever deeper, countless emotions surged within her. A gut-level longing for love. A desperate, soul-deep craving for his more intimate touch. A sudden unexpected willingness to dream about happy endings again.

Somewhere far off in another world, another time, the doorbell rang.

After a long moment, Jake leaned back a fraction, without releasing Dani. "Nurse Melinda."

Dani merely sighed.

Jake was watching her carefully. "Maybe I should drop Ty off, arrange for the sitter from downstairs to watch him, then take you home. What do you think?"

I think you just asked me to make love to you, Jake. Dani could barely find her voice. "Right now, I can't think at all." Right now, there was nothing but him. Only his green eyes, the rumble of his voice and the soft nuzzling of his lips on her neck.

His voice was husky. "Then don't think, Dani."

"Don't think?"

Jake shook his head. "Just say yes."

"Yes," she whispered.

Chapter Four

"The place isn't, uh, exactly fancy." Entering her apartment, Dani glanced nervously over her shoulder at Jake, who was leaning next to the stroller, teasing Lyssa and Kirby. Was he really about to become a guest in her home? Dani couldn't fully process it, any more than she could the kiss they'd shared in the judge's kitchen. Or the one later, in the lobby of his building where she'd waited for him. Or the one on the street.

Jake glanced up. "You don't have to impress me."

"I know, but I can't help it. I want to." She suddenly thought of the house she'd left behind in Genesis, Long Island, of the ocean view, the landscaped grounds, the original sculptures. It had impressed everybody. She shrugged. "Hey, maybe you just bring out the worst in me."

Jake's answering grin was one of pure lustful devilry. "I sure hope so."

So did she. Even as his words made her heart flutter with anticipation, Dani managed to smile back at him, her eyes drifting over his silky raven hair, her fingers itching to smooth away the curling lock that kept falling on his forehead.

She watched how his lean strong body moved as he maneuvered the stroller into her narrow living room, parked it between the sofa and crib and then glanced around. When his eyes caught hers again, they warmed, silently saying he'd like her, no matter how she chose to live. He started rummaging through the babies' bags. "So, just how shallow do you think I am?"

She smiled and kept watching him. "Just skin-deep."

Jake's lips quirked and he looked up, fixing her with that penetrating green-eyed gaze. "Is that right?"

Everything in his voice said she knew better. "Oh, okay," she conceded. "Maybe you're deep enough for wading."

Jake's soft chuckle filled her apartment. "So, have you decided to get your toes wet?"

Dani raised her eyebrows, her mouth twitching with a suppressed smile, her cheeks warming. "Maybe I'll live dangerously, and get wet all the way up to my ankles."

The sudden widening of Jake's eyes said there were some remarks even he wouldn't touch. Immediately all the color drained from her face, then flooded back in until she knew she'd turned beet red.

And then Jake simply laughed in a deep ribald laugh that was so warm and throaty it echoed in the tiny room. His sparkling eyes found hers again. "You'd better watch out," he warned.

She wasn't about to let him get the best of her. "And why's that?"

"'Cause I'm such a deep guy you might just drown."

Still flushed, she managed to roll her eyes. "I doubt it. Can I get you a Coke or anything?"

"Sure."

"Which?"

"I'll take the anything."

Yet another chuckle followed her as she went to fix some drinks. When she returned, she watched him with Lyssa and Kirby. It was obvious Jake loved kids, and not just these two, but all those at Big Apple Babies. He doted on his son, who'd already taken up residence in Dani's heart. Oh, Jake definitely went more than skin-deep. His intelligence and internal tension could be read in every glance of his eyes, in every muscle when he moved.

Sobering, Dani set down two glasses of sparkling water and watched Jake lift the girls. Kissing each nose with a playful smack, he gave hair-raising, plummeting descents into the crib, plopping the girls side by side on their behinds. As he handed each a toy, they gurgled and gazed up at him in pure adoration.

He was an easy man to fall for, all right—flirtatious, with a razor-sharp mind. So down-to-earth that material possessions wouldn't turn his head. Not even Genesis or Dani's old clothes, those bold designer outfits that had begged to be noticed.

But he'll hate me if he ever realizes I gave up a child, she suddenly thought, her throat tightening. Her secrets were piling on secrets, weighing her down, suffocating her, making her suddenly breathless.

When Jake turned his attention from the babies to her, the apartment seemed too small. Jake was filling every inch of it with his broad-chested body, his heathery scent, the slow rumble of his voice. Another kiss was in the air now, too.

But Jake's eyes merely trailed over her as if they had all the time in the world. Dani tried to fight her response—her escalating pulse, the twinges of self-consciousness, the impulse to smooth her uniform. Still, when she glanced around, she felt as if she were really seeing her apartment for the first time. She'd collected so little in these past six years—just a few books, most of which were in the bedroom. No knick-knacks or throw pillows or plants. No decorative pictures. The only objects that hinted at personality were her Rollerblades that were parked near the door.

Jake was watching her, his eyes curious. "Why haven't you fixed the place up?"

Because I've spent too much of my life worrying over fancy interiors and clothes. Besides, six years ago, when she'd been drowning in the chaos of her emotions, this low-maintenance apartment was pure relief. So was the uniform she wore now. She needed everything to be neat and orderly, easy to contain. Dani finally shrugged, wishing Jake couldn't so easily read her mind. "Too busy, I guess."

His assessing gaze merely dropped thoughtfully over her, making her heart quicken. Jake was so perceptive. Just how much about her could he guess?

A sudden shout sounded from the kitchen. "You think this is bad? You should have seen the place when she had all those roommates. It was bare *and* messy."

Jake started, then slowly turned toward the kitchen. "Ghost or friendly burglar?"

Dani couldn't have been more relieved. "Neither. My neighbor, Trevor. We talk over the air shaft. "C'mon, I'll introduce you."

Trevor waved from his kitchen, then extended a long gangly arm over the air shaft, unlatched Dani's window screen, and stuck out his hand. "You must be Jake Lucas."

"So Dani mentioned me." With an amused smile, Jake stepped forward and shook Trevor's hand. "Pleased to meet you."

"Maybe, but I've got to tell you you're my archrival." The teenager laughed and threw up his hands in mock exasperation. "I mean, you come riding in like a knight on that shining stroller, Jake. And here, I've been trying to woo the fair Dani over the air shaft for years."

Dani batted her eyelashes, smiling sweetly. "Oh, but you won my heart long ago, Trevor."

Trevor rolled his eyes, then smirked at Jake. "But it was her body I wanted. I know I'm a little young for her. But was it really too much to ask?"

Jake laughed, obviously enjoying the exchange with Trevor as much as he might one with his own son. Shoving his hands into his jeans pockets, Jake leaned casually against a wall. "So she plays hard to get?"

Trevor nodded. "I can only wish you luck."

Jake's relaxed chuckle soothed Dani's taut nerves. Until Jake said, "I might have better luck if there wasn't a third party present."

"Enough said." With a laugh, Trevor made a show of hurriedly shutting Dani's screen, slamming the Marpas's kitchen window and then pulling the blind.

Leaving Jake and her alone.

Dani wanted that, and then she didn't. When she suddenly remembered all the mail she'd stuffed into her vegetable bin, the room seemed to go slightly off-kilter. Leaning casually against the refrigerator, she assured herself it was her imagination—Jake Lucas really wasn't going to get a strange, sudden craving for a salad. He didn't move, just kept leaning against the opposite wall. For all his lazy casualness, Dani still felt nervous.

"You had roommates in this place?" he asked.

Either because he'd picked a safe topic or because of all the memories that flooded her, Dani breathed a little easier. It had been a long, rough road from Long Island to this, but she'd overcome countless obstacles. Before she thought it through, she was sharing all those crazy New York war stories with Jake. How she'd skated into The Roller Derby Diner and landed a job. And how she'd once moonlighted at an Indian restaurant where she was the only English-speaking employee.

Jake grinned. "I take it your customers didn't always get what they ordered?"

"Rarely. But then the customers didn't speak English, either." Dani sent Jake a lopsided smile. "So when they yelled at me, I didn't understand a word." As his warm eyes trailed over her, Dani realized the conversation was really nothing more than a brief interlude calculated to lead them right back to where they'd been an hour ago—kissing in a kitchen. This time, would the kiss end?

"And you had roommates?"

"Yeah. I finally got a job as a secretary over at St. Vincent's." Dani nodded in the general direction of the nearby hospital. "And I shared this place with two nurses. One took the bedroom. The other took the living room."

Jake's raised his eyebrows. "And you?"

Dani nodded toward her kitchen table. "I put a futon in the kitchen. Ran a bar between the refrigerator and the wall for a clothes closet."

Jake grinned. "I take it Trevor began to woo you during his midnight snacks?"

Dani nodded. "We shared many a pint of Ben & Jerry's Cherry Garcia ice cream over that air shaft. But you want to know the worst thing?"

"What?"

Dani's shoulders shook with suppressed laughter. "Even with three girls here, we still couldn't afford the rent."

Jake shook his head ruefully. "Only in New York."

Dani sighed. "Actually, it was fun. And things worked out. Trevor's mom, Maureen, runs a second-hand clothing shop around the corner, so she outfitted the three of us."

Jake glancing pointedly at Dani's uniform. "So far, I can tell your taste in clothes is extremely extravagant."

If you only knew. "You might be surprised."

"I'd like to be surprised."

She gazed into Jake's eyes for a long moment, thinking about their easy flirtation and about how fun it would be to primp for him, teasing him with some flighty new dress. She continued with a shrug, "The job at St. Vincent's paid for my tuition at N.Y.U. until I got a scholarship to nursing school. I graduate this term. The girls I was living with helped with my applications."

"So, you can laugh about it all now, huh?"

She tilted her head and gazed into his face. "Yeah." She nodded, her voice softening. "Yeah, I guess I really can."

"You sound surprised.

"I am."

"What *can't* you laugh about?"

Damn. Why did he have to be so perceptive? *My baby.* She shrugged. "Oh, I don't know."

In the pause that followed, Dani became conscious of the silence. She strained but couldn't hear so much as a siren from Seventh Avenue. Even though she and Jake were leaning on opposite walls—him against the doorjamb, her against the refrigerator—they were only a scant two feet apart. She wasn't nearly as relaxed as she was trying to appear, either. After all, they were alone in her apartment; the babies were safely tucked into the crib, even if they weren't changed for bed yet.

Anything can happen now.

Jake's voice was low. "Sounds like you've come a long way."

She nodded. She felt as if she'd moved mountains since she'd struck out on her own. "And I wound up here." Here, on this night, in this kitchen, sharing her past with the most unlikely man on earth. A man she'd vowed to hate on sight because he knew where her child was. A man who, in spite of that, had delivered first kisses that made her feel more complete than she ever had. A man who had all but asked her to make love.

Was Jake even aware of the effect he was having on her? Somehow Dani nodded toward the living room. "I...guess I should change the babies into their jammies."

"I'll take one, you take the other."

In the living room, they laid Lyssa and Kirby on a blanket on the floor and began readying them for bed. Jake nodded toward a table. "Your schoolbooks?"

"Yeah, I've got classes two nights a week." Dani sent him a quick smile as she sorted through outfits he'd bought for the babies. "If you'll notice, my human development book is open to the section on one-year-olds.'' Before Jake could respond, Dani giggled. ''This is so cute.'' She lifted a panda-print sleep set, which she decided Kirby could wear.

Jake was expertly tugging Lyssa's wiggling arms through a pink pajama top. ''Ever think of having them?''

This was tough territory. She felt Jake's eyes on her, suddenly too watchful for comfort. ''Surely not pandas?''

''Babies.''

Babies. Suddenly she wanted to scream that she *did* have a baby. Jake had taken hers. And somewhere out there, her child was growing up without her. Somehow she kept her voice steady. ''Sure, I want kids.'' *I want my kid.* But did she want others? As she dressed Kirby, she gazed down at the baby's guileless smile and pudgy wiggling legs. Dani had been so intent on finding her firstborn that she'd never even thought about a future.

''You'd make a good mother.''

Dani glanced up, startled. So far, she'd made for a bad one—the worst. But Jake…he was so responsible, so good with kids. ''You think so?''

Jake nodded. ''Ty really likes you. So do Lyssa and Kirby.''

Dani's heart swelled. Would her own child like her? Would they be friends? As she carefully stood and lifted Kirby into the crib, she felt a sudden rush of love and wondered what would happen when the babies' sisters were found. It was crazy, but maybe she could adopt them. She blinked three times in rapid succession, feeling sure she'd lost her mind.

Jake chuckled. ''Judge Winslow likes you, too, you know. However secretly.''

Dani forced her thoughts away from the babies. "Well, Judge Winslow doesn't count. He's not a kid."

Jake playfully tweaked his mustache. "Does that mean I don't count?"

Dani raised an eyebrow. "Do you like me?"

"Yeah."

Dani smiled. As Jake lifted Lyssa, his large strong hands nearly covered the whole back of the tiny pink pajamas. Nestling her next to her sister in the crib, his voice turned gruffly tender. "Kiss me in your dreams, girls."

He reached for the light switch, then paused, glancing toward the lit kitchen, then the darkened bedroom, as if getting his bearings. Somehow, Dani had little doubt which room Jake meant to head for once the room was dark.

When he did flip the switch, Dani's breath caught, and she watched him edge around the crib toward her. In a shaft of light from the kitchen, she glimpsed his face and realized there was something hungry in his gaze now, something predatory that made her heart pound. It had been so long since she'd made love. And the boy had only been her age, just twenty.

But now she was twenty-seven. And Jake was a man. He was divorced. Experienced. And, judging by the sudden glint in his eyes, ravenous for love. For her. Involuntarily Dani stepped backward.

Not that she voiced any protest when Jake just kept coming closer, slowly backing her all the way against a shadowy section of the living room wall. Or when his arms found her, wrapping tightly around her back like the evening itself, enveloping her in a warm, smooth velvet darkness.

Jake's voice was barely audible. "Dani?"

"Yeah?"

His breath feathered across her cheek, carrying scents of some mints they'd shared and after-dinner coffee. "I usually try to take more time. Get to know a woman."

She couldn't hide her sudden hurt. Was it only lust Jake felt? Only sex he wanted from her? "But not me, Jake?"

"That's not what I mean," he said gently. Lifting his hands, he began tenderly smoothing her hair, touching each strand that framed her face as if it were delicate, fragile. "With you, I just can't make myself wait, Dani. When I first saw you, I knew I had to be with you. I've been thinking about it all the time."

She felt exactly the same way.

She swallowed hard against the renewed dryness of her throat. Jake really felt the same chemistry that had been driving her crazy since she'd first seen him. It was scary, this combination of desire and emotional need. *And not the kind of thing you throw away by telling lies or keeping secrets, Dani.*

Should she tell Jake the truth now? Would he forgive her? If he found out some other way, he never would. *Oh, Jake, we've got to talk.*

His hands dropped from her hair to cup her chin, his thumbs grazing her mouth, feeling so warm they burned. Instinctively she licked at her lips, but instead her tongue found his thumbs, tasting the salt. And then, feeling her heart hammer, she let him dip a thumb between her lips. In the darkness, her gaze found his as her mouth closed around his thumb and suckled, her teeth grazing his skin as he ever so slowly slid it out, then rubbed its dampness in an agonizing circle around her lips.

Jake's mouth followed where his thumb had been, settling on her already wet lips, probing them apart, exploring her. After a moment, he leaned back a fraction. His breath caught, his voice both gruff and tender. "I feel like we're locked into each other, Dani."

She simply nodded. Even before he'd ever kissed her, she'd felt it. She and Jake belonged together. At least that's what she wanted to think. But maybe it only seemed that way because he knew where her child was. It was hard to say. And when Jake leaned, licking scalding wet kisses down her neck, feathering his mustache across her earlobes, Dani didn't even care. All that mattered was his husky murmurings against her skin, the hard-packed heat of his aroused body wedged against hers, and the way his mouth teased her lips, time and time again, the kisses turning ever harder, ever wetter, ever deeper.

"You really feel that way, too?" Jake murmured, his ragged breath catching between kisses. "Like we already had a past together?"

Her voice was a faint rasp. "Yeah."

Then shutting her eyes tight, she simply, silently urged his lips to find hers again, telling herself she was trying to fight the sensations he was arousing, at least until she told him the truth, but knowing she wasn't. And all the while, guilt coursed through her. Because she and Jake did have a past. And if she didn't tell him, she'd destroy their future.

"Do you want me?" he whispered.

Whatever she said next wasn't even a word, just her voice floating to the air on a needy sigh as she leaned back her head, fully exposing her neck for more kisses, gasping as his hands found her breasts, his fingers teasing the taut hard peaks. She was so ready for him. Jake was still only kissing her, fondling her through her starchy uniform, but already she couldn't wait any more than he could.

It was too much to bear. It had been years since she'd been touched, and never with such controlled passion and restrained strength. Even as her body melted, molding around him and arching toward him, she told herself to stop. And even as his hands explored her in the dark, she knew she never could. Because Jake Lucas was the one man she'd looked for—and not just for these six years, but for all her life.

Nothing could stop this fire between them.

And she couldn't risk telling the truth—or him walking away.

At the mere thought of his leaving, her arms circled his neck tightly, possessively, meaning to hold him where he stood. Shutting her eyes and breathing in his scent, the whole world seemed to disappear. But she wanted him to know everything. And she wanted to tell him she was scared. Scared because the last time she'd made love had brought such hard consequences. And scared because she knew Jake wasn't going to take her like that boy. Jake was going to take her like a man.

Need infused her whimper. "Oh, Jake..."

"Yeah?"

She moaned softly. "Jake, I...I want to tell you something."

"Tell me in bed," he returned raggedly. And then, without another word, his hard, wet mouth claimed hers again.

JAKE HAD TO HAVE HER.
Now.

Her skin was a spiced mix of flowers and salt, her lips all coffee and mint. And when her slender, shapely arms wreathed his neck in such a silent statement of total possession, his primal side took over, wanting to conquer and devour. His tongue dived between her lips, seeking her out, exploring, and everything receded into the far distance, replaced by a heated shock wave that rippled through his veins and flooded his groin with swift, powerful arousal.

"Ah, Dani," he murmured. "You torture me."

Even her sharp intake of breath seemed to knife through him, making his skin quiver. "Do I?"

"Yeah."

Since he'd first laid eyes on her, she'd tortured him like no other woman. The soft-spoken yet unmistakable need in her voice was what Jake had yearned to hear in his wife's voice years ago, and never had. But of course, Lanie never could have affected him like this.

No, Dani had come from nowhere, right out of the blue, blindsiding Jake. She was so mysterious and tantalizing. No sooner would he decide her smoldering dark eyes hid some tragic secret than they'd brighten and she'd start joking around like a kid. Oh, she'd teased his intellect....

And now his body. He moaned, his fingers twining through her hair, feeling the silken strands. Against his own scalp, her nails made him feel restless and edgy. He wanted them digging into his shoulders, his back, his thighs. Wanted them raking through the hairs on his bare chest.

He made no apology for his desire, not with his voice that loosed a soft moan against her mouth. Not with his hands that slid beneath her stiff uniform and silk slip, then between her legs, touching her through her panty hose until she whimpered and her thighs eased apart. Not when he wedged himself against her, pressing his steely length at the juncture of her thighs, or when he slowly rolled his hips against hers, loving her through her clothes.

Her moans shuddered through him, making him want to say so many things—that it had been a long time since he'd loved a woman whose need was as strong as his own. How long had it been for her? he wondered as his palms curved over her backside, pulling her flush against him. She'd said a long time. As long as it had been for him? That Dani really wanted this, needed it as badly as he did, sent another flood of awareness through him, a current so strong the arousal was almost painful. Oh, he'd meant to take Dani slow. But with her, the spark of a kiss didn't start a fire, it made things explode...made *him* explode.

"Oh—oh, no," she gasped.

His words rasped against her lips. "What's wrong?"

"I don't have any condoms."

Good. Her tone made clear she took the use of them seriously. He cupped her neck, delivering another kiss that was so deep he almost couldn't stop. Raggedly he said, "I do."

"You always come prepared?"

He could have explained Big Apple Babies gave condoms away as part of an outreach program to various schools. Or that Winston Holiday was always joking around, shoving extras into Jake's wallet. But Jake was too hot to talk. So he merely whispered, "Yeah," and pulled Dani close again, reveling in the burning heat of her skin, the salty taste of her lips, and the excruciatingly soft, steady pressure of her mound against his erection.

Finding her lips again, he drove his tongue deep, then deeper still. The whimpers Dani emitted when her tongue wasn't tussling with his made Jake want to say things a man didn't say on a first date, if that's what this was.

He wanted to say he'd never felt anywhere near this hard or hungry for a woman. That he already knew he wasn't going to be able to live without her. But he simply half dragged, half carried her to the bedroom.

The damn bed was unfortunately tiny. A no-frills wood-frame single, a side of which was shoved against the wall. Bookshelves were built right above the head-board, which meant he wouldn't have space to make love to her the way he most wanted to. But maybe nothing really mattered at this point. Even as they tumbled onto the mattress and Jake climbed between Dani's open legs, her needy hands were fumbling between them, seeking his zipper.

They barely undressed. He unzipped her uniform, pulled it down to her waist and unhooked the front clasp of her bra. Then his hungry mouth closed over her breasts, his silken tongue stroking the hard tips. Bathing her with scalding kisses, he blew on the fiery dampness until she writhed. Even through his jeans, he could feel her thighs shake as he reached between them, hurriedly rolling down her panty hose and panties. The needy tension in her body, coupled with hints of her inexperience, was making him wild. Jake kept his sweater on, and his jeans wound up somewhere around his ankles—one leg on, one leg off.

Somehow he leaned back and rolled on the condom. When his mouth found hers again, the heat of the kiss had her wrapping herself around him like a ribbon, until they were a tangle of arms and legs. He grunted when her hands slid between them, and as she guided him to her, she loosed an undisguised sob of need.

"Please...oh, please, Jake..."

It was all he needed to hear. He entered her quickly, plunging deep, again and again, catching a quick steady rhythm that made the ridiculously tiny bed move and the springs squeak. She went really crazy then—her hands clutching his shoulders, tugging at his sweater as if trying to find the bare skin beneath, her legs circling and gripping his waist, locking at the ankles. Finally her heavenly fingers scratched beneath his wool sweater and her nails dug deep into his skin.

Her voice was a pant. "Oh, Jake, I want you so much."

I want you. More than any other words, they touched Jake. He heard Dani's voice deep in his soul. "You've got me," he whispered.

And she did. Jake rocked her beneath him, able to slow for her now. Holding her tight, he kissed her tenderly as if that might soothe and stop her trembling. As his ever slower, controlled thrusts made those tremors build, her breath caught in sobs, and softer cries that rained down around his ears.

"Oh, Dani," he whispered simply when she came. She was such pure sweet magic. She pulsed around him like a strobe, each sweet spasm sucking him in, deeper and deeper, like an undertow, until he had no choice but to let go. His own release shook him so hard it scared him. Shook him until he could do nothing more than pant and gasp and rest on top of her, holding on to her tight, his heart pounding.

After a long time, Dani emitted a very shocked-sounding "Whew!"

Jake smiled. Kissing her again, he rolled beside her,

then finished kicking off his jeans. Before he could take off his sweater, or divest her of the uniform bunched around her waist, she'd nuzzled against his chest like a sleepy kitten. Against his side, he could still feel her heart pounding.

Sighing, Jake glanced down, knowing his life had just changed. He wanted to know Dani completely, to take whatever was between them as far as it would possibly go. For a long time, he merely stared at her face. Long eyelashes cast shadows over her cheekbones, and she really did have a Mona Lisa smile, her lips gently curving in a way that was wistful, knowing and yet veiled. The dark, beguiling smudges of her half-shut eyes were secretive, sensual and dreamy.

"Dani, you're so beautiful," he whispered, stroking her cheek. "I want to make love to you again. This time, slower."

She smiled up at him. "My bed's a little small."

His shrug said it was perfect. "Can you come over for dinner tomorrow night?" At that, she laughed. A deep, throaty satisfied laugh that made him feel better than he ever had.

"You really think sex like that leads to a date?"

Jake flashed her a smile in the dark. "Sex like that leads to the moon."

"Or out of orbit," she countered softly.

"Or to the altar."

Her laughter rose and fell like a beautifully played scale. "Isn't it a little soon to propose?"

He grinned. "Maybe. But if you let me make love to you again, this time real, real slow, I just might. Really, what do you say? I'll cook at my place. Mind having Ty around?"

"Heavens, no."

The sudden, surprised catch in Dani's voice told him it was true. She really liked kids, liked his son. And Jake's heart soared. He'd learned from the rocky road of experience, starting with his own biological mother, that not all women liked kids.

Dani's voice suddenly went soft. "Mind if I light a candle, Jake?"

He glanced toward her bedside table, seeing the votive. "What? Now that we've made love, you want to light a candle and pray for my deliverance?"

Dani giggled. "Or mine. You're downright wicked."

He heard the match fizz as she struck it, then he smelled sulfur and a flame flickered, better illuminating her face. As the candle burned, the scent of vanilla filled the air. Next door the babies were silent. Outside, the city lights still burned bright, but there was a lull in the street sounds, as if the power of their lovemaking had brought all of Manhattan to its knees.

When Dani snuggled next to him again, nestling her face against his sweater, Jake started to ask her to move, so he could take it off, but then he didn't want to move away from her that long, not even if it meant feeling her against his naked skin. Anyway, he'd have plenty of time to hold her naked against him. A voice deep inside him said, *Maybe even a lifetime, Jake. I think she's the one.*

Her soft smile suddenly faltered. "Jake...I—I..."

I've got to tell you something.

Sudden dread made Jake's stomach muscles clench. Was there something to bar him from seeing her? Another man? He braced himself. "You can tell me anything."

"Anything?"

He smiled grimly. "Well, I'd rather not find out you're married."

"I'm not."

"Boyfriend?"

"No attachments." Dani studied him a long moment, then her face cleared. "I...I was just going to say I'd love to have dinner tomorrow. What time?"

She was lying. What had she been about to say? His eyes narrowed. "Is six okay?"

"Fine."

He nodded toward the door. "Excuse me for a second?"

She smiled. "Coming back?"

"Oh, yeah." His devilish smile said when he did, he'd make love to her again, and this time really slow. He wanted to feel the tremors of her hot, damp skin when he held her fully naked. And he wanted to watch the agonized twist of her luscious mouth when they came together in this soft, fragrant vanilla candlelight.

"Go on, Jake," she whispered.

He started climbing over her in the tiny bed then froze. Wedged in the bookshelf right above his head was a framed snapshot of three people in front of a house.

And not just any house. Genesis. Jake would recognize those cylindrical steel buildings anywhere. Not so much because the house was of famous architectural design, which it was, but because Jake knew the man who owned it. In the picture, a young woman was squeezed between Thurman Newland and his wife, Kate.

"Jake?"

"I'm fine."

Somehow he rolled off Dani. Somehow he made it

through the dark, nearly barreling into the babies' crib. Passing Dani's purse, he grabbed it, taking it with him.

In the bathroom, he snapped on the light, dropping the purse onto the back of the toilet. When he glanced down, his shoulders started to shake with dark humor.

The condom had broken.

Not that he'd bother to tell her. He disposed of it, refusing to dwell on the possibility that he'd gotten her pregnant. That would be the worst kind of irony.

Quickly Jake started rummaging through her purse, shaking his head. Genesis. He recognized the place, all right. As well as Dani, who was standing between Thurman and Kate Newland. Six years ago, the man had come to Jake, saying his daughter had gotten pregnant by a boy in Greece during her vacation, and hiring Jake to handle the adoption of the baby.

Now Jake could only pray that Dani—*his* Dani— was in that snapshot coincidently. She just couldn't be Thurman Newland's daughter. Pulling her wallet from the purse, Jake rifled through it, then shook his head again in disgust. There wasn't a single ID. Had she anticipated this search?

Finally, in the bottom of the bag, he found a dusty credit card receipt. His fingers actually shook when he unfolded it and saw the signature. Nurse Dani *was* Daniela Newland. And seeing the undeniable evidence knocked the wind clear out of Jake, leaving him breathless.

Damn.

Had Daniela Newland been using him to find her kid?

Jake's chest was tight, his heart beating too hard. Icy tendrils suddenly slid through his veins, carrying a fear so horribly intense that, next to it, Dani's betrayal meant absolutely nothing at all.

Because Jake's son, Ty, *was* hers.

Chapter Five

"Daddy?"

Ty's sleepy whisper carried a hint of a lisp, reminding Jake of how his son had talked a few years ago, before he'd reached the advanced, all-important age of six. Jake shifted his weight on the mattress. "Go back to sleep, Ty. You've got to rest up for your karate tournament tomorrow." Jake had been watching his son sleep long enough that his eyes had adjusted to the dark, and now he leaned toward the pillow, gently brushing the shaggy bangs off Ty's forehead. "C'mon, just shut your eyes for Daddy."

"But, Daddy, I'm not sleepy."

Even as he voiced his heartfelt protest, Ty emitted a quivering yawn and his eyes drifted shut again. Realizing Ty's new stuffed tyrannosaurus had fallen to the floor, Jake retrieved it. Nestling it on the pillow next to his son's cheek, he tried to forget how much fun they'd had shopping for the toy with Dani.

Ty lifted his small fists, digging his knuckles into the corners of his eyes, rubbing sleep away. "Daddy, when Mrs. Roberts put me to bed, she said you and Dani were out on a date. Does that mean you're gonna marry Dani?"

Marry her? Anger twisted inside Jake. He never wanted to see her again. And he didn't want her anywhere near Ty. He was too afraid she'd guess Ty wasn't Lanie's son but hers. Judging from the easy fun she had with him, the thought hadn't occurred to her. But she was trying to find her child. Otherwise, she would have told Jake she knew who he was. She knew he'd handled the adoption of her baby six years ago. His signature as attorney, as well as Big Apple Babies formal stationery, had graced countless papers she'd signed.

"You think you might marry her, Daddy?"

"I—I don't think so."

"Why not?" Ty's sleep-grouchy voice was barely a whisper. "Doesn't she like kids? Doesn't she want 'em?"

What Ty meant was *Doesn't she want me?* That Ty might feel unwanted made Jake's heart ache so much that he couldn't force himself to say no. "I...figure she likes kids just fine. And I know she likes you."

"So, if we can't never find my *real* mom..."

"Can't ever," Jake corrected softly even as another rush of ice flushed through him. Because Ty had started first grade this fall, he was meeting more kids from two-parent households; either finding his biological mother or setting Jake up with a new girlfriend had become a renewed, almost obsessive theme.

And all along, you've lied. Jake had told Ty that the information about his biological parents was sealed and that Ty couldn't access the information until he was older, which was true. But Jake had also lied, saying he didn't know who Ty's parents were. Now, Ty had met his mother. In the flesh. And if he ever realized it, he'd never forgive Jake.

I can't believe this. From the moment Jake had seen the name Daniela Newland on that credit card receipt, everything was a blur. He'd never know how he'd staggered into the night without her suspecting his change of mood. Especially since a part of him—only the most male part of him, he assured himself now—had so desperately wanted to stay.

Hell, if Jake was honest about it, that part of him still wanted to go back.

When he'd returned from the bathroom, she'd changed into a white shortie gown and robe, and through thin lace cups he could see the reddened hard tips of her breasts, still aroused for him. Forcing himself to murmur an apology about getting home to relieve the sitter, Jake had simply pulled on his pants and headed for the door.

But she'd followed him. And when she'd playfully backed him against the door to kiss him good-night, he'd tried to steel himself against her touch. But nothing could stop the way her breasts teased his chest or how her arms reached out, opening for him. He couldn't stop smelling her, either. And that scent—all vanilla heat and crushed flower petals and carnal animal musk—had filled and aroused him. That lingering trace of the love they'd shared had rushed right through him, red and hot, burning through his veins until it seared something deep down, branding him.

"A kiss for the road," he'd murmured.

"Just one?"

Jake's voice had been barely audible, gruff and husky. "Maybe two."

Or countless more. Because even as Jake told himself he was furious about her betrayal and had to keep her away from Ty, his hand slid inside her robe and under her gown. She hadn't put on underwear. And heaven help him, but feeling her, still so hot and ready, he was powerless to deny her need.

He was just as unwilling to take her back to bed, in spite of how she touched him, body and soul. So he compromised. His fingers circled the nub of her desire, then slid inside the warm slick sheath of her, stroking and teasing, drawing her closer and closer to the brink even as he vowed to himself that it was over between them. Even as he swore he'd never touch her again, she'd climaxed, convulsing in his embrace, her knees giving out and his strong arms catching her.

Now, just thinking about it made Jake hard all over again, and the traitorous tug of his unwanted response further tweaked his temper. Why did loving Daniela Newland have to be so, so easy? Hell, Dani could be the wickedest woman on earth—or the only one left— and she'd still be the best damn thing Jake had ever touched or tasted. Her every kiss, every sweet flicker of her tongue, had been a fire iron, branding him heart and soul.

Jake, I have something to tell you. Had she been about to admit that she knew who he was?

Six years ago, when he'd taken Ty into his arms at the hospital, Jake had thought about Daniela Newland. A part of him felt she must love the baby—enough to give him away, to a father who wanted him. And yet, as Jake had cradled his sweet, crying son, he'd also feared she'd change her mind and try to take Ty away.

And after that, Jake never thought of her again.

Until now.

Did the woman really think she could turn up like this and lie to him and use him to find her child?

And what was a woman like Daniela Newland doing

slumming it down in the Village when her father was the richest banker in New York City? In the past, Jake had her pegged for self-indulgent and irresponsible. Not to mention easy. But after she gave Ty up, she'd apparently gone to nursing school. And she'd been living like a nun in that bare little apartment for years.

Thinking of Dani's apartment, Jake suddenly frowned, remembering that as he'd pushed through her lobby door, he'd startled a blond woman on the opposite curb. From head to foot, the woman had been dressed in black, but then a lot of artsy types in the Village wore black. It had seemed as if the woman was staring at Dani's building. At the time, he'd been too upset to think about it further, but he could swear she'd been watching it.

But she wasn't, Jake. Dani Newland's inserted herself in your life under false pretenses, and it's making you paranoid. That woman was probably just out walking.

He shook his head. Well, at least he'd bought himself time to figure out his next move. Even the way Dani had obviously wanted to argue for the rights of biological parents during their exchange in Judge Winslow's kitchen was still making his blood boil. He'd developed real feelings for her, and yet she'd only been using him. Hell, the woman didn't deserve a son.

Yeah, Jake had about as much sympathy for Dani as he did for the woman who'd tossed *him* away. Or Thurman Newland. After the adoption, the banker had tried to renege on the adoption agreement, but then not even bank accounts as fat as his could buy the law.

I just can't believe this is happening.

And why did the first woman Jake had wanted since Lanie have to be Daniela Newland? Have to be a woman who'd been using him? Have to be the mother of the child he knew he'd never share? A wry smile twisted Jake's lips. And to think he'd been so sure that no betrayal could ever be worse than Lanie's.

The Fates had sure thrown him a curve ball today.

Even worse, he couldn't look at Ty now without seeing Dani. He had her eyes, her cheekbones, the same heart-shaped face. And on a grown woman that face was sure gorgeous. How was Jake going to forget her? Even now, he wished he'd taken her back to bed. He tried to tell himself he would have punished her with his kisses, held her wrists so tight they hurt, made her writhe and beg, instead of loving her the soft, slow tender way he'd really wanted to...

She's using you, Jake.

And he'd invited her for dinner tomorrow. He'd forgotten. Now he didn't want her near Ty, but he couldn't risk arousing her suspicions. Especially since he knew what wanting a child could do to people. Some even resorted to kidnapping.

Just how far would Dani Newland go?

Apparently as far as seduction.

The thought infuriated Jake. But he guessed he could keep loving her, at least long enough to get her out of his life. He'd give her the old line about things moving too fast. Then he'd step up the action and find those two missing babies. After that, she'd have no excuse to try to see him again—or Ty.

Hasta la vista, baby, Jake thought.

"Daddy?"

Jake sighed. "I thought you were asleep."

"But why *can't* Dani be my mom?" Ty whined.

Jake bristled. *She is your mom.* The mere thought of the woman being in the same room as Ty made Jake's every last muscle tense. Suddenly his heart seemed to swell. His voice almost cracked. "What, Ty? Isn't a daddy good enough?"

Ty groaned sleepily. "But what about my school? It's the moms who gotta bake cookies and stuff. And since you can't ever find my mom..."

Jake had always known his lies would come back to haunt him. Now he told himself that not wanting to share Ty with the Newlands had nothing to do with his reasons for lying, that he'd done so solely because he couldn't risk having Ty hurt.

Six years ago the Newlands had given Ty away.

And now Ty belonged to Jake.

Case closed.

"Daddy?"

Jake's voice was edgier than he intended. "What?"

There was a long silence.

Then Ty suddenly squirmed to a sitting position, batting away the covers and flinging his arms around Jake's neck, clinging tight. "Please don't be mad at me for wanting a mommy, please, Daddy. Oh, please."

Jake's heart wrenched. "I'm not," he soothed, hugging his son tight.

"I don't really want a mommy, anyway," Ty rushed on, not relinquishing his hold on Jake. "I don't even need one, 'cause I already got me the best daddy in the whole world."

Jake's heart ached at Ty's efforts to assure him. "Ty, it's okay for you to want a mom."

Ty let go of Jake and wiggled under the covers again. "But I *don't* want one! Yuck!"

Liar.

Jake sighed. As he tucked Ty in, he suddenly remembered he'd given Dani his office key. His heart started racing. Ty was baby zero, the very first newborn ever to have been processed by Big Apple Babies, so his file was right there with all the rest.

And now Dani had access.

Had she gone to Big Apple Babies as soon as Jake left her apartment? Those icy tendrils of fear curled through him again. Did she already know Ty was her son?

"Damn," Jake muttered softly. He had to get those files.

"Daddy," Ty whispered in censure.

Jake automatically said what he always did when Ty caught him cursing. "I was thinking of building you and me a dam in the Hudson River."

Ty giggled drowsily. "You were not, Daddy."

"Were, too." Praying it wasn't too late to stop Dani, Jake leaned and kissed his son.

His son.

The son Dani Newland would never get.

JAMES SANGER, the Lou Grant look-alike Dani had once thought was Jake Lucas, walked her down the long first-floor hallway at Big Apple Babies, toward Jake's office. "It's so nice of you to come help us out."

If you only knew.

Dani's knees felt suddenly weak. How could she betray Jake after the way he'd loved her last night? He'd left her both satisfied and aching, longing to see him again before he was even gone. He'd fully awakened her, and she loved him for it. When she'd gotten out of bed this morning, she'd known there was nothing in the world she wouldn't do for him.

So just pretend you're not really breaking into his office.

Trying to push Jake from her mind, she decided to pretend this was a game. As if she were a superspy sent to accomplish a dangerous mission at Big Apple Babies.

Except it didn't really work. This was real.

Jake's office key was in her perspiring fist, and she was only minutes away from being ensconced in his office. Inside was the key to the sealed records room, which meant her child's file would be in her hands soon. Her heart hammered against her ribs, making her breath catch.

"And don't worry," James was saying. "Lyssa and Kirby will be fine in the fifth-floor nursery."

Dani's mouth was bone dry. "Thanks for helping me get them settled and for showing me the layout."

James had even assured the security guards she had free rein, although he'd mentioned that the sealed records room was off-limits to non-employees. Then he'd shown her every inch of Big Apple Babies, everything from the adorable oversize diaper pin that hung over the Waverly Place entrance and skewered the agency's banner, to the murals depicting brightly colored apples that graced all the walls. From top to bottom, Big Apple Babies was warm and homey. Yet another testament to what a great guy Jake was.

And here she was, snooping around like a thug. Her eyes stole toward the sealed records room. It was right at the end of this hallway, opposite James's office.

He stopped walking. "Well, here you are. Jake's abode. If you're still around at lunch, Winston and I usually order takeout. There's a sushi bar and a Greek place."

Why did James Sanger have to be so nice? *Just tell yourself he's the enemy. Inside Jake's office are secret encoded files that threaten children everywhere. "Agent Dani,"* she imagined a voice saying, *"you have to get those files."*

"You okay?" James said.

Dani swallowed hard. Jake's door looked like the doors of P.I.'s in the movies. Black block lettering on the frosted glass said Jake Lucas: Director. "I was just wondering where I should start looking for information…about the missing kids." About *my* missing kid.

James shrugged. "Just go through everything. I finally found Judge Winslow's relatives, Elsie and Gertie, and got a possible number for Phoebe Rutherford, so I'll be trying to find her. I think Rosita's at a place in Spain called Villa Maria, but I can't get through."

Dani felt her pulse ticking in her throat. "Well, thanks."

"I'll leave you to it. Think you'll be all right?"

"Fine."

But she wasn't. All she could do was stare at Jake's door. What she was doing was illegal. The records were sealed, and misrepresenting her purpose in coming here was a crime. Even worse, she hadn't come clean with Jake. Jake, who'd made her feel so…loved. Jake, who was an attorney, a representative of all the laws she was about to break.

It's still okay, Dani. You can turn around and leave.

But how could she possibly live without knowing what had become of her baby?

Shoving Jake's key in the lock, she went inside. On the far wall was a wooden Peg-Board from which hung countless keys, including one labeled Sealed Records.

It was that easy. Now all she had to do was wait for James and Winston to go to lunch.

I can't believe I'm doing this.

For a second, she merely stood there, now trying to pretend she was a spy on *Mission: Impossible*. She leaned toward a tape recorder, pressed Play, and a male voice said, "Agent Dani, your mission, should you choose to accept it, is to find two missing quadruplets, as well as your own child. For reasons of security, this mission has been code-named Mission: Motherhood." Slowly the tape whirred to an end. And then it began to smolder, trailing smoke toward her nostrils while it self-destructed.

But Dani knew it was she who was self-destructing.

And she was going to lose Jake.

At the thought, her insides wound into knots. For six long years she'd felt so alone. Without her family. Without her child. And then suddenly Jake had come into her life. A father himself, he was so strong and responsible, so easy to lean on.

She hadn't even been all that scared about getting pregnant again. He'd been so careful. Besides, she was stronger now than she had been six years ago. She could take care of a baby. And she knew instinctively that a man like Jake could take care of her.

Oh, his every kiss had weakened her, turning her to mush and making her feel faint. And in his embrace, she had the constant sensation she was falling. But then, time after time, Jake had been right there to catch her.

Last night, right before she'd slept, Dani had felt as though it were Christmas. The presents had been opened and the excitement was gone, and all that was left was a heavy, warm feeling in the pit of her stomach. Smelling Jake in her bed, she'd squeezed her pillow tight, wishing it was him.

Now she shut her eyes and blew out a long sigh.

"The least you can do is help look for Lyssa and Kirby's sisters," she suddenly muttered, feeling thoroughly disgusted with herself. She began a slow, systematic search of Jake's desk, his in-box, his file cabinets. After some time, her hands stilled on a stack of papers. Most were pink, but a few were yellow. Hadn't Judge Winslow said he should have received a yellow paper? One of these pertained to the adoption of Grantham Hale's twins, which Rosita had apparently delivered.

But why was a form for Lyssa and Kirby stapled to it? Dani read over the names of Grantham's twins, Stanley and Devin, then realized the papers were all Rosita's deliveries. Carefully folding them, Dani wedged them under the phone for safekeeping until Jake could look at them.

Then she settled into Jake's swivel chair, turned on his computer and started the slow, meticulous process of scanning his hard drive, now searching for something about her child. Anything.

"On Jake's computer?"

Dani started, her heart racing. How much time had passed? Hours, probably. Glancing up, she saw that James was peeking in the door. "Uh, Jake said I might find something here," she lied.

James shrugged. "Well, Winston and I are heading over to Samauri's Sushi. Want anything?"

She shook her head. She was so keyed up she couldn't swallow a bite. "I'm not really hungry."

Winston Holiday appeared behind James. The urban cowboy Dani had noticed six years ago hadn't changed much. He was good-looking, even if his tight jeans, pointy-toed boots and Stetson seemed somehow at odds with the stethoscope looped around his neck. Catching her gaze, he drawled, "Didn't anyone tell you? I'm really *Doc* Holiday. Pediatrics."

Dani squinted at him. "I thought you were a case-worker."

"That, too, darlin'. I got my start evaluating potential adoptive parents. Still do it on occasion. Especially now, since Larry McDougal quit. Any-hoo, since it's my job to red-flag all health risks, me and James here are bringin' you vittles whether you're hungry or not."

Dani's heart pounded. She could head for the sealed records room now. "Surprise me," she managed to say. "I'm not picky."

Winston winked. "Will do, darlin'."

A moment later, Dani headed for the Peg-Board. Even as she took the key, she damned herself for doing it. Was she really taking advantage of the fact that Jake's two most trusted employees were out to lunch?

Another lump formed in her throat.

Jake.

Sexy, devilish Jake, with his dimples, rakish mustache and wavy black hair that felt like silk. Jake, who'd shaken her to her core with their lovemaking. Whose green eyes heated her soul every time she looked at him. Jake, whom she desperately wanted to make love to again tonight.

Dani, get moving. This is your only chance.

As she turned toward the door, Dani's eyes swept over the framed letter that had allowed Jake to open Big Apple Babies, and she found herself squinting. She could *swear* she recognized that cursive handwriting.

But she didn't have time to think about it.

She'd waited six years for this moment, and the time had finally come.

As she headed down the empty hallway, Dani kept alert, her eyes darting every which way until she reached the door to the sealed records room.

Holding her breath, she let herself in.

She'd expected so many more obstacles. Locks, or running into one of the guards. So much for security, she thought with a frown as she headed for the file cabinet marked *N*. Her breath caught with hope even as she steeled herself for possible disappointment. Was she really only seconds away from finding her little girl? The file drawer glided open, and her nails riffled over the tops of countless green hanging files. Inside each was a purple folder.

"Newland," she whispered. It was right here.

Her fingers trembling, she yanked the purple folder. All thoughts of James, Winston and the security guards flew from her head. Squatting down, she opened the folder, resting it on her knees. Yes, everything was here. Copies of papers she hadn't seen for years. Her shaky, nearly illegible signature. Her father's bolder hand. Even Jake's signature—neat and in black ink— as the attorney.

But nothing about my baby.

Her heart thudding against her ribs, she focused on the folder itself, then pulled another for comparison. Apparently the left pocket of each contained papers pertaining to where the babies had come from; papers on the right pertained to where they had gone. Most folders had papers on both sides—except hers.

But why?

Suddenly a soft cry was torn from her throat. *Where*

is my child? Why aren't my papers here? Had someone expected her to come here and look?

Jake?

Her heart fluttered. But no. He didn't know who she was or what she wanted. He never could have made love to her the way he had if he'd suspected. Besides, she now realized, reaching into another drawer, there were other folders with missing papers. Surely there was simply activity on her file, some kind of update or processing.

But I have to find those papers today! It's my only chance!

Her eyes blurred with tears, and when they landed on her father's signature again, her heart wrenched. "I'm not going to let you ruin your life," he'd shouted six years ago.

"It's *my* life, Daddy!"

He'd merely shot her a contemptuous stare. "Oh, is it?"

And it wasn't. At least not then. She'd been such a daddy's girl. She'd loved her father more than she could imagine loving anyone, which was why she'd let him marshal her right through her own life.

Until that crazy summer in Greece. Just once, Dani had wanted to do something on her own. She'd been twenty and desperate for a taste of freedom. Desperate for a taste of the sensuality that made a woman a woman. And a man a man.

It seemed so innocent, right up until she got pregnant. Of course, the boy and his family wanted nothing to do with her and the baby. To them, she was just another loose American tourist. Knowing her father would be furious, she'd stayed away from Genesis until she was near term. But then, she'd gotten scared. She had no idea what to do, where to go or to turn.

Except to Daddy.

And Daddy hardly saw unwed motherhood in her future. He even swore he'd throw her out on the street and cut off her money if she kept the baby. Meantime, all those years of pampered living had ensured Dani couldn't do a thing for herself. She'd never even operated a washing machine, much less held a job. She had no skills, no resources.

And so she'd signed all those damnable papers her father had brought from Jake Lucas.

Suddenly a tear splashed her cheek. *How could Daddy withdraw his support when I needed him the most? How could he withdraw his love?* How could he be the same daddy who'd taught her to dance? Worried over her prom pictures? It was so unforgivable that Dani hadn't spoken to him for six years.

Not that her proud father had made overtures. It was always her mother who came as emissary. Ambassador to the king. Each time, it broke Dani's heart. But each time, Dani rebuffed her. She'd never called Margie and Baines, either.

"It's my life," she'd shouted six years ago.

And he'd said, "Oh, is it?"

Well it is now, Daddy. And I swear, by God, I'm still going to find my baby.

Dani's heart wrenched again. Even if it cost her Jake Lucas? she thought.

And then she gasped. Had she heard footsteps? Her heart pounding, she shoved the purple folder back inside the green hanging file. Footsteps *were* approaching. It sounded like a man. What if it was Jake? What should she say? It was too late to run. *Grantham Hale.*

The name was still on her mind, so she hurriedly pulled his file and stared down at it, unseeing.

The steps paused in front of the open door. "I...thought I mentioned that this room is off-limits to non-employees."

Dani glanced up. James Sanger's sincere brown eyes had just turned awfully unfriendly. He was holding a paper sack, presumably the lunch he'd been kind enough to get for her.

Dani flushed. "I guess I've got some explaining to do."

His voice was rough. "You'd better start talking."

Chapter Six

"Howdy, sailor." Standing nervously in front of Jake in her new dress, Dani cradled a bright bouquet of mixed flowers. With her free hand, she guiltily clutched Lyssa and Kirby's stroller so tightly that her knuckles had turned white. Had Jake really sounded angry on the intercom when he'd buzzed her in, or was it just her imagination? Had James Sanger told Jake he'd caught her in the sealed records room?

It was hard to tell, because Jake merely swung open his apartment door wider and said, "Howdy yourself, stranger."

When his eyes drifted from her upswept hair and the tendrils that framed her face, all the way down to her lilac suede flats and then all the way back up again, prickles washed over Dani's skin, either from the heavily lidded lazy gaze or her own guilt-ridden anxiety, she wasn't sure which. If Jake confronted her now, would she tell him the truth?

But no, she thought, her eyes settling on his dimples and the gentle curve of his mustache. Jake was smiling, and the only emotion in his eyes was so purely male that excitement tunneled through her. Placing the flowers on the lower rack of the stroller, she pushed Lyssa and Kirby inside the apartment, inadvertently brushing Jake and catching a heady whiff of his recently scrubbed skin.

Her breath caught. "Do I look all right?"

Her new dress was of velour, purple on deeper purple, printed with a subdued floral pattern. Letting go of the stroller, she found herself anxiously modeling, turning a quick, flirtatious circle for Jake, making the skirt swirl around her knees. When she was facing him again, she realized that either the impulsive spin or Jake's proximity had left her completely breathless. "I—I got the dress today in Maureen Marpas's store. Trevor helped pick it out."

Jake merely surveyed her through narrowed eyes. Then he said, "Ah, when Trevor said he liked you, I should have guessed he had good taste. But you really bought that just for me?"

Oh, yes. Last night, Jake had brought out the long-suppressed woman in her. And tonight, Dani wanted to bring out the overpowering man in him. As she'd powdered and perfumed herself, she'd imagined Jake opening this door, taking one look at her, then dragging her right into his arms. Her voice sounded raspy to her own ears. "I hear new dresses can do wonders for a guy."

"As long as it's not him who's wearing them." Jake's eyes twinkled, flickering over her again. "But let's just say this particular sailor would be glad to dock his ship in your port any day."

Dani flushed. "Beats my uniform?"

"Well, Nurse Dani—" Jake tilted his head as if considering. "Around you, I've been sorely tempted to play sick on occasion. Something about that starchy white uniform just makes me long to be bedridden."

"Just the uniform?"

Something serious suddenly touched Jake's eyes. "No. The woman in it."

Her heart skipped a beat. "Well, Jake, feel free to faint in my arms anytime."

He sent her a quick grin, his glistening teeth flashing white under his mustache. "Somehow, I'd rather play the doctor than the patient."

Just looking into his eyes made her swoon. "Want *me* to faint?"

"Be my guest."

"Okay." Dani turned, making a graceful show of leaning back against his chest. His arms circled her waist, his hands clasped across her belly, and she tilted her head and stared up at him. For a long moment, he merely swayed, holding her. Feeling his hard body behind her, how her backside was brushing against him, Dani's knees got weak and she grabbed his strong forearms to steady herself. She wanted to say, "Oh, Jake, just put your money where your mouth is and kiss me."

Before she could, he murmured, "Guess *I* don't look so hot."

"Oh, but you do!" When she realized that her quick, enthusiastic response bordered on gushing, embarrassed heat rose to her cheeks. "I mean," she corrected, still leaning in his arms and gazing up at him, "you look very nice."

Jake laughed. "C'mon, be honest. I look like hell."

"Well, you do and you don't," Dani conceded, now turning to face him, keeping her arms twined around his neck while her eyes drifted over him. Jake's threadbare jeans had been worn to the smooth texture of silk, and his tight white T-shirt sported more than one gravy splatter, but the jeans still showed off the well-delineated muscles of his thighs and his shirt molded lusciously over his pectorals.

He nodded at one of the gravy splatters. "As you can see, I've been slaving away in a hot kitchen."

"For me?"

"Who else?"

No matter how hard she tried, she couldn't quit grinning at him. She said, "Aren't you even going to kiss me hello?"

His voice was throaty. "I was thinking about it."

"Don't think too long." Heaven help her, but she loved to excite and tease this man. She wanted nothing more than to share the awakened woman he'd brought out in her. Suddenly her breath caught. Had he really stiffened against her?

Her heart missed a beat. "Is something wrong, Jake?"

He shook his head.

But even as he cuddled closer, nuzzling his cheek against hers, she felt uncertain. *Stop it, Dani. You just feel guilty about snooping today, and you're projecting the guilt onto Jake. If he was suspicious of you or if he had talked to James, he wouldn't think twice about confronting you.*

Shutting her eyes, she hugged Jake back, trying to forget the terror she'd felt when James had caught her. She'd offered some crazy, rambling explanation about how the forms in Jake's office that pertained to Grantham Hale's babies had prompted her to pull his file from the sealed records room. As nonsensical as the lie was, James had seemed to believe her.

He did believe me.

Brushing her cheek against Jake's chest, she sighed. "I missed you since last night, Jake." She wished he could have stayed with her, holding her in her tiny bed all night long. She'd missed him so much that her chest squeezed tight with guilt again. "Are you sure everything's okay?"

"Yeah."

Dani lifted her chin and gazed up at him.

He smiled back.

"Then prove it." Even as she whispered the words, she felt as if she were playing with red-hot explosives. Like dynamite or plastique, this dangerous love affair was going to blow up right in her face.

Jake leaned closer, his gravelly voice teasing the tender flesh of her ear. "You want me to prove it?"

"I wish you would."

"Be careful what you wish for."

"That's what my horoscope keeps saying," she murmured. But she only had two wishes—to find her child and to make love to Jake again. Was that really too much to ask? She tightened her hold around his neck. "Think I can't handle the likes of you?"

Jake chuckled softly. "I don't know. Can you, Dani?"

"Try me, Jake."

And he did. If she really had sensed any reluctance in Jake, it was sure gone now. There was nothing at all perfunctory in the man's kiss. Every bit as soft and slow as it was wet and deep, the kiss seemed calculated to make her remember last night—the slow heat of his hands in the dark, the way he'd entered her, so sure and quick. As the warm spear of his tongue caused a smoking thread of need to coil down inside her core, Dani's toes curled inside her lilac flats. No one had ever made her feel this full, and yet this empty. She felt pregnant, heavy in her womb, and yet so entirely ready to be filled by Jake.

Feathering kisses down her neck, his countless sweet nothings tingled against her skin. "Everything's fine," he whispered.

Leaning back her head, Dani sighed. "You think so?"

His mustache formed a smile against the sensitive skin of her neck. "I've even convinced myself."

Dani exhaled raggedly. "Of what?"

"That I'm never going to stop wanting you."

She tensed. "Oh, Jake, do you want to stop wanting me?"

There was a slight pause, a fraction too long for Dani's comfort. Then Jake's arms wrapped so tightly around her that she nearly lost her breath, and when he spoke she felt his voice, so deep it rumbled in her own chest.

"No," he said softly. "No, I don't want to stop."

Dani wished he didn't sound so leery about it. But he shot her another reassuring smile as he released her. Nodding toward a playpen beside the dining table in the next room, he said, "Dinner'll be ready soon, so I'll get the girls situated. I got Ty's old playpen out for them."

Dani chuckled. "Speaking of the devil."

"Dani!" With a gleeful shout, Ty burst from a hallway, raced across the room and grabbed her hand. "Daddy, why didn't you tell me she got here! While you go and get our dinner ready, I'm 'sposed to show Dani the whole apartment and my room. That was my big plan! And I was thinking maybe we oughta dance, 'cause you're on a date and stuff!"

Ty's boundlessly energetic enthusiasm cracked Dani

up. Jake groaned as Ty ran to the CD player. A second later "Jailhouse Rock" filled the apartment. Ty cranked the volume.

Dani gasped, laughing. Raising her voice so she could be heard, she shouted, "Elvis?"

Jake smirked and threw up his hands. "I'm old."

Thinking of last night, Dani caught his gaze and said, "Not that old." Grabbing his hand, she tugged him into the middle of the living room, where Ty was already dancing. By contrast to Jake's smooth moves, Ty's dancing was so funny that Dani doubled with laughter. The little boy made quick, finger-snapping motions that were probably soundless and crazily twitched his pint-size behind. Then, tired of that, he merely started jumping up and down.

"It's how punk rockers do it!" he squealed gleefully. "C'mon, Daddy! C'mon, Dani!"

Still laughing, Dani indulged him, jumping up and down until she was breathless. After a long time she stopped and fell into her own rhythm, dancing with Jake who caught her hand. "Jailhouse Rock" segued into something equally hard and fast and as Jake spun her against his chest, the past six years suddenly seemed to fall away. Then it hit her like a jolt. She was happy again. Really happy. At least as happy as she could be without finding her child.

"It's just Mrs. Roberts!" Ty shrieked when a series of loud thumps finally sounded on the floor. "She's hitting her ceiling with a broom. But she'll get over it!"

"No, she won't," Jake assured with a laugh. He spun Dani once more, then relinquished her and headed for the CD player, turning down the volume.

Ty groaned. "Okay, I guess I'll do Dani's tour

now," he said, taking her hand. "I'm gettin' kinda hungry, so you better go get our dinner ready, Daddy."

"Yeah, Daddy," Dani couldn't help but tease. "Go get our dinner ready." As Ty tugged her toward the hallway, she shot Jake a final, quick, playful glance over her shoulder and froze. His jaw was clenched, his eyes riveted on her and Ty's clasped hands. Just as her lips parted in shock, Jake's features reassembled. The change occurred with such stunning swiftness that Dani wound up deciding she'd simply imagined the look.

Jake smiled easily. "Go ahead, kids."

She said, "Sure you don't need help in the kitchen?"

"Nope."

Dani's unease vanished as Ty pulled her down the hallway, since it took all her concentration to keep up with his lively chatter. Apparently he and Jake had gotten a late start this morning, but they'd made it to Ty's karate tournament and Ty had won a trophy.

"This is where Daddy sleeps," Ty announced, coming to a sudden halt. Craning his neck upward, Ty sent Dani a huge grin. "See, if Daddy ever gets married, he wouldn't even have to get a new bed or anything, 'cause his is already real big."

It was definitely a far cry from the tiny, squeaky twin where they'd made love, and just looking at the king-size forest green comforter and multiple pillows piled cozily against the headboard made Dani's mouth go dry. Next to the bed was a reading table, stacked with files and books. And in the corner was a private bathroom.

"And there's lots of closet space," Ty said uncertainly after a moment. "I heard ladies like that."

Dani stifled a chuckle. "Ladies do like closets," she assured.

In response, Ty's tiny hand merely tightened around hers, and he dragged her farther down the hallway. "And this room is all mine."

"Oh, Ty!" Dani drew in a sudden, sharp breath of wonder. "It's lovely."

No wonder the little boy was so proud. Jungle foliage—magical-looking trees, leafy ferns and brightly colored flowering bushes—covered every inch of the four walls. Dinosaurs of all sorts—tyrannosaurs, brontosaurs and pterodactyls—lurked around the vegetation, as did big black panthers and bold black-and-gold-striped saber-toothed tigers with gleaming eyes. Ty's multicolored dinosaur-print bedspread was turned back, exposing the crisp sheets beneath, and a corner of his folded pajamas, also in a dinosaur print, peeked out from under his pillow.

Dani turned a full circle in the room. "Wow!"

When Ty grabbed and wrung her hand again, the pressure of the death grip almost hurt. The adorable kid was simply unable to contain his excitement.

"Pretty neat, huh, Dani?"

"It sure is." She smiled down at him. "Oh, and before I forget, I brought you something." Reaching into her bag, she withdrew a Snickers bar.

"Gosh," he said in a stunned voice, dropping her hand. "You remembered it's my favorite and everything." He took the chocolate bar and set it on his bedside table so carefully it could have been something he'd decided to frame, then he took her hand once more. "I really, really, *really* like you, Dani."

She couldn't help but laugh. "It's nice to know I rate three whole 'reallys.'"

''You really do.''

When she impulsively ruffled Ty's hair, the blondish strands felt like corn silk between her fingers. She sighed, feeling wistful. ''I think you already told me that, the other day at the police station.''

He gazed up, his eyes so round and dark and earnest that it nearly broke her heart. ''Do you like me, too, Dani?''

She brushed a thumb tenderly across his cheek. ''If I had a little boy, I'd want him to be exactly like you.''

He gulped. ''You swear? Exactly?''

She nodded. All these years, she'd been so sure she had a little girl; she'd felt it deep within her, like a premonition, though she wasn't quite sure why. But now Ty Lucas was making her long for a son. ''Just exactly,'' she whispered.

Ty flushed with pride. ''Hey, Dani, can I tell you a secret?''

She nodded, leaning down. ''Sure.''

Cupping his hand over his mouth, Ty got so close his lips touched her ear. ''My daddy *really* needs a wife, 'cause he doesn't even know how to cook anything.''

Leaning away, Dani squinted at him. ''Your daddy's cooking right now, and the apartment smells like heaven.''

''No,'' Ty insisted in a stage whisper. ''He ordered pepper steak from Charlie Mom's restaurant, then he took everything out of the cartons to make it look like he cooked. He musta heated it up again for the smell. So, see, he's gotta get married.'' Ty pinned her with a sincere gaze. ''Or else, I'm gonna have to always eat at Charlie Mom's.''

Jake's far-off shout suddenly tunneled down the hall-way. "Ready for dinner, you two?"

"Yes," they shouted back.

Once she and Ty were seated, Dani glanced through an open door to the kitchen. It was awfully neat in there. Was Jake truly passing off takeout as home cooking? As he emerged from the kitchen, tugging a clean T-shirt over his broad chest, Ty's words replayed in her mind. *My daddy really needs a wife.*

Did he? It was easy enough for Dani to imagine living in this homey apartment, with its magical jungle room and cozy king-size bed. Jake had even arranged the flowers she'd brought in a crystal vase on the table. By comparison, her own apartment seemed so bare. Yes, everything she'd ever wanted was here—a sexy man, a loving child. Babies. It was so easy to imagine the intimacy she was sharing with Jake as part of her everyday life. She guessed she'd quit looking for all these things six years ago.

Jake's voice roused her from her thoughts. "Let's eat."

While they did, she and Jake gabbed. Ty talked about his win at the karate tournament. He even rose once, ignoring all his father's protests, to demonstrate a series of lethal kicks and karate chops for Dani.

When Ty flung himself into his chair again, he said, "Hey, Dani, I'm gonna put on my pajamas early. Then you have to put Lyssa and Kirby in my bed and read us all a story, okay?"

She glanced at Jake. After a moment, he nodded his assent. "Okay," she said. Between her last bites, she continued, "This pepper steak is simply out of this world, Jake."

Ty giggled.

Jake squinted at him. "What's so funny?"

Ty didn't bother to answer. He looked at Dani. "I'm tryin' to make Dad 'dopt Lyssa and Kirby if we can't find their sisters. Would you like to have lots of kids, Dani? Or just one or two?"

Jake gasped. "Ty, c'mon. Dani might not want to answer such a personal question."

Dani chuckled. "I really don't mind." She glanced at Ty. "I...hadn't thought about it too much. But I really think I'd love to have lots of kids."

Ty beamed at her. Then his face suddenly fell. "Daddy!" he exclaimed in censure, lunging from his seat and flying across the room. Only then did Dani notice the small snapshot of a woman propped discreetly on a sideboard. It had to be Ty's mother, Lanie. She was beautiful. The shape of her face wasn't like Ty's, but they shared the same coloring, with their blondish hair and dark eyes. Ty shoved the picture into a drawer.

Whirling around, he stared angrily at his father. "What did you put that there for? May I please be excused?"

Jake glanced toward his son's clean plate. "Sure."

Ty turned directly to Dani, shutting out his father, his voice still tense with emotion. "I'm gonna get ready for our story now, Dani."

"Okay," she said.

As Ty marched angrily toward the hallway, Jake cleared his throat. "He's..."

"Temperamental about his mother?" Dani ventured.

Jake's eyes settled on her for a long moment. Something she couldn't quite define crossed his features. Indecision, maybe. Then his voice turned unusually gruff. "Yes, I'm afraid so."

Dani's heart wrenched. *Poor Jake.* Even though his relationship with Lanie was over, he'd apparently left her picture in view so Ty wouldn't ever forget his mom. "Why did you and Lanie…"

"Divorce?" Jake shrugged. "The usual things, I guess. We just kind of grew apart."

It wasn't much of an explanation. And Dani wanted to know more. "Well," she found herself murmuring, "given the glimpse I saw of her, your ex-wife's beautiful. Ty's…the spitting image of her."

A tension Dani didn't understand seemed to snap in the air. Everything seemed to pause—the hum of the refrigerator in the kitchen, the distant traffic. Then the ceiling creaked as someone walked across the floor upstairs. Dani realized she'd actually been holding her breath and slowly exhaled.

Jake cleared his throat. "Uh, yeah…Ty does look like Lanie."

"How old was Ty when…" *You and Lanie divorced?*

"Just a baby."

"Oh."

So Ty hadn't even really known his mother. How horrible. No wonder he so desperately wanted a mom. "And she didn't keep in touch with Ty?"

Jake merely shook his head.

In the following silence, Dani cast around for something to lighten the mood. There'd be plenty of time for her and Jake to share more about their pasts. *But will you tell him your secret, Dani?* She'd never told anyone she'd given away her baby. But she'd have to tell Jake. Eventually Jake would ask for her last name—it seemed odd he hadn't already—and he'd realize the truth.

But maybe not. In a flash fantasy, Dani imagined herself in a wedding dress at the altar. Jake was on one side of her in a tux; Ty was on the other, holding a velvet pillow with the wedding rings.

A minister said, "And do you, Dani, er, Dani..."

And she said, "Sorry, but I swear, I don't even *have* a last name." And then she simply smiled at Jake and said, "I do, anyway. Okay?"

"Penny for your thoughts," Jake said.

Dani heaved a playful sigh. "Nothing. C'mon. I'll help with the dishes, then we'll throw all the kids in Ty's bed and read a story."

Again a shadow seemed to cross Jake's eyes, but he grinned. "Sounds good to me."

As they entered the kitchen, Dani laced her fingers through his, suddenly giggling. "Or *are* there dirty pots and pans?" she asked, glancing toward the nearly empty sink. "Ty swears you ordered dinner from Charlie Mom's."

Jake turned around to face her, leaning against the counter. "That little liar," he said with a chuckle. "He told you that?"

She rested her palms flat against Jake's chest, then began drawing small enticing circles on his shirt with her fingernails. "I think he was trying to convince me that you desperately need a woman in your life who can cook."

"I made that dinner," Jake protested.

Dani smiled. "Ever think of getting remarried?"

Jake looped his arms around her, pulling her against him. "Yeah, but I want to make sure I'm not jumping out of a frying pan and into a fire."

"Do I look like a fire?"

He smiled, his eyes crinkling at the corners, making

no apology for his gaze drifting downward, over her breasts. "You sure ain't the frying pan."

"Well, you know what they say about fire, don't you?"

His eyes sparkled. "What?"

Her voice turned husky. "That you're supposed to fight it with fire."

"Will do," he whispered as his lips found hers for the second time that night. Heart and soul, Dani poured herself into that kiss, suddenly feeling jealous, desperately wanting Jake all for herself, wishing Jake and Lanie had never shared the most important thing a man and woman ever could—the birth of Ty, the birth of their son.

Oh yes, Dani thought, she'd kiss Jake Lucas so long and hard that he'd know he'd definitely left the frying pan for the fire, her fire.

And then, if Lanie was a problem…well, he'd never think about Ty's mother again.

"'LOOK!' EXCLAIMED the little lost prince," Dani read, "'there's the castle!' The little prince was finally home. He had searched for the lost kingdom, for the King and Queen, his mother and father…"

Jake blew out a murderous sigh. Dani's voice was so musical that it was damn near lulling *him* to sleep. This whole wretched night simply couldn't have gone more wrong. Ty had shown Dani all the family photo albums, videotapes from his birthday parties, then ascertained that Dani was perfectly agreeable to getting two dalmatian puppies. Which, of course, Ty wanted. And now Dani was cozily curled up in Jake's son's bed.

In her son's bed.

The mere thought curdled Jake's blood. No, he truly couldn't stand to look at her. Not at that sexy new hairdo, with the wispy tendrils that framed her gorgeous heart-shaped face. Or at the dress, the hemline of which had risen on her long, shapely legs. Or at the feminine little lilac flats she'd kicked off and left on the floor, so that she could cross her slender, kissable feet at the ankles without soiling Ty's bedspread.

Even more excruciating to watch was how Ty snuggled right against her ample chest. The two sleeping babies were sweetly tucked on Ty's other side, and Ty was gazing dreamily up at Dani as if she were a shooting star and he was intent on making a wish. Which he was—for Dani to be his mom.

Jake stared at them from the armchair he'd had to drag in from the living room, as if he were the family outcast. He'd been a fool to kiss her. And not just once, but twice, and so deeply he'd gotten fully aroused. Not that that was unusual. From the first time he'd laid eyes on her, the woman had kept him in a perpetual state of agony.

Now Jake almost groaned out loud. How was he supposed to get rid of Dani Newland when she kept brushing up against him and rubbing all over him, smelling like a garden blooming in heaven? Even worse, for all her duplicity, it was obvious she genuinely shared his soft spot for kids.

So why did she give Ty up?

I don't know, but I swear I'm not kissing her again.

Jake had to get rid of her, and preferably before he sank any lower. Putting out Lanie's picture was so calculating that he could barely live with himself. It had been risky, too. For a second, Jake thought Ty was going to announce he was adopted. Of course, even that wouldn't be enough to make Dani guess the truth.

Jake zeroed in on her melodious voice again.

"'Mother!' the little prince cried with joy—" Dani paused, resituating the book so Ty could better see the pictures of the all-important mother-son reunion in the story. "'Oh, Mother, I've missed you so!'"

Jake rolled his eyes. And he thought *he* was calculating. It was sure no accident that Ty had chosen this story about the little lost prince who was searching for his parents.

She is his parent.

Jake cringed, suddenly imagining her clawing through the *N* drawer in the sealed records room. The instant James had caught her going through the files, he'd phoned. Not that it mattered. The file Dani sought had been in Jake's bedside drawer since last night. The night security guard at Big Apple Babies had let Jake in.

His eyes drifted over Dani and Ty. And then he told himself to forget their dinner conversation. But listening to Dani's comments about the resemblance between Ty and Lanie had been too much to bear. Of course Ty and Lanie looked alike. All along Jake had known Ty would be genetically predisposed to look like her. But then, Lanie had never become a mother to Ty. And Dani wouldn't, either.

"Jake?" Dani whispered.

Startled, Jake glanced up. He realized Ty's eyes were shut now. "Hmm?"

"What are you thinking about?"

"You." At least that much was the truth.

Dani set the storybook aside then stood, lifting Lyssa and Kirby. "Is that good or bad?" she teased.

Jake didn't have a clue. "Good."

Ty's eyes suddenly opened in small, swollen-looking slits, and his arms shot in the air. "You forgot to kiss me good-night, Dani."

Her voice was gentle. "I thought you were asleep."

Jake found himself relieving Dani of the babies. Then his body tensed as she returned to the bed and his son's short arms wreathed around her neck. It was all more than Jake could stand, how tightly Ty clung to this woman whose hair brushed his cheeks...who smelled of flowers and a femininity that Jake could never provide in their masculine home. Even as Dani's fingers touched his son's hair, Jake himself could feel the familiar silken strands against his own fingertips.

He thought his heart would break. His voice came out sounding tight, edgy. "C'mon, Ty. That's enough. You need to get some sleep."

Only then did Ty relinquish her. *His mother,* Jake thought, guilt rushing in on him. Yesterday it had all seemed so clear-cut. Jake didn't want Ty hurt. Now, knowing how desperately his son wanted a mother, could he really deprive him?

Absolutely.

Dani Newland had signed Ty's life away. With one flourish of the pen, she'd signed the dotted line, making Ty belong to Jake. *She doesn't deserve him. She never did.*

"Night, Ty-ger," she whispered as she slipped into her flats, then switched off the bedside lamp.

The muscles of Jake's stomach clenched. She even had a pet name for him, already. Somehow it made him want to hurt her, as if she'd actually taken away his son.

"I'd better get going," she whispered as Jake walked her into the hallway, still carrying the babies.

"I'll drive you."

She shook her head. "I'll get a cab. That way, you don't have to get Mrs. Roberts to come and watch Ty."

He hesitated. He knew from experience how hard it was to load two babies into a cab. And yet, he also knew he had to foster a distance from her. So he silently helped pack up the babies and then walked her to the door.

"Thanks for everything," she said.

Those soulful dark eyes, so much like Ty's, were lit up with expectation. Jake knew he was supposed to say something about their lovemaking last night. To assure Dani he couldn't wait until it happened again. To kiss her.

Instead, he simply cracked open the door. "Well, I guess you've got everything."

She nodded. "We'll be fine. You don't need to walk us to the elevator."

I hadn't planned to. Jake opened the door wider.

She glanced down at the babies and frowned. "I was so sure we'd find out where they came from by now," she suddenly murmured. "And find the two that are missing."

Jake was more worried than he wanted to admit. Especially since the court date was barely a week away. He sighed. "I really want to step up the search for them," he said, assuring himself that working with Dani was the least of his motives. "Tomorrow, after I drop Ty off at school, I'll meet you at Judge Winslow's."

She nodded. "I have class tomorrow night. But I know the judge expects you."

"And I—" There was just no easy way to say it. "Dani, I think we should back off a little."

He'd known the words would hurt her. But he didn't expect her to look wounded to her mortal soul. The smoky depths of those chocolate eyes searched his. He tried to tell himself he was glad he was hurting her. That she deserved it for using and betraying him. But seeing the naked emotion in her gaze, Jake felt both desire and guilt tear at him. Against all reason, he gentled his voice. "Maybe we shouldn't necessarily stop seeing each other entirely, just…"

He stopped, realizing tears were in her eyes now.

"You want to see me—" Her tone was clipped. "You don't want to see me. Just tell me what you want, Jake."

"I…" *Want to carry you down the hallway, Dani. Lay you across my king-size bed and take you slow and easy. Start at your feet. Massage them. Suck your toes. Then lick wet kisses right up the insides of your thighs. I want to make you ache and burn for me like you did last night, to bury myself inside you so deep that there's nothing left in the dark but you crying out my name.*

And then Jake never wanted to see her again.

"You what, Jake?"

Damn. He should have known Dani Newland wasn't the kind of woman who'd step in and offer a guy an easy way out. Oh, no. She was going to make him suffer. "Well, like you said, Ty's got some negative feelings about…"

"His mother?"

Jake couldn't bring himself to come lie overtly and say Lanie was Ty's mother. But he nodded. "I don't want him hurt." *And I don't want you near him.*

Dani's jaw set. "So am I to expect you at the judge's tomorrow?"

He stared at her. "Yeah. I said I'd be there, didn't I?"

"You don't have to come."

With this woman, Jake couldn't win for losing. He definitely wanted the new Dani back. The smiling Dani who'd changed out of her starchy uniform and into a soft, feminine dress just for him, whose wanting arms were so quick to twine around his neck. *The sweet Dani who broke into the sealed records room today.* "The judge wants me working on this," Jake said. "So, I'll be there."

"Well," Dani said as if she couldn't care less, "see ya."

"Oh, please," Jake muttered. Whatever part of his anatomy made the decision, it probably was not his head. But he stepped close, grabbed her around the waist, backed her against the door and kissed her.

It was supposed to be a swift, hard kiss, the kind a man used to make his point. But there was too much heat between them, and too much need. Jake's blood turned thick, heat pooled in his belly, and he moaned softly against her lips. Even as he told himself he'd lost his mind, he was powerless to stop.

Until a little throat cleared right behind him.

Dani gasped, squirming away. "Ty," she croaked.

Sighing, Jake turned toward his son. "Go back to bed," he said shakily.

Ty giggled sleepily. "I just wanted to tell you I'll be sound asleep after this, Daddy! I promise I won't wake up again, no matter *what* happens!" With that, Ty hurriedly spun around and ran to his room as if the devil were on his heels.

Ty's announcement made Jake's head reel. Heaven only knew what assumptions the six-year-old was making about what grown-ups did when the lights went out.

"I can certainly see why you're worried about him being hurt," Dani said dryly. "He seems so terribly opposed to having a woman in his life."

Jake stared at her. "You think I'm using Ty as an excuse to keep out of a relationship?"

Her eyes trailed to where Jake had her pinned against the door frame. "Yeah. And since you're so anxious to avoid relationships, do you mind letting me go?"

Damn, she could be passive aggressive. But even as Jake stepped back, he already missed her—how she clung to him, her legs starting to part, the heat seeping through her pretty dress. "Don't pretend you didn't enjoy that kiss," he said.

She shrugged. "Sure I did. But if you're not interested in pursuing a relationship, then why kiss me?"

Hell, Dani, I didn't want to. I just couldn't stop myself. His voice was husky. "It was just a kiss goodbye."

"Well, goodbye," Dani returned matter-of-factly, ducking beneath his arm and out of his embrace. "And from here on out, I think it's best if our relationship remained strictly professional."

Jake's lips parted in astonishment. "Dani, wait—"

But it was too late. Dani and the babies vanished through the door. And just as Jake followed, Dani reached around and slammed the door right in his face.

A second later, Ty materialized, letting out a frustrated yowl. "Daddy!"

Jake sighed, turning toward the hallway. "What, Ty?"

"Dani was kissing you and you started talking about

me!'' Ty shoved his fisted hands on his hips. "And you put out that stupid picture of Lanie! Daddies are 'sposed to be smart. Can't you do *anything* right?'' Ty whirled around and charged down the hallway again.

Jake followed him. But his son's door slammed in his face, too.

Leaning against the wall, Jake shut his eyes. He'd done what he'd had to do. He'd gotten rid of Ty's mother. From day one, Dani Newland had betrayed him. She'd come into his life under false pretenses and used him to access sealed files at his office.

Yeah, you got rid of her, Jake.

Trouble was, he already wanted her back.

Chapter Seven

"Nurse Dani! Have you not yet noticed I am entrapped again?" Judge Winslow bellowed. "And before you to come to my aid, please ensure I am rid of all that odious junk mail!"

Dani sighed. The judge had wedged his wheelchair in the front door again, and the doorman was nowhere to be seen. "By odious," she called out as she tossed the envelopes into Evie Pope's wastebasket at the busy front desk, "I assume you mean all communications that pertain to donations, charities and fund-raisers?"

"I may be rich," Judge Winslow growled as he lifted his cane from his lap and batted angrily at the glass door, "but I didn't get that way by throwing out hard-earned money! Or paying nurses to leave me stranded!"

Dani quickly reached for the usual clipboards one by one, signing for the dry cleaning, then the pressed shirts. "Well, after what happened last Friday," she called, "I'm devoting my full attention to the correct receipt of your packages."

"Oh, that's right," the judge exploded. "I forgot you abandoned me in this doorway *last* Friday, as well!"

"And wound up with your two little next of kins for roommates," Dani retorted, turning from a UPS delivery man just long enough to shoot a hawklike glance at the stroller. She half expected her two precious charges to suddenly disappear, vanishing as mysteriously as they'd come. All week, her thoughts had turned to Grantham Hale, the widower who'd managed to adopt the twin boys. Apparently single people such as herself or Grantham Hale *could* adopt. And kids raised by good single parents could turn out beautifully, as Ty had, even if the poor little boy did so desperately want a mother.

Catching Dani's thoughtful expression, Lyssa giggled and clapped her hands. Kirby waved. And Dani couldn't help but smile. "Hey, you two cuties," she crooned.

Judge Winslow groaned. "Oh, forget about my weak heart. The sappy way you keep drooling over those babies, I'll surely perish from a glucose overdose. And speaking of my sugar, Nurse Dani, do check my groceries. Last week, I was missing a five-pound bag."

Dani shot him a long, level look. "You're not even supposed to *have* sugar. And need I remind you I was hired to be a nurse, not a *nursemaid.*"

"Ha! There you go again! Are you fighting with Jake Lucas? Ever since last Sunday night, you have been absolutely intolerable, even when the poor fellow visits."

"Visits?" Dani muttered. "We're working. Looking for Lyssa and Kirby's sisters."

Evie Pope glanced up from her book. "Oh no, something happened between you and Jake? The way you two always stare at each other, I was sure marriage was in the cards, and soon."

Dani rolled her eyes as she pocketed her pen and began checking the contents of the grocer's delivery boxes. "Just keep reading that romance novel, Evie."

"Well, somebody has to believe in happy endings."

"Better you than me," Dani returned dryly just as the doorman materialized and released the judge.

"Free at last, free at last," Judge Winslow intoned, wheeling across the lobby.

Well, maybe the judge was right, Dani thought. Since leaving Jake's last Sunday, she had felt testy. In fact, by high noon on Monday, she could have sworn the whole island of Manhattan had transformed itself into a giant postal office, chock-full of the proverbial disgruntled workers, of which she, too, was one. Overnight, and after six long years of blissful anonymity, Dani had developed a sudden love-hate relationship with all things New York. As of early Tuesday, the hate side was winning. She'd started fantasizing about fleeing all this city craziness for good.

She kept telling herself she'd go where the walls were thicker than tissue paper and where she wouldn't hear every toilet flush in a five-mile radius. Somewhere without sirens. Maybe somewhere like Akron, Ohio, where she could get a normal apartment. One with a big square bedroom and a living room without a bathroom sink in it. Maybe she'd get a sporty convertible, too, and drive it hard and fast, right down to the wheel rims.

She didn't know whether she wanted to flee because she was feeling so painfully sure she'd never find her child, after all.

Or because she felt so damn conflicted about Jake.

Or more likely, because Jake had made her start wanting a normal life again and she was scared. Could she really make things work with a man like Jake? Was she responsible enough to become a mother to someone else's little boy?

Not that Jake was asking. No, technically, they weren't even seeing each other.

Dani sighed. Maybe she hadn't confessed that Jake was the lawyer who'd handled the adoption of her baby. But Jake Lucas definitely came with his own brand of trouble. And there was no way Dani would carry a torch for a man who made love to her like he had, then turned right around and broke up with her.

Well, sort of broke up.

Trouble was, Jake hadn't really. Oh, he said they weren't together but, in reality, they'd become inseparable. They met for breakfast, lunch and dinner. Before and after her classes. And they talked on the phone late at night. Even worse, she'd borrowed one of his wool cardigans on a cool night, and it had wound up in her bed. Yes—she'd never admit it to anyone—but she was actually sleeping with the man's sweater pressed against her cheek like a lovesick teenager.

"Pathetic," Dani muttered, ruminating under her breath.

So was the way the judge kept matchmaking, keeping them on the run, trying to find the missing babies. Ty kept claiming he couldn't do his homework—according to Ty, they'd suddenly gotten lots of it in first grade—unless Dani took all her nursing books to Jake's and studied with him. Studiously Jake would don the wire-frame reading glasses he apparently wore and pore over his paperwork from Big Apple Babies.

At least until Ty and the babies were asleep.

And then Jake couldn't keep his hands off her. And Dani couldn't keep hers off him. So, even though Jake kept saying they should back off, she was usually wrapped tight in his arms when he said it. Each time he held her, that embrace had gotten more comfortable, too, until she'd started to feel they'd been together for years.

Not that she was going to sleep with him again.

No. A woman had to draw the line somewhere.

And she wouldn't have sex with Jake again unless he said he was committed. Still, every time he pulled her close and kissed her hard, she melted. And got just a little bit madder at him.

And fell for him just a little bit more.

If only they could find Rosita de Silva. After all, when the missing quadruplets were found, Dani would at least have the option of not seeing Jake. Except for Monday in court, which was now only two days away.

And today, since Jake was on his way over.

And tonight, since they were going out to dinner. And tomorrow since... Dani simply couldn't believe how hard she was falling for Jake, or how scared she was getting. Even worse, her mother had awakened her this morning with a phone call, making one more impassioned plea for Dani to patch things up with her father.

But really, the main trouble was Jake. Because now Dani knew that the mean man who'd stolen away her baby, who'd appeared in her imagination for years looking like James Sanger, had never even existed.

There was only Jake. And what he was stealing was her heart. Oh, she tried to stay mad at him for sending out all the crazy mixed signals, but then she'd see those sexy dimples deepen and those green eyes dance, and he'd take her in his strong arms and her heart would flood with happiness and all she wanted to do was to make love to him and—

"Nurse Dani!"

Dani nearly jumped out of her skin. "What!"

Judge Winslow looked her up and down. "Pardon me for mentioning it, but you've been standing there, holding that bag of sugar for five full minutes."

"Oh." She replaced the sugar in the grocery box. When her eyes dropped over the judge, she suddenly had to fight to suppress a smile. His right pant leg had been hemmed to accommodate his cast, so all Ty's wild, multicolored drawings were visible.

Nearby a man cleared his throat. Dani glanced up and found herself looking at one of Judge Lathrop's law clerks. Reaching into her uniform pocket, she withdrew her pen again, but the clerk held his clipboard protectively against the front of his steel gray suit.

"Uh, no offense," he stammered, "but after what happened last Friday, well, Judge Lathrop insisted we have the judge sign."

At the hint of Dani's possible incompetence, Judge Winslow chuckled gleefully.

"Oh, ha, ha, ha," Dani said. Flicking the end of her pen, she offered it to the judge.

"A ballpoint?" Judge Winslow sniffed, then drew an elegant black fountain pen from his shirt pocket. Leaning forward, while the clerk held the clipboard, the judge very carefully signed his name. Dani moved behind the wheelchair, ready to push the judge to the elevator. Suddenly she gasped, her eyes riveting on the signature.

That's where she'd seen it!

It was the same hand that had penned the framed

letter in Jake's office, which meant the honorable Judge Tilford Winslow was Big Apple Babies' secret backer!

COCKING HER HEAD toward the newscast that blared from the living room TV, Dani backed against the closed kitchen door, guaranteeing that neither Judge Winslow nor the babies could disrupt her discussion with Jake. "I didn't say anything to him," she assured in a hushed tone.

Jake stared at her, still looking shell-shocked. For the first fifteen minutes after his arrival, he'd merely sat on a stool at the kitchen's island, chewing moodily on his mustache. Now he leaned beside Dani, wedging a powerful shoulder against the door. "But I still don't get it," he whispered. "Why me?"

"I don't know, Jake, but it's true."

He stared down at the grocery list in his hand, one Dani had filched from the judge's writing desk, his eyes drifting over the shaky cursive. "Well, there's no mistaking his handwriting. It's too distinctive."

"Oh, Jake," she whispered. "I...I don't know why I didn't recognize Judge Winslow's writing before." But, of course, she did. If she hadn't been so selfishly intent on finding her own child at Big Apple Babies, she'd have made the connection. Maybe the lost babies would have been found by now, too. Guilt flooded her and only the fact that she still wanted to find her child kept her from confessing every last one of her miserable transgressions.

Jake thoughtfully toyed with his mustache. "And you didn't say anything?"

"No. I thought you might want to protect his privacy. I mean, the judge did give you seven million dollars, and he obviously wanted to do so anonymously."

Jake frowned. "Judge Winslow's rich, but I don't think even he has that kind of money. There must have been other secret contributors." Jake shook his head again. "But who? And why would they give the money to *me?*"

Dani's hands crept around his neck. "Because you're such a swell guy?"

Jake smiled. "There's got to be more to it than that."

"I haven't the foggiest. But the more I think about it, I guess you'd better confront the judge, Jake. I mean, I know his donations were anonymous, but what if Lyssa and Kirby aren't Judge Winslow's next of kin at all? What if there was some kind of…" Dani paused, blew out a quick sigh and shrugged. "Well, I don't know, some kind of paperwork mixup, and those girls were delivered here because of Judge Winslow's secret connection to Big Apple Babies?"

Jake's eyebrows raised as if to say she had a point. "And there's another possibility."

Dani realized her eyes had momentarily strayed, dropping from Jake's eyes to his chest, to his soft-looking emerald V-neck sweater. "What?"

"Maybe the quadruplets are his kids."

Dani's eyes narrowed. "Are you kidding?"

Jake shrugged. "Men can have kids at any age. Maybe they're his and he's been trying to cover it up. Maybe something happened to the mother."

"They do have his blue eyes," Dani murmured. "Given Judge Winslow's winning personality, do you want to be the one to ask him?"

Jake chuckled softly. "You're going to make me do the talking?"

Dani sent him a long, sideways glance. "You're the one who's about to get sued."

When Jake smiled again, the corners of his eyes crinkled and green lights shone in the irises. "Yeah. But you know him better."

"Jake," Dani said, and scowled. "You have a bad habit of trying to weasel out of things that might be difficult."

"I knew this would come back around to us."

"I didn't say a word about us."

But hadn't she meant he was trying to weasel out of a relationship with her? She glanced away uncomfortably, then forced herself to go on. "Maybe I do want an explanation of why you say you want to back off when you obviously want to be with me."

Dani swallowed hard and raised her eyes again. Jake merely lifted a finger and brushed an imaginary lock of hair from her forehead. She thought of countless things she didn't have the nerve to say, that Jake wasn't the kind of man who hedged. That the night they'd made love, he sure hadn't asked. All he'd taken for a permission slip was her needy kisses. "Well, Jake? Why say you want to back off if you want to be with me?"

His lips parted, but instead of speaking, he sighed. Something flickered in the depths of his eyes. Caution, maybe. "I have my reasons."

Dani's pulse suddenly raced. Jake knew who she was. She was sure of it now. Had he been hoping she'd come clean of her own accord, proving herself honest so he could love her? Maybe James Sanger had called Jake, after all. She gulped around the lump in her throat, trying to steady her nerves. *Don't be a fool, Dani. If Jake knew something, he would have said so.*

"Does it have anything to do with…your ex-wife?"

"Lanie?" The surprise in Jake's voice said his ex-wife wasn't an issue. So did his eyes, caressing Dani now, and his body that suddenly pressed closer, warming her side. His voice turned throaty. "Look, Dani, right now, you and I are here…together."

"Well, for a man who's not dating me, you've sure come on to me a lot this week."

Jake smiled, lazily arching an eyebrow. "You don't come on to me?"

She chuckled softly. "I don't initiate."

His voice dropped. "Oh, you're a paragon of virtue."

She wasn't. So she searched his face, expecting to find proof of a double meaning. All she saw were eyes that drifted downward and settled pointedly on her caressing hands. Smiling, she merely continued to rub circles on his chest. "You call this initiating something?" When Jake chuckled, the soft rumble sent heat through her.

"I've been initiated, Dani. I call this getting to know the ropes."

"Ropes bind," she warned softly.

"But aren't binds made to be broken?"

Maybe some. But not those between a man and woman who loved each other. Or between a mother and child. Sadness twisted inside her. "I thought rules were made to be broken."

He smiled. "Let's break those, too."

Dani's fingertips suddenly tingled. They had a memory of their own and recalled the thatches of his thick dark chest hair, and a long line she'd traced yesterday from between his pectorals, all the way down his flat, taut belly to his belt. She forced her fingers to still.

Jake laughed, as if to say her resolve wouldn't last. She knew he was right, too. He'd haunted her mind for six long years, and now his body held an even greater power over her. So much so that she knew he could break her heart. "Jake, I...I can't pursue a relationship that's going nowhere."

He angled his head downward. Right before his lips closed over hers, he gently murmured, "No one's asking you to, Dani."

Slow and probing, the kiss was as pure as a white satin sheet. It made Dani think of timeless things...of wind and air. And the ocean near the house in Genesis. How the curtains of her old white canopied bed used to lift gently in the breeze, carrying scents of sea salt and the cry of gulls. When Jake drew away, she gazed dreamily into his eyes.

He grinned. "So, are you going to do the talking?"

She smirked. "Was that kiss just a bribe?"

"Nothing more," Jake said lazily, though his eyes said different.

Dani suddenly sobered. Jake could play her so easily. He wasn't above using his kisses as bribes, but what else did he want from her? And what were his other mysterious reasons for not wanting to see her? She edged backward a pace.

His voice was still husky. "What's wrong?"

That I want nothing more than to stay in your arms, and I know I can't. "I'll talk myself blue in the face if you'll just let me go."

"You didn't feel all that desperate to leave a second ago."

"Well now it's a second later," Dani returned tartly.

"Sure it's not you who's trying to weasel out of a relationship, Dani?"

Color heated her cheeks. "I'm just trying to protect myself. C'mon, lets talk to the judge!" She pushed gently past Jake.

But he was right behind her. Even as she stepped carefully around Lyssa and Kirby, who were playing on the living room floor, she felt his chest, that delectable wall of strength and heat, pressing against her back.

Judge Winslow muted the news with his remote, then swung his wheelchair around. His usually acerbic tone softened with concern. "Nurse Dani, your face is flushed. Oh dear, have you taken ill?" Judge Winslow's piercing blue eyes suddenly crinkled with amusement, tweaking her temper. "Now, don't tease her too much, Jake," the judge crooned. "Nurse Dani's got a very sharp tongue."

And the judge was about to hear it. Dani mustered her sweetest smile. "Since we're being so direct, may I get right to the point?"

"Please do."

The judge looked so sanctimonious that Dani simply came out with it. "Judge, are Lyssa and Kirby your babies?"

Judge Winslow looked positively mortified. He stared at Dani as if he'd never seen her before. "Excuse me. Do you mean as in *mine?*"

Dani nodded. As Jake put his arm around her waist, her eyes shot to his. Was he about to ask the judge about his status as the secret backer of Big Apple Babies?

Jake cleared his throat. "Judge Winslow, we have some surprising new information."

"Information?"

Dani sighed, suddenly feeling guilty. "I'm sorry, but we have to ask. Are you the father?"

"No! And what's your purpose in asking? Are you trying to give me a heart attack, Nurse Dani? Are you out of your mind?"

"So much for that avenue of inquiry," she murmured.

Judge Winslow gaped at them. "What on earth gave you two such a preposterous idea?"

Jake was squinting cautiously at the judge. "Sir, when you signed for Judge Lathrop's package today, Dani recognized your handwriting. She had also seen it on a framed letter in my office, which means that you're a secret backer for my business."

The judge colored slightly but otherwise didn't react. "That's all you know?"

Dani leaned forward curiously. "There's more?"

Judge Winslow glared at her. "Not that I'd divulge."

Jake's hold around Dani's waist tightened. "Judge, I know you wanted to be anonymous, and I respect that. But now, since I know this much…why me? Can I ask that? I mean, I'm sure we never met."

Judge Winslow's eyes settled on Jake, then he sighed. "Jake, you were the best prosecutor we'd seen around family court for years. Oh, you never came before me, but I was aware of your background, that you were adopted and had an emotional investment in your work. But then, so do many lawyers.

"You were special, though. I heard you worked ceaselessly, sixteen-hour days, and fought like a dog for your clients. You always won, too, taking people to hell and back on the witness stand. Because of you, a lot of helpless kids were spared horrible abuses.''

"But I quit."

Judge Winslow shrugged. "If you hadn't, you would have burned out and been unable to do anything for anyone.''

Jake shook his head. "And that's it? That's the reason I was the recipient of that check...and those that followed?''

Judge Winslow stared at him. "Isn't that enough?''

Jake's voice was low. "I just don't know what to say.''

The judge pursed his lips sourly, but a twinkle remained in his eyes. "Nothing would be my preference. But you must promise me that you...and you—'' he glared ferociously at Dani again "—will never divulge my identity. Nor attempt to discover the identity of any other backers. Each has personal reasons for anonymity.''

Dani's voice softened. "What was yours?''

Judge Winslow rolled his eyes. "If I were identified as a philanthropist, I'd be hounded by fund-raising socialites. My reputation as a mean old judge, a reputation it took me nearly a century to build, would be utterly destroyed.''

Dani scrutinized him, her mind running wild. Did Judge Winslow have some other, undisclosed, connection to Jake? Something that had to do with Jake's paternity, maybe? "I don't believe that's the whole reason for one instant.''

"Oh, yes," began the judge. "If anyone knew I gave away a million dollars—''

"Ah!" Dani interjected. "Since Jake's facility was

seven million, does that mean there are six other backers?''

Judge Winslow looked suddenly livid. "I'm quite serious, Nurse Dani. Cross me on this one, and I won't ever forgive you."

"Sorry," she murmured demurely. "It won't happen again."

Jake still looked stunned. "So, you really weren't going to sue me?"

"No! I just wanted to encourage you to do everything possible to bring this affair to a speedy resolution. Of course, Suzanne Billings is going to make your life miserable come Monday morning." The judge paused and wrung his hands. "I just wish we knew who hired her. At any rate, as you've guessed, Lyssa and Kirby's arrival may have to do with my backing of Big Apple Babies. Quite possibly, they're not related to me." Judge Winslow cleared his throat. "And," he added drolly, "they are definitely not my daughters."

Jake voice was firm. "We're doing everything we can, sir."

But they weren't!

Dani gasped, her hand flying to her mouth as if to capture the sound. "I forgot," she said hurriedly, glancing between Jake and Judge Winslow. "I found some yellow papers in Jake's office for babies Rosita had delivered, including for Lyssa and Kirby."

Jake groaned. "Was there anything useful on them?"

Dani shrugged guiltily. "I don't know. I wedged them under your phone so they wouldn't get lost." She waited for Judge Winslow to make some snide remark about her burying the clues. But it was Jake who spoke.

"Why didn't you tell me?"

Because she'd been so intent on sneaking inside Big Apple Babies sealed records room, then so mortified at getting caught. "I...forgot," she repeated, pressing a hand to her heart. "Oh, if anything's happened to those babies, I'll never forgive myself."

Jake and the judge merely stared at her.

Then as if by consensus, their lips curled downward in displeasure. Not that Dani blamed the two men. Jake was about to be sued. And the judge had a vested interest in the business that Jake could lose. *And then there's you, Dani. You were selfish and irresponsible enough to give up a baby. A living, breathing human being. And you're just as selfish now. Two babies are missing, and you're sneaking around, lying to Jake and burying the clues!*

Dani clasped her trembling hands in front of her. Suddenly she wanted to cry.

"C'mon," Jake growled. "Get your pocketbook."

Dani stared warily up at him. "Where are we going?"

"You say that like I'm taking you to a dungeon."

Jake sure looked angry enough. "Just wondering," she said weakly.

He blew out a long, exaggerated sigh. "Big Apple Babies."

"You ARE ALL STILL perfectly anonymous!" Judge Winslow assured for the umpteenth time. "I am merely phoning to inform you that Jake Lucas knows about *me.*"

There was a silence.

Then a unified gasp.

Then six people other than the judge began chattering in six extremely well appointed living rooms in Manhattan.

"Winslow, you're my best friend. But you never should have handwritten that letter," accused a shaking, elderly male voice. "As a lawman, you know better than to leave such a clue!"

"Now, it's not the end of the world, you old-timers." The youthful, soothing female voice was strangely undefinable, but hinted at Southern roots. The identity of the woman to whom it belonged was a complete mystery to the other backers. While they knew each other socially, the woman had insisted she could never meet face-to-face.

Judge Winslow's best friend sighed. "Well, since we're gathered on this conference call, we must discuss my replacement."

The words saddened the judge, who wished his ninety-year-old friend wasn't so ill. "I won't hear of it."

"Absolutely not!" said another aged voice, spoken by a man who had made his great contributions to New York City back in the days when it was still safe to sleep on the fire escapes on long, hot summer nights.

"Sorry, but I've only got time to discuss Jake Lucas and those missing quads today, folks. I've got a couple of babies of my own to worry about, and a tennis match in a half hour. And you know me, I like to keep in shape."

Judge Winslow rolled his eyes. "Rub it in."

The deep tenor chuckle of response belonged to the city's hottest bachelor, and the sound was every bit as rich as the thirty-something man's bank accounts.

"But I want my replacement decided upon!"

"Darling, you're irreplaceable," crooned the woman with the strangely undefinable voice.

"You certainly are," agreed two other previously silent voices, including a Wall Street baritone.

"Well, we need cash flow." Judge Winslow was determined to change the subject. "Especially since we'd all like to see the opening of a facility for teens. And so, I was thinking…"

"Yes?" the other six voices chimed.

"What about Thurman Newland?"

"Thurman detests both Jake Lucas and Big Apple Babies," protested Judge Winslow's best friend. "We all know they processed his grandson. Winslow, he's approached both you and me, seeking legal representation for getting the kid back."

"I know that!"

For six years, the situation had been intolerable. All the wealthy secret backers knew the Newlands socially; even the mystery woman seemed aware of the Newlands' situation. Because they'd all naturally taken a personal interest in baby zero, it was only a matter of time until they'd become painfully, secretly aware that Tyler Lucas was Thurman and Kate Newland's flesh and blood. So, when Dani Newland had shown up on his doorstep, Judge Winslow had hired her immediately, hoping to right past wrongs. The poor girl was a wonderful nurse, he'd decided, but her personal life was a real disaster area.

In fact, Judge Winslow could think of only one other young lady in worse straits—his great-granddaughter Phoebe Rutherford. Of course, she was beyond all hope. Telling himself not to dwell on the wretched Rutherford gene pool, Judge Winslow cleared his throat. "Well, the two babies are still missing, but Jake and Dani are dating."

Somebody echoed, "Jake Lucas and Dani Newland?"

Then the voices came in an indistinguishable rush. "You can't be serious!" "Does Jake knows she's Tyler's mother?" "Does Dani know he handled the adoption?"

Judge Winslow sighed. "I'm sure she knows who *he* is. But he keeps his cards so close to the vest that I've no idea what he's up to. She doesn't know Tyler's her son, though. Otherwise, more sparks would have flown by now. Which is why we need to vote on my plan."

"Plan?" his best friend echoed.

"I want to force everything into the open. It's the only legal way Thurman and Kate will ever get their grandson back."

"Not to mention their daughter," reminded the mystery woman. "Why, she hasn't spoken to her poor daddy in six whole years."

The judge's voice gained enthusiasm. "If Thurman gets back his grandson, then maybe he'll be willing to part with enough money for our facility for teens."

"What about the quads?" someone asked.

"We'll vote on my plan, then come back to them," Judge Winslow said. "Because I also think I've found a way to circumvent Suzanne Billings."

"But you're retired now, so what can you do?"

Before the judge could answer, a male groan sounded. "The sitter's here, and I'm late for that tennis match, so can we please hop to it?"

"I'm not hopping anywhere with this cast," Judge

Winslow said. "Now, is everyone amenable to a vote?"

Six voices murmured yes.

And then the old judge began to take roll call.

Chapter Eight

"Sure you're through eating?"

"Yeah." Jake nodded, shoving the phone receiver between his jaw and shoulder. As worried as he was about finding the babies and safeguarding his business, the mere sight of Dani soothed him. Right now, she was straightening his office. It was Sunday, and for the second time today, someone had actually answered the phone at the Villa Maria, where Rosita's family thought she might have gone. Earlier, a man with a heavy Spanish accent had taken Jake's name, listened to his predicament, then disconnected him, seemingly accidently. Now, hours later, Jake had gotten through again.

"Rosita's got to be here," he said. "The woman who answered kept repeating her name like she'd heard it before."

Dani's resigned sigh seemed to say that might simply be because Rosita and her husband had spent their honeymoon at the villa. "Fortune cookie?"

Jake sent her a worried smile. "Sure."

"Here, open mine, too. Ty took his upstairs to the nursery." Pushing two cookies across the desk, Dani continued bustling around, tossing out empty Chinese takeout cartons from Charlie Mom's. Early this morning, when she'd arrived at Judge Winslow's wearing a curve-hugging black-and-white-striped jersey dress, Jake realized from the judge's comments that her starchy white uniform had never been required attire.

And a lot of Jake's questions had been answered.

Oh, he'd wondered at Dani's many contradictions, about why such a rich girl would live in that bare, cramped apartment, and why someone so gorgeous would be content to hide behind a sexless uniform. Now he figured it was self-imposed penance for giving Ty up. She was repressing her womanhood, feeling she didn't deserve to experience it because she'd run away when it brought the ultimate responsibility—her pregnancy. The realization had just about brought Jake to his knees.

He sighed. For six years Dani had been denying herself the full sexual life she was made for—and all the emotions that went with that. She had such a woman's body, too—ripe and lush. Made for sin. For *my* sins. As Jake's eyes drifted over her high, full breasts and firmly rounded backside, then down the tight black opaque stockings hugging her long legs, he felt that he'd die if she didn't let him make love to her again soon.

Not that she would.

At least not while she still sensed his emotional reserve. He frowned again, as his concern over finding the missing kids crowded his thoughts once more.

Dani suddenly paused at his office window. Close enough that Jake could finally reach out from the swivel chair and draw her gently to him. She came without hesitation, so easily that Jake swept his palm over her backside in a caress that might have been accidental but wasn't. When he pulled her onto his lap, her dress and his jeans suddenly seemed such a thin barrier between them.

He realized her eyebrows were furrowed. Readjusting the phone, he nuzzled her neck, smelling her, teasing her with his mustache. The touch of her skin soothed his worries, just as the sight of her had. "What?" he said.

"Some woman was out there. Just staring up at your office window. She looked like she might be lost or something."

"What did she look like? I saw a blonde outside your building the other night."

"Outside my building?"

Jake shrugged. Holding her waist more tightly, he drew her nearer, wedging her hip hard against his belly. "I didn't mean to alarm you. It was probably nothing...just that she seemed to be looking up at your place.'

"I couldn't tell if she was blonde," Dani murmured. "It's too dark." She sighed as if to say she had more than enough on her mind already with the missing babies, that seeing the woman was probably just a coincidence. "Well, I just wish those yellow papers I found had contained something useful. I can't believe we raced down here Friday, and they didn't even help."

Jake shrugged, running a hand beneath her silken hair. His other dropped lower, gliding from her waist over the curve of her hip to her outer thigh. "Forget the papers."

Dani's gaze met his, her dark eyes narrowing seductively. "You always have only one thing on your mind, Jake Lucas."

It wasn't true. He was worried sick about the missing

babies. Still, he huskily said, "You know me well."
And then, pressuring the back of her neck, he angled
her head downward, his mouth settling over hers. He
felt her lips part, the honeyed heat of her breath, the
lazy, leisurely mingling of their tongues. The whole
long, wet kiss was like a slow sigh; her body relaxed,
her hip warming his groin, one of her breasts brushing
his chest, the tip hardening and peaking. Desire pooled
in his belly, just lazy circling waters building to a
strong, swift current.

Gliding his hand along her leg, Jake slid it beneath
the hem of her dress, then shifted his weight again, so
she could better feel the stirrings of his arousal. It was
long moments before Dani edged away, emitting a sudden
sharp intake of breath.

Not that Jake let her go very far. "I want to be inside
you again, Dani," he murmured against her neck, feeling
he wouldn't rest until she was completely his again.

Dani swallowed hard, faint color suddenly tinging
her cheeks. "Well…right now, we've got to find those
kids. We've only got until tomorrow morning, Jake."

She was right. He also wished the yellow papers
she'd shoved under his phone had turned out to be
more significant.

"I can't believe court's tomorrow," she murmured
worriedly.

The phone receiver had dropped to his shoulder. Jake
raised it to his ear again and rubbed her shoulder in
reassurance. "We've made calls all weekend, Dani.
We're doing everything we can." But everyone was
still missing—Rosita, the quadruplets, Phoebe Rutherford,
Larry McDougal. It really was a nightmare.

Last night Jake and Dani had torn apart the sealed
records room. The paperwork pertaining to Ty was still

safely hidden in Jake's bedside drawer at home, so there was no danger of her finding it. While the yellow papers she'd left under his phone hadn't turned out to be significant, she *had* found other misfiled papers indicating Lyssa and Kirby had been delivered to the correct address.

"At least you found out Judge Winslow really is next of kin to those girls," Jake reminded Dani now, hoping that would make her feel better.

"Yeah, but I still don't think he believes it. I just wish we knew who their parents were. And what exactly happened to them."

"Well, it was clear from the paperwork that the only living guardian had died."

Sympathy touched Dani's expression. She obviously felt terrible for the judge. "But which of Judge Winslow's relatives died, I wonder."

"Phoebe Rutherford?" Jake suggested. "It seems that she's been living hard and fast." But maybe not. After all, Jake had imagined Dani as being loose and easy, when nothing could have been further from the truth. Still, Phoebe Rutherford really had broken leases, bounced checks and danced naked in public fountains, just as the judge had said. But had she died, leaving the judge guardian of her girls?

Dani said, "I'm just so sure we're missing something."

When she leaned forward to grab the stack of yellow papers on Jake's desk, her backside wiggled against him, and he sighed wistfully. He watched her read over the papers, even though all they contained were names of babies, and of the parties to whom they had been delivered. "C'mon," he murmured. "Lean back."

She did as he asked, but in a perfunctory fashion,

then she read his watch. It was already six o'clock. "Jake," she said, "no one here told Suzanne Billings the quads were missing, so who do you think hired her?"

Jake shrugged, his palm rubbing slow circles on her waist. "Guess we'll find out tomorrow. Anything's possible." Maybe even a real future between himself and Dani. He leaned around her and snapped open one of the two fortune cookies. "Ready for your fortune?"

Dani turned and gazed at him, her expression softening. "Sure."

"'Don't be afraid to take that big step,'" he read, then glanced at the second. "Mine says, 'Be careful what you wish for.'"

Dani groaned. "No, that one's mine. I told you. All my fortunes have been saying that for months." A smile suddenly curled her lips. "So, what big step are you avoiding?"

Telling you Ty's your son. Jake had come close to doing so countless times. Especially in the past couple of days.

"Who knows?" he murmured now.

He wasn't ready to share Ty. But he didn't want to lose Dani, either. And if he waited too long to tell her, she'd never forgive him. Pushing aside the thoughts, he continued, "I just wish this woman would take me off hold. What kind of hotel is this anyway?"

"It's a villa," Dani corrected absently, still staring at the yellow papers in her hand. "Think I should check on Ty in the nursery?"

Jake nodded his head. "Sure. We'll both go in a minute."

Ty was fine, since there were adults upstairs. Still, the pressure he'd exerted on Jake this week to find his mother was…unnatural. Ty wanted to know how Jake could spend so much time looking for missing quadruplets, but not for his own son's mother. And he wanted to know what Jake's intentions were when it came to Dani.

Good question, kid.

Ty's footsteps suddenly pounded down the hallway, then Ty lunged breathlessly into the office, collapsing against Jake and Dani. "Daddy!" he gasped. "Hey, Daddy, I gotta tell you something!"

But the phone suddenly clicked back on, so Jake held up his hand for quiet. "Be with you in just a second, Ty," Jake whispered. Raising his voice, he said. "Hello? Is this Rosita?"

"You wanta Rosita?"

"Yes." He'd asked for Rosita countless time, and now he was starting to feel more than a little testy. Somehow he kept his voice even. "I need to speak to Rosita de Silva."

"Oh—" The woman's voice took a downswing. "de Silva."

Dani whispered something soothing to Ty, but Ty's groan filled the air. "Da-addy! C'mon. Get off the phone."

Jake covered the receiver. "Please, Ty," he whispered in censure. Then he raised his voice. "Yes. Please. This is Jake Lucas. I'm from Big Apple Babies."

"Rosita de Silva, she goes home, *sí?*"

Jake's fingers tightened on the phone. "Has she left, then?"

The voice sounded very frustrated. *"Sí! Sí! Sí!"*

And then the dial tone sounded.

Jake sighed, recradling the receiver. Maybe Rosita

was headed home. Or maybe, given the communication problems, she and her husband had never even been at the villa. Feeling tired, he glanced at Ty. "You know better than to interrupt me when I'm on the phone, Ty."

"But, Daddy, I…"

"You what?" Jake asked.

"I found the babies!"

Jake stared at him. "The—"

"Babies," Ty said again.

In the next heartbeat, Ty was racing down the hallway with Jake and Dani close on his heels. "Good, there's an elevator," Ty called out. "It wouldn't come before and I had to run all the way down the stairs!" Ty leaped inside, holding open the door with both his small hands. "Daddy and Dani, hurry!"

Jake grabbed Dani's hand, pulling her into the elevator. "Where are they?"

Ty jabbed the fifth floor button. "In the nursery."

Dani gasped. "Here? The babies were here all along? How do you know it's them?"

"It's just gotta be them." Ty doubled at the waist, rested his hands on his knees, then blew out deep breaths. "I ran all the way down the stairs," he explained again raggedly.

Jake stared at the overhead bar, watching the floor numbers light as they passed. Then he glanced at Dani. The hope in her eyes touched him. It was for him. And for this business he'd spent six years building.

Ty righted himself. "They're boys! Maybe that was the big mixup, 'cause we were 'sposed to be looking for girls."

Dani's eyes widened. "I—why, I just assumed they

would be girls because they were quadruplets, but of course, the girls could have brothers.''

''They look a lot like Lyssa and Kirby,'' Ty continued. ''Somebody helped me put 'em all in one crib for comparison.''

When the doors swished open, Jake strode into the nursery, heading straight for two adorable boys who were playing with Lyssa and Kirby. But when he reached the crib, disappointment twisted inside him. The boys were the right age, and they resembled Lyssa and Kirby. But their eyes were brown, their hair sandier. Jake righted the ID bracelets on their wrists.

'' 'Stanley and Devin,' '' Dani read over his shoulder.

And then she gasped. Quickly she shuffled through the yellow papers that were still clutched in her hand. ''I thought Stanley and Devin were…''

Ty groaned. Putting his fists on his hips, he stared at Lyssa and Kirby in glum apology. ''I thought I'd found 'em.''

Jake squeezed his son's shoulder. ''You did, sort of. Stanley and Devin are twins.''

''Rosita was supposed to take them to Grantham Hale,'' Dani finished in a rush, reading from the yellow paper. ''And since we know Grantham recently got his twin sons…''

''That means he accidently got Lyssa and Kirby's little brothers,'' Ty finished.

FEELING UNSURE OF Grantham Hale's reaction, Dani and Jake tried to make Ty wait in the apartment foyer, but he wound up plastered to Dani's side, perched on the edge of a white sectional sofa, while Jake talked to Grantham.

''It's a delicate issue,'' Jake was saying.

Maybe. But Grantham Hale was apparently nothing if not cool as ice under fire. Jake explained the mistake while the medium blonde-haired man with the amber eyes simply remained in his dark leather armchair with Lyssa and Kirby in their stroller next to him, and their baby brothers snuggled against his broad chest. The resemblance was undeniable. The boys had the same bright blue eyes and white blond hair, and Grantham said they'd come with bracelets bearing the names Langdon and Nicolas. Rosita had said they were his twins.

But they weren't. And when Jake was through explaining, Grantham's only reaction was the barely discernible tightening of his fingers on the boys' two small backs. His eyes held a slight touch of sadness, too, either a perpetual sadness because of the wife he'd lost or because of this new development concerning the babies with whom he'd already bonded. Dani wasn't sure which.

His voice was measured. "Jake, you know that to get two babies I've patiently played by the rules and endured more scrutiny than the president. But now I have them, and even if they're not the right ones, I hope you realize I'll use all my power and connections to keep them."

No doubt, the man would succeed. Given the opulence of this East Side high-rise, which offered seemingly infinite suites of rooms separated by French doors from the round living room and a splashy skyline view, the man's net of influence probably stretched far and wide. Except for a messy, open gym bag near the door, the place was a showcase of good taste. Framed posters from Grantham's ad agency's national accounts graced the walls, but Dani realized he probably had other business holdings. In fact, his name was ringing a bell. No doubt, he was some name around town, but then Dani had been out of circulation for six years now.

"Grantham, I can't promise you anything," Jake said carefully. "However, the legal guardian of the quadruplets, a judge named Tilford Winslow, has already been informed of this situation. He's in his eighties, hardly interested in parenthood, and he says he's willing to work out an adoption agreement."

Grantham nodded thoughtfully. "You say the name's *Winslow?*"

Jake nodded.

Grantham suddenly blew out a sigh. "Well, then," he said as if everything were decided.

"There's still the issue of their sisters, Lyssa and Kirby," Jake said softly.

Ty scooted away from Dani and pointed at the girls, his voice rising hopefully. "Yeah, we can't split 'em up, so maybe you could get them, too, Mr. Hale."

"Take two little girls?" Grantham murmured. He looked at Jake. "I'd be glad to, you know."

Jake nodded again. "You're already approved through our agency—I know James Sanger's scrutinized you carefully—and, as I said, Judge Winslow is amenable to an adoption agreement."

As Grantham leaned, pulled the stroller nearer and took a closer look at Lyssa and Kirby, Dani's heart wrenched. So much for adopting those little girls. *But maybe I'll still find mine. Or have another.* Even so, she couldn't stand the thought of never seeing Lyssa and Kirby again. Her voice broke. "Oh, I—I'll miss them so much," Dani said in a rush. "If you ever need anything…"

Grantham glanced up. When their eyes met, there

was something so wonderfully friendly and warm in Grantham's gaze that Dani decided she liked him very much.

"Great," he said. "Just give me your number. Business takes me out sometimes, and I like the idea of having a nurse-slash-baby-sitter on retainer."

"I won't be a full-fledged nurse until the end of this term," Dani said, feeling delighted. "But I'd love to sit."

Ty groaned, plopped down beside Dani again and put his arm around her waist. "But the twins, Mr. Hale. This was 'sposed to be *their* house. The nursery over at Daddy's 'doption agency's nice, but it's not *this* nice."

Grantham chuckled. "So you like my place?"

"Yeah. It's really neat. And it looks like there's lots of room for the twins, too."

"Well, now that you mention it, those twins did have my name on them, didn't they?"

Ty's eyes widened and he began counting on his fingers. Just watching him made Dani smile. Ty needed a haircut, but the way his shaggy, sun-streaked bangs fell in his eyes was thoroughly endearing. Impulsively she reached up and brushed them away so he could see.

When Ty finished counting, he stared at Grantham, looking impressed. "If you got the twins you were 'sposed to get, plus Lyssa and Kirby and their brothers, that makes five kids."

"Six, honey," Dani corrected softly.

Ty merely shrugged, as if to say it was a matter of apples and oranges. "Would you really take six of 'em?"

Grantham shrugged. "I guess I'd have to hire an

extra nanny, but I bought a house last year in the suburbs and now I'm thinking of moving in, so the kids
would have enough room.''

Jake was eyeing Grantham, clearly relieved he was
taking this so well. "A new place?''

Grantham nodded. "In Genesis, Long Island.''

Dani's eyes widened. Grantham was going to be a
neighbor of her parents. Sadness knifed through her. If
only she were on speaking terms with her family, she'd
probably see the quadruplets frequently, if Grantham
was allowed to keep them all. *Six children.* Heavens,
she still only wanted her one child. In reflex, her arm
snaked around Ty's shoulder. When she drew him
closer, he came so easily against her side that he really
could have been hers.

She shook her head, feeling as impressed as Ty.
"You'd really consider taking in six orphaned kids?''

Grantham winked. "I guess I'd have to quit my day
job.''

The man might be her age, but he was obviously
wealthy. She glanced around, her eyes landing on his
gym bag again, then on a tennis racket propped against
the wall. "Guess you won't have much time left to
play.''

Grantham laughed. "Oh, I always find time to
play.''

Dani smiled. "I'll bet." *And pity the poor woman
who falls for you.* Somehow, Dani imagined there had
been many. And only one had caught Grantham Hale,
the wife who'd left him a widower. Not that Dani had
taken a personal interest. All the world's Grantham
Hales would never stand a chance against Jake.

Jake crossed his arms, then lifted a hand and toyed
thoughtfully with his mustache. "Well, Grantham,

there are clear legal precedents for not splitting up the quadruplets, Tilford Winslow is amenable to an adoption, and the twins already legally belong to you. I don't think I'll have any trouble getting you custody of all six, if you're serious. Is it what you want?''

Grantham grinned. ''Can I pick up my twins tonight?''

''Oh, Mr. Hale,'' Ty gushed, ''I really, *really* like you.''

Dani chuckled.

Jake smiled. ''You should wait and take the twins tomorrow. You'll need time to settle them. And you've got to bring Langdon and Nicolas to court tomorrow morning. I'll bring the twins.'' He glanced at Dani. ''You'll still bring Lyssa and Kirby. They should stay with you tonight since they're in your custody.''

Grantham shook his head in amazement. ''After a year of intensive interviews and practically living with James Sanger, I can't believe I might wind up with six kids instead of two. I mean, why would a court system so previously determined not to give me any kids at all suddenly turn around and give me six?''

Jake smiled. ''Because circumstances just made you lucky.''

''I feel like I won the lottery.'' Grantham leaned back in his armchair, his wide hands supporting Langdon and Nicolas. Then he sighed the satisfied sigh of an all-around contented man.

Only later, when they were headed down in the elevator—with Jake's arm wrapped around her and a very tired, if excited, Ty leaning against her side for support and Lyssa and Kirby sleeping in the stroller—did Dani suddenly realize she'd found Grantham's same familial contentment with Jake and Ty.

"Hey!" Ty's voice was as drowsy as it was surprised. "There's one of those little Snickers bars in my jacket pocket!"

Dani chuckled. "Guess the Snickers elf must have snuck it in there. Did you see him, Jake?"

"The Snickers elf?" Jake shook his head. "Not hide nor hair."

Ty giggled sleepily. "Daddy, there's no Snickers elf. Dani put it there."

She laughed. "Did not."

Jake tsked his tongue. "No Snickers elf? Next thing you know, you won't even believe in Santa Claus."

Ty glanced up with a wicked little smile. "I'll always believe in Santa 'cause he brings presents."

In mid-laugh, Dani suddenly tilted her head and frowned. How had Grantham Hale known she was a nurse? She wasn't wearing her uniform, and she was sure she'd never met him before.

Deep in thought, Dani scarcely noticed the woman watching them from across the street. She resembled the woman outside Big Apple Babies, but half the women in the city wore dark clothes and trendy black scarves. Her mind still on Grantham, Dani suddenly relaxed and smiled. Surely Jake had mentioned her to Grantham in a previous conversation, probably when he'd asked Grantham to help Big Apple Babies with its possibly impending image problems.

"What put that Mona Lisa smile on your face?" Jake murmured.

The fact that you're talking to people about me. "You."

"You make me 'n my dad smile, too," Ty offered.

As if to prove it, Jake sent Dani a grin, one so devilish that her heart suddenly fluttered and her knees got weak and her toes actually curled in tandem with his mustache.

DANI SANK ONTO the plump cushions of Jake's sofa and glanced toward the adjacent room where Lyssa and Kirby were sleeping in Ty's old playpen. "Finally," she said on a sigh, "peace and quiet."

Jake reached over her. Just as he flicked on a lamp, he kissed her so softly and tenderly that when he drew away, the warm, cozy glow in the room was something Dani felt from the inside out. Sighing, Jake stretched his arm along the sofa back, letting his fingers dangle right above her shoulder, a whimsical smile touching his lips.

He said, "I can't believe Grantham wants to adopt six one-year-olds." He shrugged. "Well, almost one-year-olds. I think the quads turn one next month."

"Well, they're awfully cute." Dani snuggled closer, resting her cheek against Jake's shoulder and feeling his soft sweater soothe her skin. "Do you really think you can get him custody?"

"Under these circumstances? Sure. I think they'll all be his by tomorrow afternoon. Basically, we only need Judge Winslow's signature." He glanced down, shooting Dani another slow smile. "In quadruplicate."

Dani smiled back. "No problem there. I know he's still upset and desperate to find out which of his relatives has died, but he knows those kids need a good home and that Grantham can provide it." She sighed. "I guess I'll need another job for the rest of the term, too, while I finish school and start sending résumés to area hospitals. Judge Winslow's cast should come off any day now. It's just too bad there's no way to save Ty's artwork."

Jake pressed a kiss to the top of her head. "Why not ask Grantham for a job, at least until he heads for the suburbs?"

Her heart skipped a beat. "I'd love to watch those kids, and Grantham did say he'd be looking for someone."

Jake chuckled. "What that man's going to need is a wife."

Dani's smile turned wistful. Did Jake need a wife...need her? Maybe. After all, it was funny how things turned out, how seemingly dire circumstances could suddenly, magically, reverse. "Suzanne Billings probably won't be able to sue," she said, her voice turning drowsy. "Your business is safe. Grantham's going to be a father..." *And maybe you'll forgive me for not telling you everything about myself, Jake.*

"A father six times over," Jake murmured, his voice becoming deeper. "The excitement of hearing Grantham say he'd take the kids really wore Ty out. It's actually earlier than his usual bedtime."

"It feels later." Dani smoothed Jake's sweater with her palm, wanting to tell him how good it felt to relax against him.

Instead she said, "I loved putting him to bed." She loved how Ty's little arms had shot in the air, demanding her hugs, how softly his mouth pressed kisses against her cheek, and how sweet and creaky his voice had sounded as he'd whispered, "Isn't everything turning out just great, Dani?"

Jake's arm dropped from the sofa back, his palm curling around her shoulder, then gliding down the length of her arm. "The poor kid was awfully tired, though."

So was Jake. It was in the deep, chesty rumble of

his voice, in how his luscious green eyes drifted shut as he rubbed circles on her side. Dani imagined stretching out on Jake's king-size bed, her arms splayed wide as she reveled in all that luxurious space, then she'd nestle next to Jake until they were so close they might as well be in *her* tiny bed. "Hmm," she hummed.

Jake lazily raised his dark eyebrows. "Hmm?"

She shrugged. "I just hope everything works out for Grantham. He's so nice. Even though I only met him tonight, I've been thinking about him all week."

Jake smoothed her hair. "And here I was," he teased softly, "so sure you were thinking about me."

She gazed into his eyes, her own saying he was right about that much. Nudging him playfully, she said, "No...I mean, I started thinking about adopting."

Jake's eyes widened. "You...adopt?"

Her chest squeezed tight. Could she really let go of her own lost child, begin life with another? Wasn't that what she was thinking about when she fantasized she and Jake were together permanently and that she would become a mother to Ty? She would never forget her baby, but Dani now knew that somewhere, some truly loving parent such as Grantham Hale had taken hers.

Dani shrugged, glancing up. "You sound so surprised."

Jake was watching her carefully. "You'd go through months of agency interviews and scrutiny to get a child?"

"Yeah, I guess I would," she murmured. Maybe she hadn't known it until this very second, until she'd spoken the words. "I want children more than anything, Jake. I...I'm not sure, but I think I'm ready to move on with my life." Suddenly she sat up and turned fully toward him. "Oh, Jake."

Their eyes met and held. He was perfectly still, his eyes impossible to read.

"Yes?"

Dani's throat suddenly ached from restrained emotion. "Jake, I—I have to talk to you. I have to…tell you something. And you're not going to like it."

He was going to reject her cold, but she owed him the truth. "I'm going to say this, Jake," she continued quickly. "I'm just going to come right out with it. And, uh, if you want me to get up and leave when it's over, it's okay. I…"

She paused, knowing there were no real words, no way to prepare him. She tried not to imagine his horrified reaction, the disappointment when he realized she'd been using him. Already she felt bereft and heartbroken, sure that Jake's gorgeous eyes would never sparkle again with warmth when he looked at her.

His voice was barely audible. "Sounds serious."

"It's real serious. And it's about you and me."

He merely watched her, waited.

Oh, Dani, be brave. You've got to believe that whatever's between you and Jake is strong enough to weather this. If she didn't, she could never tell him. She was too afraid of losing him.

"You've never asked me, but my last name's Newland. I'm Daniela Newland. You were hired by my father, Thurman Newland, six years ago to handle the adoption of my baby."

There. She'd said it.

When she saw Jake pale, tears stung her eyes. Mindlessly she reached out, grabbing his soft sweater in fistfuls, as if that could keep him from throwing her out of the apartment. Maybe she hadn't known it—not even a second ago—but she wanted this man so badly that she couldn't care less about her own pride. "It was so wrong of me," she pleaded. "That day we met in Judge Lathrop's chambers, I—I decided to try to use you to find my baby. But, Jake, oh Jake, things between you and me became so much more." *You're becoming everything to me.*

She waited for him to scream. To yell. To tell her to get the hell out of his apartment. But when he spoke, his voice was so low and controlled that she had to strain to hear him.

"Why did you give up the baby?"

"I was young and confused..." Dani began. And then the whole rambling story poured out. She told Jake how much she'd once loved and respected her father, until he'd withdrawn his support because she was in trouble. And how her father's overprotectiveness had insured her helplessness, but how she'd overcome that and arrived in New York, haunting the street near Big Apple Babies, hoping to glimpse Jake. She told him how she'd heard someone yell at James, so all along, she'd thought James Sanger was Jake, and she admitted to searching the sealed records room. She finished by saying her relationship with her father was completely severed.

Jake looked shocked. "You haven't spoken to your father in six years?"

Dani's cheeks heated with defiance for the father against whom she'd rebelled. "No, and I never will." Before Jake could respond, her grip on his sweater tightened. "Oh, Jake, I know everything I've done is wrong. But I didn't find out anything, I swear. And I would never look again. Not now. But please, oh, Jake, please try to understand, it was my child. My *child*..."

She was pleading now. "You have Ty, so surely you

can understand. What if, in one stupid moment of panic, you signed his life away, and then you could never get him back?'' Dani paused, tears clinging to her eyelashes.

"I would never do that," Jake said softly.

Her voice caught. "I know it, Jake. You're so strong, so responsible. But I—I did what I could. I never gave up looking for my baby. Every year I would light a birthday candle and make a wish to find my baby. And I...I know you can't tell me anything. That it's your job not to tell me..." A hot tear fell, splashing on her cheek. "I—I can only hope that one day—somewhere, somehow—my child will grow up and come looking for me." Her voice broke. "Be-because I'll be here. I'll *always* be here."

Dani's heart broke in the silence that followed.

Jake hated her. She'd lost him.

Half pulling him by his sweater and half leaning, she pressed her cheek against his. "Please, Jake," she whispered, "*please* say something."

She leaned away again, her dark eyes imploring. And then his lips parted, as if he were about to say something terribly important, maybe even something horrible, or just something for which he couldn't find words.

"Please," she said again.

But instead of speaking, Jake leaned forward, wrapped his arms around her and hugged her tight. Dani was so shocked she couldn't move. Not even when all his strength and warmth seemed to infuse her. She could swear she didn't deserve this wonderful man or his forgiveness. But apparently he was hers. And suddenly her arms circled him, hugging him back with all her might.

"Oh, Jake, you're so good, so kind." He'd raised a child alone, where she had walked away. As her tears fell in earnest, the words she'd held closest to her heart tumbled out. "I want to be with you. I've got to be in your life, Jake. I...I think I could love you."

Chapter Nine

"I could love you, too," Jake whispered.

Did love her. Jake knew it by the way his heart swelled when he said it. He hadn't wanted it to happen. But it had. Tonight Dani's honesty had touched him. And now everything was different. He and Dani were falling in love and because of what they'd begun to share, maybe nothing else mattered. Maybe all the joys and sorrows of parenthood that Jake had borne alone could be his and Dani's together. She'd given Ty up, but in all these years, she'd never quit looking for him. "Dani, I want to be with you."

Her voice was husky. "You really mean that, Jake?"

His answer was the touch of his mouth, her response the slow, velvet-warm parting of her lips. And then they were conversing in another realm, with a kiss so liquid that its intoxicating heat sent streams of slow-moving molten lava through Jake's veins. "Oh, yeah," he murmured right before his lips captured hers again. "I mean it, Dani."

And I have so much to tell you. He'd tell her Ty was hers. And share every story he could remember about her son, everything she'd longed to hear for all these years. He'd tell her how tiny and wrinkled Ty was when he'd come home from the hospital, and about that first birthday when Ty blew out the candles on his own cake, while only blocks away, Dani must have been lighting a candle for him, making a birthday wish.

Oh, Ty was Jake's son.

But he belonged to Dani, too. Ty possessed her dark eyes, her small mouth, her mysterious smile. And as Jake silently vowed to share Ty completely, an excitement that had been buried deep inside him suddenly broke through. For six years, all those wonderful stories about Ty were bottled up inside, and Jake had longed to tell someone. *To tell Dani.* After all, who could better understand Jake's pride than his son's mother?

And there were stories about Dani's father, too. Oh God, Jake *had* to tell her about her own father.

And he would. But they had so much time to talk. Right now Dani was too close, clinging to him so sweetly. Her full, firm breasts were crushed against his chest and her heart was pounding. The fiery hot sword of her tongue dueled with his. No, Jake couldn't talk now, not when his palm pressed the delicate small of her back and nothing more than that gentle touch made a soft, strangled cry tear from her throat.

When she arched against him, no power in this world or the next could stop Jake from kissing her. He told himself to get to the bedroom, where he could lock the door in case Ty awakened, but he still couldn't stop. No man—not even Jake—could control real passion. Untamable, its kisses begat kisses. And each new kiss flared under its own intense heat, until there was only one wild, burning kiss that raged on and on long after it turned deep and hard and their skin was on fire, long after they'd kicked off their shoes and Dani was stretched on top of Jake on the couch, her endless, lovely legs weak and loose and straddling his hips.

One of her slender feet dipped over the side of the sofa, her toe on the carpet as if to anchor her in the raging sea. But Jake knew it wouldn't…couldn't. Because the dam holding back the flood of their need had broken, and he and Dani were spinning in gushing currents, swept away on a relentless tide of lust and emotion. Like a drowning man, Jake longed to release the cries he bit back. His throat ached with the restraint, even as his groin ached where he'd become so stiff with his need for her.

"Oh, Jake…Jake."

At the senseless rasp of his name, he cupped her backside and squeezed, pulling her firmly to his erection. And then Dani began to move on top of him, shaking so uncontrollably that Jake thought he'd burst from the sweet, torturous pleasure. Dani, his lovely Dani had so obviously punished herself all these six years, working and studying around the clock. Wearing those starched-stiff uniforms. Going home alone to that barren little apartment. Always living for her lost child. Living without a man. Like a nun.

Yes, Dani had deprived herself so long.

But no more. Tonight Jake would give her what she needed, what she was silently begging for as she clung to him. And in giving, Jake would take what he most craved, too. Something only Dani could give, that Lanie had always withheld, a woman's total response. Her total love.

And because Dani could give that, Jake was determined to love her as she'd never been loved. To capture her and take her to the brink, holding her there until she was love's hostage and there was nothing left in her but pure want for him, pure need.

To that end, Jake rose, took Dani's hands and led her inside his darkened bedroom. Locking the door, he lay her across his king-size bed and, in a crack of light from the window, he stared at her silhouette, at how her dress had risen high on her thighs, at how her knees trembled, parting ever so slightly in silent invitation.

She was just waiting for him to take her. So he dropped onto the mattress and crawled upward from the foot of the bed, his hands gently parting her knees further, making room so he could settle between them. At her soft whimper, at how her quivering knees raised and her fingers tightened on his back, renewed heat coiled inside him.

"Shh...shh," he whispered.

She gasped. "Ty and the babies..."

"The door's locked, but yeah, we have to be quiet."

They didn't have to rush, though. This time Jake meant to claim her completely. So he kissed her until her mouth was slack and wet and her body relaxed. By the time he knelt again, his eyes had adjusted to the dark. Gently he pulled her dress over her head, caressing her breasts, rolling her tights away from her silk bikini panties, lifting her bare feet one by one and tonguing the arches.

Cradling one of those gorgeous feet against his heart, Jake finally took his full gaze, moaning softly, almost soundlessly, at the mere sight of her, at the pebbled peaks of breasts that strained her lacy low-cut bra. Her curved belly and full, round hips. The precious dark mound that was visible through her panties, the hairs tangling in a soft, warm-looking V.

Jake's hand followed the entire path of his eyes, until

it molded over the mound, letting her feel the warm pressure of his palm, feeling her respond without moving, just her throbbing heat through the silk. When her breath caught in another soft sob, an excruciating pull of arousal gorged him with blood. Jake lifted his own sweater by the hem.

Before he'd even bared his chest, Dani's hungry fingers were twined in the curling hairs. Jake covered her hand with his, tenderly lifted it and kissed her fingers, drawing them between his lips. And when she didn't protest, he flattened her palm on his chest and slid it ever so slowly downward, over a nipple that grew hard at the damp touch, over each hard ridge of his ribs, then across his taut belly and protruding belt buckle, and then finally, blessedly, between his legs.

Sucking in a breath and shutting his eyes in ecstasy, Jake squeezed her shaking fingers around where his burgeoning arousal strained the zipper of his jeans. Not that she needed coaxing now. She was already exploring the ridge with a touch that was more than Jake could stand, that had him clenching his teeth tight against his sighs. Suddenly leaning, he buried those sighs against her breasts, kissing her through the cups of her bra until he found the catch and the warmth of his mouth met her silken skin.

Even as Dani managed to unbuckle his belt and free him, Jake's tongue was drenching her breasts, and he was divesting her of the bra and panties. Kicking free of his jeans, he wetly tongued every blessed inch of her until his mouth finally settled at the sweetest, dew-drenched part of her.

She was so ready. Deliriously feverish. So unlike anything Jake had ever felt, much less tasted. Dani wanted it so much, tremors of need shook her legs and her silken, open thighs were alive and pulsing with it. But she didn't make a sound, only clutched his headboard with one hand and pressed the other against her lips, suppressing her whimpers.

Jake heard her anyway. Heard her plead for him with fitful breaths. And yet he took his time, moistening her thighs with sugary, wet kisses, lazily teasing her, tonguing the nub of her desire with a drizzled honey meant to take her on a long, slow ride into oblivion. When Dani began to protest, to try to writhe away, Jake merely held her fast and kept loving her in a way that would be a true claiming. And then she was arching toward him, her hands grasping and releasing his hair, and the way she moved under his mouth became a voice in itself that called out for him, strengthening his need to make her want in a way she'd never wanted before.

He heard only one soft sob, "Jake, Jake."

And that one cry of need nearly destroyed him.

Not that he'd let her come. Not yet. He wouldn't until he was deep inside the dew-filled glove of her, sheathed in all her slick warmth. Right before she shattered, Jake moved upward on her body. Oh, Dani clutched at him. Small animal-whimpers she simply couldn't contain met his ears and she tried to force his mouth back to her.

But Jake merely knelt naked in front of her, slid his palms beneath her damp knees and lifted her quivering legs. Lithely leaning, he slid open the beside drawer, got a condom and quickly rolled it on. His breath ragged, he edged nearer, his own knees momentarily weak as his sheathed erection grazed the opening he was seconds from breaching. Then he reached out his hand and gently, ever so slowly, stroked Dani's cheek.

"I love you," he whispered.

Her breath caught, one knife-sharp inhalation that quivered through him, then she become utterly still, her eyes on his face. And slowly, with one long, deep, torturous thrust, Jake slid inside her.

She came as he entered her, shuddering all around him. His mouth closed hard and hot over her lips as he drove deeper and deeper still, feeling the slippery, hot velvet glove of her, like pulsing fingers, capturing and releasing him over and over, as if her pleasure would never end.

Dani whimpered, not saying words, just other-worldly sounds against his neck. And then she softly sobbed, "Jake," and her arms clung to him in as thorough a possession as that which he now had to claim. His excruciatingly slow thrusts sharpened and quickened, until he wanted to beg Dani to end this agony. It had to end soon. Jake knew he'd die if it didn't. And yet he held on to the blissful torment until Dani writhed beneath him again, straining toward another peak. Until his pleasure was almost pain. Until everything but her vanished.

The second she shattered, Jake's whole body tensed and he exploded with a hard spasm that shook him completely. It was seconds before he could even feel the shock wave of ripples, that sweet pulsing that was a lifeblood they now shared. And then he was kissing her again, his mouth claiming hers over and over, until those kisses became nothing more than shared sighs and vague brushings of damp, blistering lips.

Only much later did she flick on the bedside lamp. For a second, Jake merely marveled at her dreamy, drowsy, dark smudges of eyes, her soft seductive smile and the dampened tendrils of hair that swept her fore-head.

She nodded toward the bathroom. "I've got to get up," she whispered in an endearingly creaky voice.

"Me, too." He nodded. "But you first."

When she rose, Jake watched her, still possessing her with his eyes. A voice inside him kept thinking, *She's mine.* And he knew he'd never be able to let her go. His lazy eyes trailed upward, caressing the woman who belonged to him now, traveling over her buttery thighs and her silken backside that was flushed a deep rose color in the lamp's soft light. Lovingly he traced the hourglass curve of her hips and waist.

Then he realized she hadn't moved.

And suddenly Jake's lips parted in silent protest. Because Dani was gaping down into the bedside drawer he'd left open when he'd gotten the condom. The adoption papers were right on top, not even in a file.

"You bastard," she whispered.

And then she slowly turned toward Jake.

"I was going to tell you."

Dani barely heard. Her mind racing, she lifted the loose papers from the drawer. She had to concentrate. To block out the sensations that still rocked her. Even worse than Jake's hard heat or the fevered burning of her skin or the shaky weakness of the legs she was standing on, was her raw emotional vulnerability.

Jake had made her feel so open and fragile. And she'd been such a fool.

Ty. The name pounded in her head, in rhythm with the dull thudding of her heart. Was Ty really her son? Dani simply couldn't believe it. It made no logical sense, but it was right here, in black and white, as unmistakable as Jake's betrayal.

But what about Lanie? she thought in shock. Jake's ex-wife had Ty's same blond hair and dark eyes! *And so do you, Dani.* Oh, how could her assumptions have been so wrong? How could she have betrayed her son by being so sure she'd given birth to a girl?

God, forgive me, she thought as the truth sank in. For six long years, she'd imagined a blond, dark-eyed daughter—taking her first steps, leaving for school, blowing out candles on her birthday. And now the reasoning hit Dani like a revelation.

No, she'd never seen her baby.

But she'd wanted a girl, because a boy wouldn't need her. Boys were strong. But Dani meant to teach her little girl how to care for herself and make her own decisions. And how to stand up to men. Especially to men like Dani's own father.

Or Jake.

Jake, who'd known the truth and hadn't told her.

Oh yes, she'd wanted to teach her daughter to stand up to men like her father and Jake. So if Dani's little girl ever got pregnant, she'd know how to keep her own baby.

"Oh, no," Dani whispered now, covering her mouth. If only that fantasy image of her daughter hadn't been so fixed in her mind, maybe she would have recognized her very real son. Bone-deep shock made Dani powerless to move. Like a soldier blinded in a field of war, she merely stood, unseeing until she finally realized she was still stark naked and staring right at Jake.

"How could you?" she finally said. Then she began

moving, her free hand snatching her clothes from the floor.

"Dani..."

She couldn't look at him. "Don't even talk to me."

He didn't. But as she slipped on her tights and dress, she could feel those burning green eyes, the heat of the gaze on her damp, well-loved body, making her skin prickle. In the periphery of her vision, she sensed Jake's powerfully lithe movements as he shook out his jeans, then stepped into them, not bothering with his shirt. Feeling him right behind her, she headed for the living room to find her shoes.

"Dani, slow down." Jake's voice was both tense and tender. "Everything's okay."

"Okay?" The word hit her like a blow.

Shoving her feet into her flats, she whirled on Jake so fast she nearly lost her balance. Reaching out and grabbing the sofa back, she stared at him. "Ty's my son and you think it's *okay?* You *knew* and didn't tell me. And he's my baby and he's all grown-up. Six years old and I've missed his life! I thought he was a girl. I thought..."

"A girl?"

Dani's eyes darted to the hallway. She could run, grab her little boy and go. Instead, her eyes snapped back to Jake. He came into sharp focus, looking sleek and powerful, like a well-satisfied animal just come from a mountain lair. Even as she tried to turn away, her eyes fell over his sweat-slick shoulders and the dark unruly hair on his bare chest. That he looked so well loved fed her fury, and her gaze burned down the length of him, stoking the inner fire of her own rage.

"You thought you'd had a girl?"

Not about to share another damn bit of herself with

Jake Lucas, Dani wordlessly headed toward the play-pen and started packing Lyssa and Kirby's belongings. She had to get away from Jake so she could think. And she couldn't try to take Ty now. That would be crazy.

Even though pure fury coursed through her, Dani lifted the babies into their stroller so gently they didn't awaken, then she pushed them toward the door. With her hand on the knob, she paused. She started to turn around to warn Jake, to say she'd be back and, next time, by damn, she'd get her son. *Or maybe I really should take him now. Just go to his room. Grab him and take off.*

She would dare Jake to stop her.

No. If you do, you'll blow it. You've got to be craftier than that. Jake's a lawyer. He'll cream you in court and you'll never see Ty again.

Ty. Once again the insanity hit her. Ty Lucas was her son. *Impossible.*

Suddenly she felt Jake behind her. He had the nerve to come incredibly close, his naked chest just inches from her back. Unbidden, she throbbed, suddenly conscious of the most intimate part of her own body, still warm and moist from Jake's heat.

Almost against her will, she let go of the doorknob and turned around, and he leaned against the door, his palm splayed on the space right above her head. His slightest movements—the narrowing eyes, the flare of his nostrils, how his tongue darted out flicking his mustache—fueled her temper even as her knees weakened with renewed longing. Watching him, she damned her own body for betraying her. But her breath caught and an almost painful ache for Jake pulled at the core of her.

The emerald slits of his eyes were slowly turning as

watchful as a panther's, and as predatory. They swept over her, his mere glance, a claiming. His voice was low, controlled. "You've got to believe I was going to tell you."

"When?"

"Tonight."

"How could I believe that?"

"Because I said it's true."

When he leaned a fraction closer, she tried to steel herself against the unbearable heat of him, but the musk of their lovemaking clung to the air. She felt it catching in her hair, enveloping her. With each breath, she was inhaling raw memories of his fiery tongue flickering under the cover of darkness, of how wanton she'd become under the knowing ministrations of his hands, his lips, his tongue.

Heat flooded her cheeks. Her voice was suddenly so dry it cracked. "Jake, back up. Get away from me."

But when he moved, it was only closer, trapping her against the door between the cool wood and his hard heat. His voice was barely a whisper. "You're being damn sanctimonious."

"I have every right to be." She felt the blood drain from her face. "Ty's my son." Even now it seemed so impossible. Her pulse began to race, and the words pounded in her head. *My son, my son, my son, my son.*

"I raised him."

When Jake's jaw suddenly clenched, the sculpted rigidity of his face chilled Dani so much that her breath caught. So this was the killer prosecutor. The man who'd once worked tireless, sixteen-hour days. Who pushed things to the wall and always got his way. He'd realized how angry she was, that she might threaten his total right to his child, and she guessed she'd just become the enemy.

But she wasn't about to back down. Instead she narrowed her gaze and stared hard, piercing right through Jake with her eyes. "I've waited six years. Six long years of not knowing where my child went. Of not knowing if he was healthy and happy." Tears threatened, tears of sadness and betrayal, angry tears. But somehow Dani blinked them back. Her eyes darted to the hallway. "Oh, yes, Jake. He's mine."

Jake's eyes turned as hard as cutting gems. Incisive and full of insinuation, they raked over her. He was trying to stay calm, but his temper was aroused. His voice was deceptively soft. "Guess you weren't thinking about the possibility of your *son* during that summer in Greece."

Dani's head was pounding. So Jake even knew how Ty was conceived. And now he'd apparently use the information against her. "Tonight I told you what happened. And that I'd been looking for my baby." *For Ty.*

Jake's low-voiced words carried a warning. "You were willing to break a few laws to find him, too."

Her eyes turned flinty. "I would have broken every law in the world." But how could Jake's son be hers, too? she wondered numbly as the reality hit her again. How could her son be a boy she already cared for? A boy she'd imagined would become hers if she married Jake? She drew in a sharp, involuntary breath, hating Jake. Really hating him. "How could you let me get to know him like this, Jake? How could you—" Her voice broke, her dark eyes suddenly searching his face. "How could you make love to me without telling me?

Listen to me pour out my heart tonight, without telling me?''

Anguish was in Jake's eyes, but his voice was hard. ''Having you in my life means *I've* got to give him up.''

Dani could merely stare at him. ''He's my son, Jake. How did you even find out who I was?''

''The picture of Genesis in your room. I recognized your parents…you.''

It must have been after they made love, when she'd lit the candle. Even now, she could smell that sweet vanilla mingling with Jake's masculine scent. But he'd had known that long! Had known when he'd said good-bye that night, touching her so intimately, making her climax at the door. Her shocked tone was laced with accusation. ''What if we'd never wound up in bed, Jake? What if I was just some woman who you weren't interested in sexually, would you have told the truth then?''

No.

His silence said it, even if his lips didn't.

Her eyes glazed in fury. *My God, I could have gone to my grave without knowing.* When she looked at Jake again, his face was livid, a mask of controlled emotion.

''My actions were justified, totally le—''

''Legal?'' Her word sliced the air like a razor. ''What about your code of ethics, Jake? About what's right?''

''Was giving up your son right?''

Oh, that was low. She could scarcely believe she'd been lying in Jake's embrace just moments before. To-night she'd felt ready to share her life with Jake. She'd shared everything, including the pressures that had driven her to give Ty up. Jake had understood, forgiven her. And then he'd loved her like she'd never been loved.

Now he said, "I can't have Ty hurt."

Pain arrowed through her, and this time the tears that stung her eyes splashed down her cheeks. And to think she'd felt guilty about lying to Jake! "You think I'd hurt my son?" She thought of Ty again, right down the hallway, within her reach. She could run to him, hold him, kiss him. "I'd sooner die than hurt him."

"Six years ago you wanted no part of him."

"That's a lie, Jake! And you're trying to push me away from you right now, so I'll have no claim on Ty!"

"Oh, that's what I was doing tonight? Pushing you away?"

She really did want things to be okay between them. She wanted him to love her again, while she fantasized about getting married and being a mother to Ty. But renewed anger filled her. "You said Lanie was his mother."

Jake was staring at her, his eyes watchful and intense. "I never said that. You just thought—"

"You made me think Lanie was his mother."

Jake reached for her then.

"Don't touch me."

But his movement was swift. When she snatched away her hand, his body simply pressed down the whole length of her. Just as surely as she'd yearned to be in his bed again, she wanted escape from his body that carried both seduction and threat. And from his words, which she knew would only carry self-justifications.

"Lanie doesn't even belong in this discussion."

Jake's sudden derisive chuckle caught Dani by surprise. "Or maybe she does."

"What's that supposed to mean?"

"It means she was just another woman in a long line of women who've used me and don't want children."

Pain knifed through Dani. All she'd ever wanted was children and Jake knew it. "You have a child." Her voice pulsed with anger. "My child. So don't expect me to start playing violins."

He leaned close, so close that the gentle kiss of his breath touched her face, making traitorous heat curl in her belly. His voice was terse. "More than anyone, Lanie knew I wanted to be a father. I wanted kids so bad I could taste it. So we spent two years trying to get pregnant. When we didn't, the doctors said there were no physical problems, so we kept on trying and trying, doing everything we could."

Unbidden, jealous rage unfurled inside Dani. It was illogical, but she couldn't stand the thought of another woman mothering her son. "Even if Lanie couldn't get pregnant, she got Ty."

Jake's sudden twist of a smile didn't meet his eyes. "Turns out, Lanie just wanted to be married to a hotshot prosecutor. She didn't think Ty's adoption would really go through. The day we brought Ty home, I found her birth control pills. All along, she'd been taking them. Making damn sure we didn't conceive. She was a cold woman, and out of my life by that night for good."

Dani's heart wrenched. So that's what had happened with Lanie. But Dani couldn't afford to sympathize, not when she wanted some kind of rights to her son. That's what she had to get. "Look, Jake, I'm not Lanie. I didn't use you the way Lanie did, either. And I doubt there's really been some 'long line' of women in your life who don't want kids." When he said nothing, Dani found herself nodding swiftly. "Who else?"

Jake's eyes flashed fire. "My damn mother."

That stopped her cold. The tears in her eyes dried up, and she felt suffocated, couldn't breathe. So that's how Jake saw her. She was like the mother who had given him up, because she'd given up Ty. She thought of her life these past six years, so lonely, so full of hope she'd find her baby. "Maybe your mother is like me." Her voice was meant to cut deep. "Maybe she's been out there all these years, just looking for you, Jake."

His eyes widened and Dani's heart squeezed at her own cruelty. "And don't twist things around," she continued. "You're the one in the wrong right now. I came clean with you tonight. But you—"

"You gave Ty up. And you can't waltz in here under false—"

"I didn't waltz anywhere! And I didn't know he was my son!"

She hadn't meant to shout. But the sound had rocked the room. Jake was so impossible, so self-righteous. God, she'd looked for years. And he'd known it. Oh, he was probably going to keep lying to her. He might never have told her Ty was her son. She steadied her voice. "I didn't know he was my son," she repeated.

"But now *I* know."

The small voice sounded behind them.

Dani suddenly pushed at Jake, moving him aside. Her son, her baby, was standing at the mouth of the hallway. He was wearing his jean jacket over his dinosaur pajamas, and his backpack was strapped on. A yellow knit hat that was pulled down low over his ears indicated he meant to be gone long into the winter. In his hand, he clutched the handle of a small brown suitcase.

"I heard everything." His lower lip trembled. "I know you're my mommy, Dani."

"Oh, God, go back to bed, Ty." Jake's voice sounded from a million miles away. "Just go back to bed."

Ty didn't move. His round dark eyes filled with murderous tears of rage. "You said you didn't know who she was, Daddy. You said you tried, but you could never find my mommy. You said my mommy didn't even want me."

"Ty! I never said she didn't want—"

"My mommy was looking for me!" Ty shrieked. "Dani wanted me! She wanted me!"

Dani cried out, "Of course I wanted you, Ty! Oh, Ty, I wanted you! I always wanted you!"

Then Dani simply ran. Her boy needed her. The baby to whom she'd given birth, who'd been whisked away, stolen by Jake Lucas from her womb and heart. She flew to Ty, kneeling down, circling him with her arms. Holding him tight, hugging him to her, she did what all new mothers did, felt for his fingers, pressing each of them to her lips, letting her hands rove over every inch of him, all the while knowing she'd never let him go again.

"Da-Daddy lied." Ty wept now, his small shoulders racking with sobs. "Take me away from here, Mommy!"

Instinctively Dani lifted him. As his legs wrapped around her waist and his ankles locked behind her back, she cradled him, tears coursing down her own cheeks—of fury at Jake for hurting her son, with love for the baby she'd finally found. She ran past Jake. ''Oh, Ty, of course I'll take you away!''

Chapter Ten

Jake knew he could call the cops, but he couldn't move.

Oh, Ty, of course, I'll take you away!

The empty room felt like a vacuum; Dani's words and Ty's cries of betrayal echoed in Jake's mind and in the hollowed-out silence. Something was pounding—Jake's head or heart—he wasn't sure which. And he still couldn't move. He could only stare at the empty space where Ty and Dani had been.

I'm a grown man, he thought. *So how could a voice as tiny as my son's hurt so much?* More than hurt. The questions Ty had left unvoiced were still killing Jake inside. *How could you lie to me, Daddy? You knew Dani was my mommy, so how could you lie? Daddy, were you ever gonna tell me Dani was my mommy?*

Yeah, as a daddy, Jake had done it all wrong.

As a lover, too.

Even now, Dani seemed to be running across Jake's living room, kneeling in front of Ty, bundling him in a tight hug, while tears streamed down her face. Jake could still see her eyes staring at him over Ty's sobbing shoulder, looking so haunting in their perceptiveness, so venomous in their accusations and so unwilling to forgive. Jake's heart wrenched just thinking of the way Ty and Dani had clung to each other, a mother and son reunited, while he'd just stood there, the mean old bad daddy who'd lied, keeping them apart for so many years.

If only Jake could lie to himself now. Convince himself that his worst nightmare had just come true. That Dani, who had no legal right to Ty, had just criminally removed the boy from his home.

Sure, Jake could call the cops.

They'd see it as kidnapping. Especially since Jake could prove that Dani had misrepresented herself when she'd come into their lives, and James Sanger would swear to her illegal search of the sealed records room.

Legally Dani *had* kidnapped Ty.

But Jake's code of ethics said Dani had a place in Ty's life now, that the past six years had given her the absolute right to claim her son. Six years ago she'd done something she'd regretted, but she'd paid the price. Cutting herself off from parents she loved, she'd had to start her life over again. And in all these years she'd never once stopped looking for Ty.

Jake blinked away what he told himself was nothing more than dust in his eyes. But he knew the sting was from tears he was too much of a man to shed. He just couldn't stop thinking about Dani. She was so right for him. He couldn't live without being able to feel the open readiness of her body, without having the right to hold her naked and trembling. But more than anything, he couldn't stop thinking about how she'd kept searching for Ty all this time or about what she'd said—that Jake's own birth mother might have kept searching for *him*.

Before tonight, that thought had never once even crossed Jake's mind.

The woman who'd raised him would always be his mother. But now the horrible truth Jake had lived with for years had surfaced. He secretly felt unwanted in such a bone-deep way he couldn't even talk about it. He'd simply always assumed that his birth mother hadn't wanted him. But now, for the first time, he was thinking, really thinking, of her.

Maybe she was still out there somewhere, like Dani had been for Ty. A nameless, faceless woman who lit candles and made heartfelt wishes every year on Jake's birthday. A woman he might have passed unknowingly on a city street, the way Dani and Ty had almost passed like ships in the night. A woman who'd never once stopped loving Jake, but who had silently stood vigil from afar.

Oh, God, that hurt so bad.

Why was it so much easier for Jake to believe that the woman who'd borne him was weak and self-centered and hadn't wanted him? He sighed, already knowing it had made him feel justified in holding Ty so selfishly tight. Jake had always needed to prove that, unlike his birth mother, he was the parent who would hold on.

But now he had to do something even harder—let Ty go.

He had to share.

Dani had taught him that. Tonight, while he'd loved her, she'd reached him in places he hadn't even known existed, making that hurt deep inside him break free. Because what if, just like Dani, his birth mother had never stopped searching? Or, what if she'd let Jake go, not out of weakness or for her own convenience, but from a well of maternal strength, giving Jake a better life, her own heart breaking all the while? The thought of that woman, committing such self-sacrifice on his behalf, made Jake's whole soul ache as he'd never known it could.

And it was all so possible, so terribly, painfully possible.

Yeah, maybe his mother had wanted him, after all.

God knows, Dani and Ty had loved him since.

And so tonight, Jake let them go, praying he wasn't losing the two people he now knew he loved most in the world.

"OH, BABY...sweetheart...oh, Ty."

For a long time, Dani murmured nothings while she hugged and rocked her sobbing little boy. They sat on her couch, with him in her lap, his legs wrapped tightly around her waist, his ankles locked behind her back. She touched him, smelled him, removed his hat and ran her fingers and lips across his corn silk hair.

The trip to her apartment was a blur, seen through tears. She'd hailed a car and lifted Ty inside, thrusting money at the cabbie and forgetting her change. They'd driven past a dark-clad woman in the street, maybe the same one Dani had seen outside Big Apple Babies and Grantham Hale's place. Maybe the same one Jake had seen outside her apartment. And although seeing the woman again worried Dani, her only real thought now was for her son.

From the second he'd called her "Mommy," she'd been unable to relinquish him. She'd even carried him bodily up all five flights of stairs to her apartment, moving on pure, adrenaline-driven emotion, the kind that allowed mothers to perform far more miraculous feats, such as lift cars to free their trapped young ones. Whether the energy came from Dani's rage at Jake or her love for Ty, she didn't know.

All she knew was that Ty was hers. He was right here, safe and secure, healthy and alive, wrapped in her arms. The tiniest things about him—his fingers, his little boy smell, the deep wrinkle in his pajama top— were all miracles. Because he was hers.

Hers.

Just as she was his.

For an hour, they didn't even speak.

They sat in darkness, because Dani couldn't force herself to let go of Ty long enough to reach over and flick on a lamp. When she finally did, Ty cried out, as if she might abandon him.

"It's okay." Her arms swiftly circled him again and his tightened around her neck. "I'm just turning on the light."

Ty nodded, burrowing against her chest. By degrees, he stopped crying. Growing silences, punctuated by hiccups and sniffles, outdistanced his sobs. Dani became slowly conscious of the heaviness of his arms on her shoulders, that her thighs were tingling, having gone to sleep because of his weight on her lap. Suddenly she realized she hadn't relocked the apartment door. She'd left her jacket at Jake's, too. And Ty's suitcase. And the babies.

Not that it mattered. Regardless of what was happening between them, Jake would take care of Lyssa and Kirby. Ty roused his head from her shoulder. It swayed, almost as if he'd gotten dizzy from all his crying.

His eyes were puffy, his voice a faint rasp. "I hate Daddy."

Dani's throat was so tight with unshed tears that it had almost swollen shut, but she held back her own sobs now for her son's sake. Gently smoothing his bangs, she whispered, "No you don't, Ty. You don't really hate your father."

"I do."

Even as Ty said the words, rage bubbled inside Dani again. *I do, too, Ty.* She thought of how carefully Jake must have set Lanie's picture out for her to see, of how Jake had actually wanted to make her believe Lanie was Ty's mother. Dani could have died without ever holding this boy, without ever realizing Ty was her son.

Careful not to betray her emotions, Dani leaned and kissed Ty's rosy, tearstained cheek. Somehow her voice came out sounding soothing. "Your daddy was trying to do what's best."

Ty gasped. "He lied."

Yes, he did. And it's killing me, Ty. Gathering her son even closer in her arms, Dani pressed her cheek to the top of his head; in spite of her fury at Jake, her heart still ached for him. He'd betrayed her, something she could never forgive, but he didn't deserve to lose Ty's love.

When Ty started crying again, this time more softly, she felt a rush of empathy, and she wished she could do more than simply share her son's grief. She wanted to take it all inside herself, to make Ty happy again. Sadness suddenly twisted inside her. "Please don't hate him," she said again.

After all, Dani knew how much it hurt to hate one's own father.

"Ty, I know it's hard to understand, but your Daddy's not perfect, any more than I am. And even though

he lied, you've got to understand that he did it because
he loves you.''

''He doesn't love anybody.''

''He does.'' *And I thought he could love me. I can't
believe he'd let me think Lanie was your mother, Ty.
Not even for an instant.*

''But I hate him.''

''Please try,'' she whispered.

Then she sighed. She had no intention of forgiving
her father. Or Jake. The two most important men in
her life had kept her away from her son.

''Mommy?''

Just hearing Ty call her that made new tears spring
to her eyes. She could barely speak. ''Yes?''

Ty didn't answer, merely shrugged. When he lifted
his head and stared reverently into her eyes, she realized he'd only wanted to say the word. He needed to
say ''Mommy'' just as much as she needed to hear it.

Mommy.

She said it in her mind. Then she stared deeply into
Ty's eyes, her eyes. Her voice still carried a faint trace
of surprise. ''You're my son.''

''You *really* are my mommy,'' Ty whispered.

''Really, really,'' she whispered back.

And now she could see herself in his face. How had
she ever looked at this boy without realizing the truth?
Any stranger on the street would have known. Her
baby shared her dark eyes, the shape of her face and
her mouth. His long-forgotten Greek father wasn't even
visible; every inch of Ty was hers.

And Jake's.

She wanted to deny it, but she couldn't look at Ty
without seeing Jake. Ty had learned Jake's gestures and
mannerisms. It was in how his mouth pulled when he

was lost in thought, and in the way he tilted his head when he smiled. Even in looks, Ty was as much Jake's as hers. Jake had paid his dues, too. It was Jake who'd taken care of life's small details—doctored the skinned knees, cooked daily meals, cleaned Ty's clothes.

Ty uttered a shuddering sigh; the sobs that had racked his body had completely worn him out. "I can live here with you, Mommy. Right?"

An hour ago, Dani actually might have said yes.

Now her eyes flitted around her tiny, bare apartment. As much as she needed to be in Ty's life, Jake was his father now. And not just legally. He and Ty had made a stable life together, a home. She felt her heart stretch to breaking. She'd given Ty up once. Could she do it again, this time because it was best for him?

Seemingly reading the answer in her eyes, Ty's lower lip trembled. Dani gently lifted his chin, then stared into his eyes as hard as she could, wanting her son to feel the truth of her words. "I love you more than anything in the world, Ty."

He blinked, making a tear splash down his cheek. "So, why don't you want me?"

Her heart broke. "I want you so much," she whispered. But just blocks away, her boy had a real home. "Ty, right now we've got to see what we can work out with your daddy." *If anything,* she thought in panic. Keeping her voice even, she tried to sound reasonable. "And there's only one bed here."

Ty's eyes pleaded. "We could share, Mommy. I'm not very big."

She wanted to weep, to indulge her emotions, to break down and confess how desperately she wanted Ty to stay. "I think you might miss your own room...at home." *With Jake.*

"I wouldn't."

"C'mon." It took all she had, but she could still barely hold back tears. Her nose stung, her chin suddenly quivered. "I...left Lyssa and Kirby at Daddy's."

"I don't care about them!"

"You're hurting right now." For his sake, she kept her voice calm. "But, Ty, I know you care about them. And you care about your Daddy."

"Why can't you marry him?"

"I...I don't think that's going to happen, Ty."

"I'm 'sposed to forgive him, so why don't you gotta forgive him?"

"It's...different with me and your daddy."

Ty stared at her for a long time, his eyes dark and big and round and beautiful. Teardrops caught in his eyelashes, glistening. Sighing heavily, he simply leaned forward and hugged her tight again. "I'm never gonna talk to him again 'cause you mighta married him if he wasn't a liar."

It was true. Dani's heart wrenched so unexpectedly that she almost cried out. Full force, it hit her that she'd really lost Jake. But she couldn't forgive him for the lies he'd told. *Be careful what you wish for.* Her own fortune came back to haunt her. She'd finally found her baby. But when she gained her son, she'd lost the man with whom she'd been falling in love.

Suddenly Dani felt bone weary. She was tired of crying. And tired of losing all the men in her life.

First she'd given away Ty.

Then she'd walked out of her father's house.

And now she had to leave Jake.

She suddenly said, "You love your daddy." And then her breath caught. Because Dani wasn't just talking about Ty's love for his daddy now, but about her love for her own.

Not that she'd forgive him.

Ty leaned back in her arms. She stared at him, and he stared back as if he'd never see her again.

"Mommy," he said simply. Then, with new tears welling in his eyes, he lifted his small hands and gingerly cupped her cheeks. Leaning forward, he stared deeply into her eyes, in exactly the way she'd just stared into his, and he whispered, "I'll do anything for you, Mommy. Even go home to Daddy."

"Oh, Ty." She lifted her fingers, and as she pressed his hand more firmly against her cheek, she shut her eyes and exhaled a soft sigh.

When she opened her eyes again, Ty wordlessly reached into the pocket of his jean jacket and brought out the bite-size Snickers bar she'd left there. Biting his lower lip hard to stop its quivering, he carefully ripped the wrapper, then painstakingly split the candy in two, blinking away tears as he held each side up for comparison.

"Here, Mommy," he finally whispered, offering her half. "I think I got it even."

Dani's eyes stung again. She wanted to scream that she didn't care if it was even. She didn't need a perfect half. Jake could have 99.9 percent of her little boy. She only wanted this, just a fraction of her son.

Somehow she managed to take the chocolate. She could never forgive Jake for lying, but if she wasn't involved with him, would he still let her see her Ty? Her voice was scratchy. "Thank you, Ty."

"You're welcome, Mommy."

As Ty started eating, he sniffled and his tears dried. When he licked at the smears on his still-quivering lips,

Dani suddenly found herself thanking God for small favors—for Snickers bars, and the fact that her young son's deepest woes could still be cured, however temporarily, by nothing more than a half inch of sweet chocolate.

HE HADN'T PUT ON A SHIRT. In fact, when he swung open the door to the apartment, it didn't look as if Jake had done anything but stand there since Dani and Ty had left. The babies were still sleeping in the stroller beside the door.

"You came back."

He sounded surprised. And the faint implication made Dani's blood boil. *Where did you think I was going? To Canada or Mexico with Ty?* For Ty's sake, she kept her voice calm. "Of course I brought him back."

Jake's eyes were alive with emotion—surprise, relief, wariness. But when Ty stared meanly up at his father, murderous rage turning his smoky eyes black as coal, all emotions but concern vanished from Jake's face. Leaning, he tried to help Ty take off his jacket, but Ty flinched and stepped back a pace. Jake looked positively stunned.

"I'm gonna tell you one thing, Daddy," Ty snarled. "And then I'm never gonna speak to you again."

Jake eyed his son, as if weighing how to handle this. "What?"

"I hate you. And I only came back 'cause Mommy made me."

Jake sighed. "Please, Ty…"

Making a show of shutting his mouth tight, Ty gave Dani a quick hug. Almost against her will, knowing this wasn't helping, she dropped to her knees and hugged him back. "Don't worry," she whispered, "we'll try to work something out."

"Tell Daddy he better." Ty stepped back, shot one last angry glare at Jake, then stomped down the hallway. A moment later, his door slammed.

Just looking at Jake, Dani felt as angry as Ty. Especially when she saw Jake's eyes flare with danger, a sudden spark that fizzed to life like a match. No matter what he might say, Jake saw her as a threat because she might take away his child. *Having you in my life means I've got to give him up, Dani.*

To her surprise, Jake said, "We've got to talk. We can get past this." He leaned back, ushering her inside the apartment.

She stayed put. "Sorry, I've got to go."

Jake merely stared at her. "Dani, I love you."

Did he really think it would be that simple? Her voice was barely controlled. "Jake, you put Lanie's picture out for me to see. When we talked about her, you let me think she was his mother. If we hadn't wound up in bed, you never would have told me."

Suddenly Jake moved toward her, coming too close again, making the air snap with the living energy between them. His voice was so low, gruff and persuasive that it trembled through her. "But we did wind up in bed. We've been in bed tonight. And you have to believe I would have told you."

"I don't."

"You've got to."

She shook her head.

His green eyes turned flinty. "Ty's never going to forgive me. Now you're not. But do you know who you really won't forgive?"

His tone infuriated her. So did the fact that he wouldn't admit it when he was wrong. "Who?"

"Yourself."

"You're the one who lied!" she protested. "The one who didn't come clean!" She lifted her finger and pointed it right in his face. "I want some arrangement where I can see my son, but I am not going to let you railroad me. The issues we have about Ty are one thing. What's between you and me is another."

Jake's voice was deathly calm. "Aren't you listening?"

She stared at him, fury pumping through her veins. "Did I miss something you said?"

"Yeah."

"What?"

"I love you."

She wanted to say that was his tough luck. But her knees suddenly weakened and her heart squeezed. *Oh, Jake. I don't know what I feel, but I don't think I can live without you.*

"Dani, forgive me. Forgive yourself."

"I don't know what you're talking about!"

"I'm talking about how you live alone in that cramped little apartment," he answered, leaning a fraction closer. "About why you wear starchy oversize uniforms when you don't have to. And don't date. And work around the clock."

Realizing her jaw was hanging open, she snapped it shut. "This isn't about me! It's about you and your lies. Don't you dare try to turn this argument around."

His jaw was clenched, and his voice dropped to a near growl. "I know you want to be with me."

Her cheeks flushed with heat. Even now she wanted him. She was thinking about reaching out and running her fingers through the thatch of black hair on his chest. Of brushing her cheeks against him, and pressing kisses to his skin. About pleasuring him in the secret ways he pleasured her. After Jake, she couldn't imagine ever wanting another man. She could barely find her voice. "I want you. But sex doesn't matter."

It did, though.

Sex, at least the kind they had together, mattered more than most everything else. And they both knew it. So did the fact that they shared a son.

Dani drew in a sudden, audible breath. A panic she didn't quite understand had started fluttering around inside her like butterflies. It felt like the flapping of wings, or like something beating inside her, trying to get out. Suddenly she had to get out of here; she didn't even know why. "Look, I—I'll just make arrangements to talk about Ty through a lawyer."

Jake nodded. "I'll be my own counsel."

As she turned to go, he caught her hand. "Before you leave, Dani, I've got to tell you something."

She stared at him warily, that strange panic still jarring her insides, making her want to run. "What?"

"It's about your father."

Her heart seemed to miss a beat, then pump too hard, making blood surge in her veins. "My father?"

"I didn't get a chance to tell you that, after the adoption went through, your father tried to get Ty back damn near any way he could. He used his connections, hired attorneys. I figured he just wanted his grandson back. And maybe he did. But when you said you'd cut off all ties with him, I thought…" Jake shrugged. "I just thought you might want to know. Your father might have been trying for you, realizing his own mistake."

She'd been holding her breath and now she slowly exhaled. Pressing her hand to her heart, she still couldn't believe what Jake had told her. She barely heard his next words.

"I'm sure your father wanted what's best for you, just like I want what's best for Ty. That's why I'm willing to work something out, so you can see him."

Shock and relief mixed together in her system, making her feel a little faint. Jake had just said she could see Ty. That was the important thing. In a sudden rush, she realized she'd been half convinced she'd never see her son again after tonight.

"I can see him?" she repeated.

"Yeah."

Her eyes slid past Jake, to the cozy home where he was raising her boy. "Even if we're not together, Jake?"

At that, Jake uttered softly, "Damn." Anger sparked in his eyes again. And then, without warning, he leaned and caught her face in his hands, cupping her cheeks so tightly it almost hurt. He stared deeply into her eyes. "I'm only going to say it one more time. I love you."

She almost melted. Almost said she loved him, too. But the words didn't come.

"Please, Dani," he said. "Quit punishing yourself. Try to love me. Let me love you."

And then, still cupping her face between his palms, Jake kissed her hard. There was no movement, just the steady pressure of his mouth. And it lasted a long time, him just cupping her face, kissing her hard like that.

Dani wasn't even sure what it meant.

Either it was a kiss meant to impart all Jake's hope and strength. Or it was a kiss goodbye.

DANI WAS CRYING AGAIN when she entered her apartment. She just felt raw and wrung out; the night had been too full of emotion. Gently she put Lyssa and Kirby to bed. After tomorrow, when she took the babies to court, she guessed she'd give their crib to Goodwill. She'd certainly have no need for it.

Already she missed the little girls, but she knew Grantham Hale would get custody and that he'd be a wonderful father. Dangling a hand inside the crib, she rubbed the babies' backs until they were sound asleep again, knowing that soon, once the arrangements were made, she'd be spending time with her own son.

Her father's grandson.

Was it really possible that her father had hurt the way she had? That he'd realized, only when it was too late, what he'd forced her to give away?

"Forced me?" Dani suddenly whispered.

No, it was she who'd given Ty up. She, and only she, had signed the dotted line. Hers was the final word. She had to accept that now. It wasn't her father's fault. Any more than it was her mother's or Jake's.

Her eyes filled with tears again. Somehow she had to quit thinking about Jake. She still couldn't believe he might have let her go thinking Lanie was Ty's mother. And Jake was dead wrong. Dani had forgiven herself.

Hadn't she?

Dani glanced around, taking in the bare living room. The lack of plants and pictures, the hard little bed in the room beyond, the simple blinds. But she didn't have much money, and she'd been so busy with work and school.

Punishing herself? No, she had no idea what Jake was talking about. Tonight he'd just wanted to take the focus off himself and all his lies. But at least he'd told her the truth about her father.

Slowly Dani stood. She walked across the room, picked up the phone, then punched in a number. Three rings sounded before someone picked up.

"Hello?"

At the voice, Dani's eyes blurred and her heart flooded with renewed emotion for the man she'd missed so much all these years. Her voice caught as she said, "Daddy?"

Chapter Eleven

It was a horrible morning.

As if sensing their lives were about to change again, the babies wouldn't stop crying. Lyssa spilled juice on her best outfit, then Kirby needed a last-minute diaper switch. Dani calmed the babies, taking them downstairs and settling them in a cab, only to remember she'd left her keys dangling from the lock in the front door. She'd had to carry Lyssa, Kirby, the stroller, and all the baby bags back inside, up all five flights, to retrieve the keys. By the time she'd finally reached Judge Winslow's, she was fighting serious tears of her own.

And then she found out Judge Winslow had vanished.

Dani had no idea where he might have gone. She just couldn't think straight. All night long, she'd stayed awake, crying and thinking about Jake. As dawn broke with soft yellow light slanting through her blinds, Jake's lies didn't even seem important anymore, only the strength inside him, his capacity for loving her.

She wanted Jake so much. *But what if I let him love me? What if I can't take the responsibility? What if I crush under the weight of it and run away, like I did six years ago? This time I won't just hurt Ty, I'll hurt Ty and Jake.* Wasn't that what she really feared?

Dani pushed Jake and Ty from her mind, and the stroller down a tiled hallway in the family court building. Her heart was beating too fast, pumping out energy she no longer really possessed in a redoubled effort to hurry her tired body along.

Court should have started ten minutes ago.

Quickly she wrestled Lyssa and Kirby's stroller through the double doors of the courtroom, then sighed in relief. Nothing was happening yet. She'd made it.

Now all she had to do was face Jake. She wouldn't cry or break down. And after that, her duty here would be done. Later, by the time she met with the lawyer and Jake to arrange visits with Ty, her emotions would be entirely under control.

Or they wouldn't be.

Already she knew Jake wasn't here. She felt his absence in the room, as if he'd just hugged her hard, then left her. Still she paused inside the courtroom doors. As her eyes pointlessly searched for him, she wondered if courtrooms were usually so crowded for cases such as this. Some of the people even looked like media types.

Her eyes darted over the pew-style seats, then to the gated area up front, with its elevated judge's bench, witness stand and jury box. To the left, the judge's clerk, a thin, middle-aged black woman in a gray suit, was seated behind a scarred wooden desk. Behind the prosecution table was a tall white woman in a navy dress who wore her chestnut hair in a French twist. Probably Suzanne Billings.

James Sanger was at the defense table. He was facing a stenographer who was beneath the witness stand, but he was sizing up Suzanne and looking hell-bent on proving beyond any reasonable doubt that Big Apple Babies wasn't liable for negligence in the mixup of the quadruplets.

Dani didn't see Jake anywhere.

Even as relief flooded her because she had more time to prepare herself for seeing him, her heart squeezed with crazy, irrational fear. Was Jake all right? Had something happened to Ty? Why was Jake so late? He was always so punctual.

Just thinking about Jake caused a tremor inside her. As surely as if he were actually here, Dani suddenly felt him grab her. She felt last night's swift, strong kiss goodbye; once again, the never-ending pressure of his lips so firm and hard shook her soul.

She realized Grantham Hale was waving from the first row of seats. He'd turned himself out in a chocolate suit, cream shirt and stylish wide tie, and he looked rich, respectable and definitely responsible enough to raise six kids. Mustering a smile, Dani returned his wave and started pushing the stroller down the center aisle. Parking Lyssa and Kirby's stroller next to Langdon and Nicolas's, Dani slid next to Grantham.

"Hi!" Grantham whispered with merry excitement, his cologne wafting toward Dani as he leaned, kissing and tickling the girls until they giggled. "Jake got Judge Winslow to sign the documents last night. It's all settled. I'm taking the twins and quadruplets."

When Grantham's eyes raised to Dani, the spark in them flickered out. "Oh, no," he whispered in a rush. "You look so upset. Is it because of the girls? I meant everything I said about letting you see them."

"I'll miss them." Dani reached forward and

squeezed Grantham's forearm in assurance. "But no. I'm fine. Just tired."

And bracing herself for Jake. As her fingers fell from Grantham's suit sleeve, the rich texture of the fabric comforted her. She'd debated about what to wear, herself, and she'd finally decided on her uniform, white stockings and Reeboks. In spite of all the nasty things Jake had said about her wearing the outfit to punish herself, she'd wanted to look professional. Like someone who wouldn't do something so foolish as unwittingly sign a document giving her custody of two babies.

Glancing down at the uniform's starchy fabric, Dani thought of the soft, feminine purple velour dress she'd bought especially for Jake. And of the black-and-white jersey dress she'd found way at the back of her closet and of how Jake had carefully lifted the hem, preparing to love her, his large warm hands molding around her hips, cradling them.

She heard him say, *Please, Dani. Quit punishing yourself. Try to love me. Let me love you.*

Even now his voice trembled through her, a slow husky rumble that thrummed her, stroked her. She fought the urge, but finally turned, glancing over her shoulder again. Where was he?

And the judge? Judge Winslow had promised he'd be waiting at his apartment this morning, so she could help transport him, Lyssa and Kirby downtown to the family courthouse. But he hadn't been there, and neither Evie Pope nor the doorman had seen him leave. Surely James Sanger would need the judge's testimony to prove he'd already given custody of the quadruplets to Grantham. Especially if Suzanne Billings was as lethal as everybody said.

Suddenly Dani did a double take. At the back of the courtroom was a woman about her own age, in a dark dress, with a fashionable black scarf draped over her head. Dani was sure it was the same woman she'd seen at Big Apple Babies, outside Grantham Hale's, and then from the cab last night.

Who was she? Had she been following Dani? Or Jake? And why?

Suddenly all the questions vanished. Because the doors opened and Jake walked in. Nothing could have prepared her. The instant Dani saw him, the whole world stopped revolving. Like lasers, his eyes immediately found hers. There might as well not have been another soul in the room. Or in all of Manhattan.

She'd never seen Jake in a suit and tie. And he looked good. As he started pushing Stanley and Devin's stroller down the aisle, she took in how his charcoal jacket made his hair look blacker and accentuated his broad shoulders and his lean flat torso.

Then her heart wrenched. Ty trailed a few paces behind his daddy, dressed in an uncomfortably new looking navy blazer and pants, his arms crossed meanly over his chest, his head downcast.

I bet he didn't talk to Jake all last night. Probably, out of concern, Jake kept Ty home from school. She felt so responsible for the rift. Her inability to help hurt all the more since Jake's words last night had allowed her to call her own father.

Right before Jake reached the first row, Dani's pulse accelerated. Would Jake turn right and face the jury? Or left and sit beside her?

He nodded at her and Grantham and turned into their aisle. Just as he started to sit beside her, Ty inserted himself in the spot and grabbed her hand in what felt more like a death grip than a gesture of affection. Jake's jaw clenched, as if he'd had about enough of Ty's surliness, but he scooted over, giving their son space.

Ty peered up at her, his eyes red, probably from crying and lack of sleep. "Hi, Mommy," he croaked. It definitely sounded as if his voice hadn't had a workout this morning.

Everything inside her chest swelled. "Hi," she whispered.

Ty scooted closer, leaned against her side and shut his eyes. She glanced at Jake.

He shot her a brief smile.

That was the worst.

As his mustache lifted, hints of his dimples showed, and the tiny wrinkles at the corners of his bloodshot green eyes deepened. Just that one fleeting smile made her long to feel the strength in his arms when he wrapped them so tightly around her. She wanted him so badly. *But you'll blow it, Dani. You'll screw things up again. You'll hurt Ty. Jake's a good father. You've got to leave them alone, let them patch things up.* She'd given up her boy once out of fear. Now she had to let go out of love. Because Jake was the strong, responsible one. The one who was best for their son.

She looked away, forced herself to stare forward. How was she was going to get through this? Just sitting here with Jake and Ty made her want to run. She could feel Jake's eyes drifting over her, willing her to look at him.

She wouldn't.

Up front, three knocks sounded. Dani glanced toward a door at the farthest corner of the courtroom. As it opened, the middle-aged black woman stood and

Dani could now see that the nameplate on her desk said Ms. Cooke. Ms. Cooke smoothed her gray skirt, then circled her desk and faced the courtroom.

"All rise!" she called in a regal voice.

Dani's heart fluttered as she stood. Judge Winslow still wasn't here! As one of Jake's secret backers, she'd expected the judge to try his very best to help Jake by offering his testimony.

"Case forty, part thirty-eight now in session," Ms. Cooke continued. "The Honorable Judge T. Winslow presiding."

Dani stared at the empty doorway. Ty emitted a soft gasp. Jake raised an eyebrow. Next to her, Dani could swear Grantham Hale uttered a soft chuckle, as if at an inside joke.

And then, sure enough, Judge Winslow came through the doorway. He was fully robed and the cast had been removed; walking shakily, he used the cane he'd been carrying for weeks.

As he approached the bench, you could hear a pin drop.

As if only now realizing the proceedings were under way, the dark-clad woman suddenly started tiptoeing down the center aisle. Just as Judge Winslow took his seat, the woman in black reached the gate to the inner sanctum of the courtroom and whispered to a uniformed court officer, who let her through. As she seated herself next to Suzanne Billings, her dark veiling scarf dropped to her shoulders, revealing a mass of blond hair.

Who was she?

Dani's eyes shot to Jake again as they reseated themselves. Catching Dani's gaze, he whispered, "Must be Suzanne Billings's assistant."

"It's a court, Mommy," Ty whispered meanly. "Tell Jake he's 'sposed to be quiet."

Jake. Ty wasn't even calling him Daddy anymore.

Dani flushed, still feeling Jake's gaze, like a caress, and wishing Ty wasn't trying to use her to get at Jake. "Ty," she murmured in soft censure, her arm tightening around him as she watched Suzanne's assistant. All this time, the woman must have been spying, trying to find out where the babies were, searching for signs of negligence. Dani's color deepened. How much of her relationship with Jake had the woman witnessed?

Dani's mind flooded with things she could have seen. Stolen kisses and telling caresses. The deepening green of Jake's eyes when he looked at her. Dani tried to quit torturing herself with memories as Suzanne Billings called her witnesses. The prosecution's argument was astonishingly brief.

Then, one by one, James Sanger's people were led through a side door and took the stand. All testified to how busy Dani had been the day the babies had been signed for—the man from UPS, the grocery store and the dry cleaner's, as well as the bike messenger and the law clerks. Then the lawyers made a stipulation that Larry McDougal couldn't be found.

And Rosita de Silva was called.

Dani's lips parted in surprise as Rosita took the stand.

"She and her husband came back from Villa Maria last night," Jake whispered. "James found her."

At the sound of Jake's voice, Ty's hand tightened around Dani's. Because it squeezed Dani's heart even more than her fingers, she missed nearly all of Rosita's halting testimony. The poor woman was clearly mortified, but she'd been operating on the instructions of

Larry McDougal. She offered to resign from Big Apple Babies, something Dani was sure wouldn't be necessary, judging from the compassion in Jake's eyes.

As Dani's eyes slid away from him again, unshed tears made her nose sting. Surely Jake couldn't really love her, not completely. He'd get over her in time. He and Ty would patch things up. Jake was such a wonderful father. The best.

"I really will resign," Rosita said.

"No such thing will be necessary." Judge Winslow gave her a quick once-over and slammed down his gavel. "The witness may step down."

A very stricken Rosita left the witness box and was led out. No doubt, she'd be fine. Jake wasn't the kind of boss who placed blame if things turned out right in the end. Further haggling up front determined that the mixup was due to negligence on the part of Larry McDougal, and since he couldn't be found, the suit against Big Apple Babies would be dropped. Of course, that was all on the condition that Suzanne Billings could introduce another, related matter, to which the judge returned, "Ms. Billings, please. You shall have your turn."

Near Dani, Jake was blowing out a long sigh of relief.

Then the county clerk said, "The court calls Daniela Newland."

Dani's eyes widened.

Ty stared up at her. "Mommy?"

"I guess I have to go up," Dani whispered.

Not that she understood. She hadn't been served a subpoena, or told to go to the witness room. Did this concern the "related matter" Suzanne Billings wanted to introduce? Well, this was a court of law. Dani could hardly refuse.

Feeling self-conscious, she smoothed her uniform and stepped the few paces to the gate. The room fell silent again as a court officer let her in. Passing the stenographer, she entered the witness box, feeling as if a thousand eyes were on her, but really noticing only two green ones—Jake's.

As a court officer placed a Bible on a corner of the witness stand, the court clerk raised her hand.

"Raise your right hand."

Dani did so, placing her other on the Bible.

"State your full name for the record."

"Daniela Newland."

"Daniela Newland, do you swear to tell the truth, the whole truth and nothing but the truth, so help you God?"

"I do."

Once seated, Dani turned toward Judge Winslow. She wanted to scold him for keeping her out of the loop. His cast was off, he wasn't home this morning, and he'd apparently come out of his short-lived retirement. But then Dani's eyes caught the painting behind the judge. It was of a lady, veiled and robed in white, holding high the golden scales. And suddenly Judge Winslow—wearing his black ceremonial robes and scowling down at her from the bench with those piercing blue eyes—seemed less like a man and more like angry Wrath incarnate.

Dani kept her mouth shut.

And turned her eyes to Jake. She couldn't help it. Right now she needed his strength, just the way her growing son would need his father's strength all his life. Jake nodded, barely perceptibly, giving it. *He really does love me,* she thought.

Suzanne Billings shot from her seat. "This witness isn't on my roll sheet."

James Sanger shrugged. "Judge, I didn't call her." He pointed toward a corner. "Should we have a sidebar on this?"

Apparently that meant James wanted everyone to confer more privately in the corner, which they did. Dani's ears strained to hear why she'd been called, since the suit had already been dropped and it was arranged last night that Grantham would have custody of the babies.

While Dani's ears strained, her eyes stayed on Jake.

And Ty. Her baby. Facing them, she could see how unhappy they both looked. Jake tried to touch Ty's shoulder, but Ty scooted all the way over to Grantham Hale. It brought tears to Dani's eyes again. *Oh, please. Don't sit up here, like a fool, and start crying for no apparent reason in front of a whole courtroom full of strangers.*

But she wanted to help her son. It was hurting him to be this mad. She thought of last night, of how her mother had gotten on the phone, then her dad again. Except for telling him about Ty—she wouldn't do that until concrete arrangements were made—she'd let her dad know what she'd been doing with her life.

Her daddy had been so proud. His voice had caught. "You know what I said all those years ago? That your life wasn't your own?"

Dani's throat had shut tight. "Yeah, Daddy."

"Well, it's really yours now, baby. You've made it your own."

And she had. She'd made it, after all. But could she ever trust herself to share her life with Jake and Ty?

She suddenly blinked, realizing Judge Winslow was addressing her. Suzanne and James were back in their seats.

"What?"

"I said do you love Jake Lucas?"

Dani gasped. Jake's eyes widened. Wrenching her gaze from his, she stared at Judge Winslow in outrage. "Excuse me?"

Judge Winslow stared back, his piercing blue eyes as cold as ice. His voice, heavy with the weight of the law he represented, was so resonant that it seemed to come from the bottom of a deep, echoing well. "Do you love Jake Lucas? It's a simple question, Ms. Newland. Yes or no."

Dani's jaw went slack. She barely registered that the judge had called her Ms. Newland instead of Nurse Dani. Why wasn't someone objecting to this? Dani stared around the room. Suzanne Billings merely returned her stare, expressionless. It must have been the judge's idea to put her on the stand. Was this some kind of joke? Angry tears welled in her eyes.

Her voice was low. "This isn't funny."

Judge Winslow merely peered down at her. "No, it certainly is not. Whatever our previous relationship, we are now in a court of law, Ms. Newland. *My* court. *Family* court. And because this is a family court, its interest is to best enable all citizens to negotiate family matters. I am well aware—as are you, Ms. Newland—that Tyler Lucas is your son."

Dani abruptly turned away. All along, Judge Winslow had known! She felt as if the breath had been punched out of her.

Judge Winslow continued, "Your illegal intervention into the Lucas home has caused dissension between the boy and his adoptive father, Jake Lucas."

Dani had never wanted anything so bad as she now wanted to run. This was crazy! She was in a courtroom full of strangers! And now Jake wasn't going to help her. He was merely waiting, tugging on his mustache. Not that he was afraid to tell the judge to back off. But Jake wanted to hear her answer.

The room was dead quiet.

Judge Winslow sighed heavily. "Ms. Newland, may I remind you you're under oath?"

The horrible panic Dani had felt last night was coming back. She was suffocating. Something was sitting on her chest. Wings were flapping in the pit of her stomach. And she had to get out of here. She didn't know why. But she had to. Her eyes flew to the door. Then she glanced down at her white running shoes.

Everyone was staring at her now. Everything was so quiet.

Jake and Ty were waiting, wanting the truth.

She could bolt from the box, run down the hall. Would the court officer catch her? Make her stay? Her eyes flitted between him and the clerk. Oh, no, what was happening inside her? Why did she feel so crazy? So panicked? What was this beating inside her that felt like wings?

And what should she say? She loved Jake. But if she said it, Ty would never understand why she and Jake couldn't be together.

Why can't we be together?

Those wings beat more furiously against her insides until the mad flapping became almost a pounding. Suddenly she wasn't even sure. Just knew it couldn't be. *I have to get out of here. Right now!* Her eyes welled with tears, making the faces in the courtroom blur. Everything, including Jake and Ty, turned into a smear of colors.

"Ms. Newland!" Judge Winslow thundered.

The slam of the gavel made her blink, and the tears fell, rolling down her cheeks. Quickly Dani ducked her head, swiping them away.

"I remind you once again, you are under oath. You have sworn, so help you God, to tell the truth."

I have sworn to God, Dani thought in panic.

"If you perjure yourself, I will send you straight from this courtroom to jail. So answer now. Do you, or do you not, love Jake Lucas?"

Run, Dani! Just run!

Dani's legs moved before her mind.

She was halfway to the door before she even realized she'd fled the box and darted between the defense and prosecution tables, then past Jake and Ty. Tears she didn't even bother to control were streaming down her cheeks now.

She hit the doors at a dead run.

As she burst through, she heard Ty shriek, "Get my Mommy back!"

A sob tore from her throat, but she kept running. Kept running even when she heard footsteps pounding behind her. She didn't stop until she slammed into the wall at the end of the hallway and couldn't go any farther. Whirling around, she expected to find the court officer.

Instead, she found Jake.

He looked so calm, so strong. His voice was soft. "I know you love me."

She could barely hear him. The flapping inside her

was deafening, like the wings of a huge trapped bird against a cage, trying to get free. And suddenly she realized that loud flapping was really the incessant pounding of her own heart against her rib cage. And with a final pound, what was deepest in her heart came out, and Dani suddenly cried, "Oh, God, Jake, I really gave him away. Oh, Jake, how could I have done it? How did I ever give away my baby? Our baby? How?"

Jake's strong arms caught her then. He hugged her so tightly she could barely breathe, and Dani wanted him to hold her tighter still. Because only Jake's arms were strong enough to squeeze out all those crazy deep truths inside her. How she'd been trying to become a trained nurse just so she could better take care of her baby if she found it. And that she *was* punishing herself. And that she didn't think she deserved Jake and Ty's love.

"It's okay," Jake whispered over and over, against her cheeks, in her hair.

And finally it was. Somehow Jake made it okay. That horrible panic lifted. The incessant pounding ceased. And the flapping wings suddenly took flight, as if all Dani's caged-up fears had been set free.

"I could have taken care of Ty by myself," she whispered.

Jake's voice was as gentle as a breeze. "But then you never would have found me. And both your son and I love you, Dani."

This time she really heard him. She nodded, and just let Jake hold her, absorbing his strength.

"Mommy?"

She looked down, barely able to see Ty through her tears. Her son was so perfect. His teary eyes were big and sincere and his earnest voice was meant to be so helpful.

"It's okay, Mommy," he said softly, "I was real little when you gave me up. And no matter how hard I try to 'member it, I can't or anything."

"Oh, Ty." A final sob was wrenched from Dani as she dropped to her knees and held him tight. "I don't know what to say. Maybe I never will. But I—I'm just so sorry, baby."

Ty blew out a brave, quavering little breath, and his eyes brimmed with fresh tears. "I just need you to be my mommy now," he murmured. *"Please."*

After all she'd done, her son still wanted her. And if Ty could forgive her, Dani knew she could completely forgive herself. "I *am* your mommy," she assured. As she stood, Jake lifted Ty into his arms. And this time, Ty went willingly, wrapping his arms around his daddy's neck, burying his face in his shoulder.

Dani gazed into Jake's eyes. "I love you," she said tenderly. "And I love Ty. I want to be in your lives."

Jake's voice caught with emotion. "You'll marry me?"

Dani merely nodded, too overcome to speak. When she finally found her voice again, she whispered, "Oh, yes." And then she stepped forward. Wrapping her arms tightly around her two men, Dani squeezed hard, with her whole heart.

"We're really gonna be a family?" Ty whispered.

"Really, really, Ty-ger," Dani whispered back.

When she looked up again, Jake's luscious green eyes met hers over the top of their son's head. Shifting Ty on his hip, Jake smiled and angled his head downward. And then, ever so softly, his lips brushed hers with a kiss so feather light that only Dani's soul could really feel it.

Dani's soul, that after six long years, was healed.

Epilogue

It was funny how things came full circle. How Dani had set out from this house six years ago to find Jake and her baby, and how she'd found them both, though not in the way she'd expected. How it was the search for two missing babies that had finally led Dani back to her own missing child.

Funny, how Jake had fallen so in love with her. And helped bring her home to Genesis.

Jake's dad clapped him on the back. "Son, she's gorgeous."

And she was. Swirling in front of the orchestra, dancing with her father under an illuminated white tent on the landscaped lawn of Genesis, Jake could swear Dani had never looked so beautiful. His eyes trailed over her long white gloves, to the low-necked, fitted beaded bodice of her sleeveless wedding gown, then down to the full skirt that, with the train draped over her arm, swirled as she turned gracefully in her father's embrace.

Thurman Newland had aged in the six years since

Jake had first met him. His salt-and-pepper hair was now a silver mass. But his face was lit up, joyous. And Dani's glowed. Her skin was as clear as this starlit night, her eyes dark, vibrant and alive.

Jake wanted nothing more than to dance with her.

His wife.

But he could be patient. He could share. Because later tonight, Dani Lucas would be all his again. For now, Jake merely touched the heavy gold band on the finger of his left hand, trying to get accustomed to the feel of it. Besides, he enjoyed seeing the restored closeness between Dani and her father. The two had something so special; it had been apparent ever since they'd made up. And both Thurman and Kate doted on their only grandson.

Yes, Dani loved her daddy.

And Thurman loved her.

It was never more evident than this evening, when Thurman had taken his daughter's arm and led her toward the man she was about to marry. Jake's heart had wrenched when he'd seen how badly his father-in-law's hands shook. Right before he relinquished Dani, Thurman's eyes had met Jake's in a sudden, silent plea, saying, *Please Jake. Dani means the world to me. Please be careful with her.* And Jake had stared back, his own eyes steady, making that vow and promise.

And then the all-powerful Thurman Newland had done what all men who father daughters have to do someday: given away his little girl.

So now Jake let them dance their final dance. And his eyes suddenly searched the crowded tent for Ty, who'd run off with his grandmothers. Because, like Thurman, Jake would someday have to let his son go. But then, love was always in the giving away. Jake knew that now. Each day, Dani taught him. And he taught her.

Beside him, Jake's father chuckled, then pointed. Ty had resurfaced, tugging on Grandpa Newland's tuxedo tails, and the ever indulgent grandpa quit dancing with the bride, leaned and listened to Ty.

Jake's dad laughed. "You missed your chance. Ty's cutting in."

Jake tweaked his mustache and chuckled as Ty stretched his arms around Dani's waist, letting his mother lead, while people stepped back and pointed, commenting on how cute Ty was.

Thurman approached with a playful shrug. "If you want a dance, you've got to be downright aggressive."

Jake smiled. "I guess her own husband has to cut in."

"Guess so."

Jake shook his head. He'd watched half the wedding goers have a spin. Winston Holiday and James Sanger. Trevor Marpas, who'd come with his mother. Escorted by Evie Pope, Judge Winslow was still unsteady on his feet, but he'd managed a turn. Even Thurman's driver, Baines, got both a slow and a fast dance. Then Baines had returned to the arms of a comely widow he'd married a few years back, the housekeeper Margie.

Just watching Dani, Jake sighed with deep satisfaction. Then he took another deep breath, savoring the sea salt that traveled on the late autumn breeze. Over the music, he could suddenly hear the rushing waves breaking on the beach.

The wedding had been amazing. Kate Newland's forte was parties, and in just a week—which was all Jake, Dani and Ty were willing to wait—musicians, florists, caterers and cake makers had magically appeared. It was as if Kate had kept them on retainer for years.

Maybe she had. Clearly Dani's wedding had been on Kate's mind since the day her only daughter was born. Not that Kate wasn't flexible or that Anne Lucas hadn't put in her two cents. When the weather had suddenly changed, bringing an unseasonable warm spell, both women promptly moved the wedding outside.

And so Jake and Dani had exchanged vows on the beach.

Now Dani was really his. Suddenly Jake felt wistful, thinking of his biological parents. Were they really out there somewhere? Would they be proud of him tonight? Were they lighting a candle, sending a silent good wish his way?

His eyes traced over his father beside him, his mother chatting merrily with Kate near a punch table. Maybe Jake really would seek out his biological parents. Not now, but sometime when he felt more ready. The parents who had raised him would understand.

They always had.

Meantime, Jake had a family of his own to think about. There was Ty to raise. And the brothers and sisters he was demanding, the babies Dani wanted so desperately. And might already be carrying, Jake thought with a sudden grin, thinking of the condom that broke the first time they'd made love.

"I've about had enough," he suddenly said on a playful sigh.

Clapping both his dad and Thurman on the shoulders, Jake headed into the fray to claim his bride. Leaning, he tapped Ty's shoulder.

"Daddy!" Ty giggled. "Does that mean you want to dance with Mommy?"

"Sure does."

A second later, Jake's wife was in his arms. But he'd barely begun to hold her when she found his hand and started leading him from the tent. "What?" Jake said with a laugh. "I don't dance as well as Ty?"

Dani chuckled wickedly. "Oh, I assure you, you're my favorite dance partner of all."

He draped his arm across her bare silken shoulders and then, feeling the coolness of her skin, slipped off his tux jacket."There," he said gently, putting it over her wedding gown as they stepped into the night.

"Thanks," she murmured. "Oh, Jake, isn't it beautiful out here?"

"Yeah."

It was perfect. The romantic night sky was midnight blue, lit by a full moon and a scattering of bright, twinkling stars. In silence, he and Dani walked over the lush green grounds, toward the beach, wending through the ethereal, monolithic sculptures. When Jake glanced over his shoulder, he saw the great chrome and steel house, and how the moon and stars reflected on the walls, making it appear as if it were lighted from deep within. It was a living, breathing place.

Genesis.

Tonight it was a place for new beginnings.

Keeping her train draped over her arm, Dani lifted it higher as they walked onto the sand.

"Your shoes?" Jake said simply.

"I don't care."

Jake didn't, either.

A little sand never hurt anything. Besides, the reception was nearly over. And they were alone on the beach now, under the moon and stars, on this clear, starlit night. They didn't stop walking until the foaming surf rushed close to their toes. Jake felt the salty breeze against his face, the last loving fingers of autumn's warmth waving goodbye before the cozy winter. And suddenly he needed to feel Dani's heat.

Turning, he tilted her chin, then leaned and kissed her hard and deep. And while his tongue dove between her lips, Jake thought about how wanted she made him feel. How she'd sworn to have and hold him. To love him until death. Oh, she wanted him so much. His babies. His touch. To share his bed for the rest of her life.

Jake had never guessed he could feel so wanted, so loved.

He moaned against her lips, her quick response to him already flooding him with desire. Her hips brushed his, and his brushed back, letting her feel his need. And then he deepened their kiss until it threatened his control and he had to draw away.

Jake's voice was husky. "I need you. I need you because of the way you always want me."

Dani lips were well kissed and slack, her eyes glazed with arousal. She smiled. "I know. I love you, Jake."

"I love you, too."

For a long moment, they gazed at each other in the moonlit darkness. He felt the soft touch of her hand around his waist, saw the breeze lift her hair and the love in her eyes, and he marveled at the freedom in his heart.

And then, without another word, they silently turned together, arm in arm, and faced the sea. *I'll always need her to want me,* Jake thought. *And she'll always need my strength.*

Together, Jake knew, they were ready to face the world.

Verdict: Parenthood

The courtroom drama isn't over yet! Awarded custody of both quadruplets *and* twins, wealthy widower and man-about-town, Grantham Hale is thrilled to become the father of Lyssa and Kirby, Langdon and Nicolas, *and* Stanley and Devin....

At least Grantham *was* thrilled—until Judge Winslow's great-granddaughter, the mysterious dark-clad Phoebe Rutherford, turns out to be the biological mother of the quadruplets! Phoebe claims her image problem is a hoax, created by her now-deceased husband. And she's determined to get her babies back from Grantham—in absolutely any way she can. But, as usual, when the gavel finally comes down, it's matchmaking Judge Winslow who gets the last word. He sentences Grantham and Phoebe to be parents—together!

* * * * *

Don't miss #699 VERDICT: PARENTHOOD
only from Jule McBride and American Romance!

HARLEQUIN®

AMERICAN ◆ ROMANCE®

COMING NEXT MONTH

#697 SPUR-OF-THE-MOMENT MARRIAGE by Cathy Gillen Thacker

Wild West Weddings

Cowboy counselor Cisco Kidd never expected to be a fifteen-minute fiancé in a client's matchmaking plans. His intended, Gillian Taylor, was certainly anxious to say "I do." While her sexy sass turned on his every desire, her eyes held secrets—secrets he'd spend their required honeymoon seducing from her.

#698 PLEASE SAY "I DO" by Karen Toller Whittenburg

Three Weddings & a Hurricane

Rik Austin wouldn't let wedding planner Hallie Bernhardt disrupt his plans to disrupt this wedding. He knew just what to do—a little tequila here, a little seduction there. Before she knew it, Hallie would be bewitched and bewildered—and the wedding would be history. But a funny thing happened on the way to disaster....

#699 VERDICT: PARENTHOOD by Jule McBride

Big Apple Babies

Overnight, the "Sexiest Man in Manhattan," Grantham Hale, became the adoptive daddy of quadruplets *and* twins! But his real troubles start when the quads' presumed-dead—but very much alive—biological mother reappears and the judge sentences Phoebe and Grantham to be parents... together!

#700 MR. WRONG! by Mary Anne Wilson

Guardian angel Angelina had worked hard to turn Melanie Clark into the proper mate for "Mr. Perfect." But *now* Angelina finds out Melanie is destined for Mr. Perfect's rougher, tougher, untamed brother...a guy Melanie can recognize at forty paces as Mr. Wrong!

AVAILABLE THIS MONTH:

Look us up on-line at: http://www.romance.net

Let's Celebrate!

LOVE & LAUGHTER™

invites you to
the party of the season!

Grab your popcorn and be prepared to laugh as we celebrate with **LOVE & LAUGHTER**.

Harlequin's newest series is going Hollywood!

Let us make you laugh with three months of terrific books, authors and romance, plus a chance to win a FREE 15-copy video collection of the best romantic comedies ever made.

For more details look in the back pages of any Love & Laughter title, from July to September, at your favorite retail outlet.

Don't forget the popcorn!

Available wherever
Harlequin books are sold.

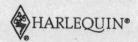

HARLEQUIN®

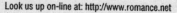

LLCELEB

HARLEQUIN WOMEN KNOW ROMANCE WHEN THEY SEE IT.

And they'll see it on **ROMANCE CLASSICS**, the new 24-hour TV channel devoted to romantic movies and original programs like the special **Romantically Speaking-Harlequin® Goes Prime Time.**

Romantically Speaking-Harlequin® Goes Prime Time introduces you to many of your favorite romance authors in a program developed exclusively for Harlequin® readers.

Watch for **Romantically Speaking-Harlequin® Goes Prime Time** beginning in the summer of 1997.

If you're not receiving ROMANCE CLASSICS, call your local cable operator or satellite provider and ask for it today!

ROMANCE CLASSICS

Escape to the network of your dreams.

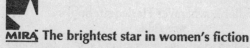

The condom had broken

Not that Jake would bother to tell her. He disposed of it, refusing to even entertain that he'd gotten her pregnant. Otherwise, he'd just barreled from her bed, past the babies' crib—and now he started rummaging through her purse, looking for ID's.

Nurse Dani simply *couldn't* be Daniela Newland.

Six years ago her father had hired Jake to handle the adoption of his daughter's baby. Now Jake could only pray that Dani—*his* Dani—was someone else. His fingers actually shook as he unfolded a dusty credit card receipt....

Daniela Newland.

Seeing the signature left him breathless. So, Dani had been using him to find her kid. Icy tendrils slid through Jake's veins, carrying a fear so horribly intense that, next to it, Dani's betrayal meant nothing at all.

Because Jake's son, Ty, *was* hers.

Dear Reader,

I'm pleased to present the first book in my new miniseries, BIG APPLE BABIES, to be followed by *Verdict: Parenthood* next month and two more titles in 1998!

These New York love stories are set around an adoption agency named Big Apple Babies, which is backed by anonymous matchmaking millionaires, one of whom will be unmasked in every book! While each story stands alone, much-loved characters—especially those from the New York family courts—will pop up their heads in the future, so we can see their lives progressing. You'll meet Manhattan men with lots of attitude and heart, and some adorable tykes, the Big Apple babies themselves.

Mission: Motherhood is set mostly in my own neighborhood, a cozy corner of Greenwich Village where mounted policemen still clip-clop by on horses, passing tree-lined sidewalks and stately old brownstones. But Manhattan's special magic can be felt everywhere—from brightly lit Broadway to glamorous Fifth Avenue, from the high-rolling excitement of Wall Street, to the old-world charm of downtown's Little Italy.

Please share this magic with me as Big Apple Babies' characters take on lives of their own, and we discover how—no matter where they are—people who were meant to be always magically find each other and fall in love.

All my best,

Jule McBride